THE PAISLEY HUNTER DETECTIVE FILES:

THE BUTCHER, THE TAKERS, AND THE MONEY MAKERS

(Book 1)

ALAN W. HOUNSHELL

Copyright © 2022 by Alan W. Hounshell

All rights reserved. No part of this book may be reproduced in any form or by any electronic or mechanical means, including information storage and retrieval systems, without permission in writing from the author, except by a reviewer who may quote brief passages in a review.

ISBN: 9798405818573

DEDICATION

For those diagnosed with multiple sclerosis and who've experienced strokes, continue to hope, and take one day at a time.

In memory of Lady Lu Lu, my furry corgi companion, who will be missed by all, but not easily forgotten.

DISCLAIMER

The characters and events in this book are fictitious. Any similarity to real persons, living or dead, is coincidental and not intended by the author.

ACKNOWLEDGMENTS

With grateful appreciation to my son Will who took the time to snap my picture for this book, my cousin Renee Ciancio who provided preliminary proofing before publishing, and my favorite and reliable book cover artist TK Palad.

A special thanks to Mireya Hernandez and Paul Stratton for providing initial feedback on this book and for family members such as Janet Hurt who continue to read my drafts and encourage my writing.

A NOTE FROM THE AUTHOR

After finishing this book, please provide feedback on Amazon or Goodreads. Share your recommendations for this book with friends — this is how independent authors grow an audience of readers. If you enjoyed this book, please check out my other novels which are available through Amazon below:

- *The Antique Dealer*
- *Bingo Baby*
- *The Witch Detective: The Fire & Brimstone Bourbon Trail Case*
- *Ancestry: Awakenings* (under the pseudonym of Cullen Kit Alexander)
- *In The End* (under the pseudonym of Cullen Kit Alexander)

For those of you looking for a casual podcast targeted primarily at those of us who are 50 and older (or anyone that will listen), I do an amateur periodic podcast called *Get A Life 2*. You can subscribe to this podcast through Podbean, Apple, or Audible.

Enjoy and go throughout your life in peace and harmony.

Alan

CHAPTER ONE

The cry of a newborn child — sounds of new life. That was the scream heard from the small cabin in the middle of nowhere. The child's mother lay lifeless as the baby was taken to the incubator. The midwife was quiet as she went about her work. She checked to ensure that the baby was healthy; she noted the birth weight, height, and date of birth which she carefully recorded on a counterfeit birth certificate. Baby boy #1019 was perfect with ten toes and fingers. He had a perfect Apgar score. She picked up her cell phone and quickly texted someone about the child. She then rolled the baby into the other room of the cabin. What was coming next was something that she did not want to see.

A few moments later, a person wearing a hazmat suit with a mask covering their face entered the room with a set of classic butcher tools (i.e., cleaver, saw, and several sharp knives). The mysterious person examined the incapacitated parent. This creepy, insidious person was called the "Butcher" by staff that lived at the cabin. No one knew who was in the suit — male or female, and no one wanted to know for fear that the Butcher would kill them. The Butcher had already had another girl become conscious last week, resulting in a bloody mess. She tried to escape, even with her stomach unstapled from a C-section. She ran for a mile holding her insides together before the Butcher shot her through the head from fifty yards with a Remington 7600 rifle.

The Butcher ran their gloved hands through their newest victim's hair. "So pretty, Rebecca. They said you were the best piece of meat in the whole house, and I never sampled you because I don't like to play with my food."

The gruesome killer checked the fat content in their victim's arms, hips, legs, and breasts and decided how they would cut her apart. There was an art to carving up an animal — a mammal in this case. The Butcher felt the limbs and decided they were too skinny to keep. Like a skilled cutlery artist, the Butcher cut the victim's arms and legs off and finally her head. The remains of their victims were thrown into a 55-gallon garbage can. These would be liquified later using a technique to dissolve all flesh and bone, and then any residue would be dumped into the river or burned to ashes.

The Butcher turned Rebecca over and spread the adjustable table apart, exposing her abdomen. A garbage can was slid under her torso. Then they sliced her open, proceeding to gut her like a fish. Once everything was cleaned out, they peeled her flesh off and began filleting the muscle and remaining fat like fine cuts of meat. After the filleting was done, they vacuum-packed the meat and dated it. Each freezer bag's contents were identified and dated and placed in a freezer in the back of the room. The Butcher cleaned up the splattered blood captured by the large thick millimeter plastic drop cloth and wiped down the room. The remaining body pieces were tossed into the garbage can. The process of destroying the evidence had begun.

Darcie had been a midwife for twenty years. She was a medical school student but dropped out. She felt a higher calling that involved saving these unborn children and putting them in the hands of people who could raise them better. She wanted to make sure that these children got better than she did growing up. She had seen what had happened to her mother and sisters. Their lives had been cut much too short due to their reckless lifestyles. Her mother and sisters were in and out of jail for drug trafficking, assault, and prostitution for the most part. All of them were dead now, and she was lucky that she had left home to escape that world.

Darcie had no remorse for these young women. They usually got pregnant by being high or stupid. Her previous job at the local health department helped prepare her for dealing with this population. She knew the type of environments these girls came from and the lives they were living. She was doing her part to rid the world of these tiny parasites who kept social services busy and brought another generation of welfare recipients into the fold. She knew what the Butcher did with the mothers. She was repulsed by it, but at the same time, she felt that this gruesome flesh carver was eliminating a life that had served its purpose and did not deserve to live. She didn't have any idea who the Butcher was, but she knew that whoever they were — they were someone sick and twisted who would kill her if she screwed up.

As far as all the young kidnapped pregnant girls who had ever been in her care, Darcie lied and manipulated them and sedated those that would not comply. She told them whatever they needed to hear.

She swore they were in a "special program" to turn their lives around that included one-on-one and group therapy to address their substance use and mental health needs. Darcie promised no law enforcement or child protective services would be involved. To make things more convincing, she faked being a therapist and offered daily groups to know what these young pregnant girls were thinking. She even had forged degrees on the wall, giving herself prestigious credentials such as an M.D. and Ph.D. It didn't matter if the girls believed that she had earned the degrees because it made her feel important.

Most of these young teens were poor, naïve, and desperate. The majority had legal charges, and they didn't ask questions for fear of being turned over to the cops. As part of the program, they were not allowed to contact anyone until birth. In return, they received the program for free and a generous stipend with the promise of more money once the delivery occurred. The organization that Darcie worked for always looked for young women who were more likely to be compliant. Most of the pregnant captives believed they were kept in chains because of their AWOL histories. Darcie told most of them that being shackled would prevent them from leaving before collecting their money.

The pregnant teens were kept in an isolated area near the Red River Gorge where the chances of a collaborative escape were improbable. Regardless, the cabin's location was almost impossible to find, and no one would ever think about coming to a forty-year-old abandoned strip mine reclaimed by the forest. The only means to reach the reclaimed area was by the river, and even then, you had to know how to get through the thick forest. It was the perfect hiding place in the middle of Wolfe County.

Darcie would typically nurse a newborn for two weeks, and by then, the baby would be more robust, and a new adoptive home would be ready. All the legal documents would be legitimate looking with no chance of any future legal challenge. In exchange for her diligent work, Darcie would receive a seventy-five-thousand-dollar payday for each child successfully sold. All children sold had a 30-day money-back guarantee. Darcie knew if any of the adopted infants under her initial watch died within 30 days, she would either be killed or have a financial penalty.

The pregnant girls came from all over. Most came from the other 119 counties. Lately, Darcie had been getting out-of-state trash, which did not appeal to her. Her pay had increased, but she didn't like people outside her home state — even if they fit the criteria. These were all people that no one would miss or care about because they were poor and offered little to society besides fast food service. Darcie took her payment in cash and kept it in a steel safe in her house. No banks or investments were used to avoid any suspicion. She had a long-term plan for a short-term job. Darcie's motivation may have been financial, but the Butcher's motivation was always about the next meal.

CHAPTER TWO

Paisley Hunter was brought back to the world of the living like she had been for the past twenty-seven years — with a big cup of black coffee along with the local and state newspapers. Life had indeed come full circle since she left small-town life decades ago. In the past year, Paisley traded her dreary apartment in Chicago for a large farmhouse across from Quaillan's Dairy Farm in Wolfe County, Kentucky. Instead of waking up and looking out at a brick alley, she drank her coffee and read her papers while viewing magnificent sunrises in a large sunroom adjoining her kitchen.

Besides cleaner air, no traffic jams, and less crime, her new home came with a rogue rooster named Doodle who belonged to no one. Doodle crowed on the hour every hour, starting at four every morning, come rain or shine. Not to be ignored, the cows welcomed Paisley by mooing and ringing the bells around their necks as they grazed from spot to spot, just as the first cup of coffee hit her mug. Being up early did not bother Paisley. She was used to being up all hours of the night when she worked homicide in Chicago. The animals were a warm welcome to a stake out in the middle of a Chicago winter and a criminal with an itchy finger. Right now, she just wanted to soak up the sun, drink her java, and know how terrible things were in the world.

Today was a better day than the last two days. Her multiple sclerosis had been flaring up, and she had been experiencing some balance issues, and her vision was beginning to blur. However, she still muddled through chores and ran the ice cream shop with a smile that hid her problems. Her left hand had also become partially numb, but she had learned to compensate over the past couple of years. She had also experienced a cascade of electricity shooting from her right shoulder, which continuously ran down her right arm. Still, her body never allowed her to discharge the electricity from her fingertips. If she could do that, she'd have a superhero costume and would be lighting up criminals.

Paisley had seen her MS neurologist in Chicago about a month ago. Thankfully, her most recent MRI showed a slowdown in her spine and brainstem lesions. Although the medication and the infusions had contributed to slowing the progress of the disease, there was no cure. The worst thing was the unexpected MS hugs that she received, which felt like an angry bear hugging her and squeezing the life out of her. At least she could still control her bladder and bowels. When she was first diagnosed with multiple sclerosis, Paisley had difficulty controlling those two functions. Her first neurologist, Dr. Myron Axon, told Paisley that she would most likely never be able to walk without a cane or walker. She proved Dr. Axon wrong on that prognosis.

Once upon a time, Paisley had been a Chicago detective and a damn good one. At the time of her MS diagnosis, she was a senior detective. Before becoming a detective, she had been an eager beat cop who shot through the ranks like a rocket. In all her years working in law enforcement, Paisley had been able to earn and retain the respect of supervisors, peers, and most of the criminals she had arrested. She made every attempt to close all her cases by working long hours, often at the loss of family time and sleep, to catch criminals and follow up on leads. She had only fired her gun fifty times while in the line of duty, but she made sure to tell everyone that she did not fire first. Paisley had to only kill someone once, and that was fairly traumatic. Paisley was given no choice when the perpetrator created a situation that put someone's life at risk. Some of her cadet friends were not as lucky. Over the years, five of them had been killed in the line of duty. Paisley knew that she was blessed, and she thought that she could continue to work without placing herself or others at risk, even with MS.

Then things started to go south. Paisley began having problems using her fingers, and her legs started going numb at year 23 on the job. Her ability to concentrate and think through cases often became impaired, or she became more forgetful. She was still good at solving cases, but things came to her slower. Days of running down thugs were left to the younger detectives trying to make a name for themselves or beat cops who wanted to get recognition. Her glory days on the force were now just memories.

Chicago Dr. Gloria Applegate had been Paisley's general practitioner for over fifteen years before Paisley moved back to Wolfe County, Kentucky. Dr. Applegate initially treated Paisley's complaint as a sciatic nerve issue. However, when Paisley woke up one morning six months later and had pain and numbness in her feet, and she had lost control of her bladder, she knew something was serious. Dr. Applegate had CT scans ordered, but nothing on the initial scans indicated a significant issue. It would be two months later that the answer would be known. It took a fall while getting out of the shower for Paisley's doctor to begin understanding her medical issue. If it had not been for her daughter's nagging to see the doctor again, Paisley's condition would have been addressed later, causing her treatment and setbacks in recovery. As soon as Dr. Applegate found out about the fall, she admitted Paisley to the hospital. Six days into the hospitalization, she had been put through numerous tests, including a spinal tap and multiple scans, but nothing conclusive. She was discharged before an answer could be provided.

    It felt like a sharp knife being plunged into her heart a million times when the diagnosis came. She was told that she would receive treatment for relapsing-remitting multiple sclerosis. Dr. Applegate further informed Paisley that her physical and cognitive abilities would be impaired at times, and her symptoms would worsen, improve, and then reappear again. Paisley was in denial of her condition and its ramifications on her work and family, and she was anxious to get back to work. She was referred to a young and cutting-edge neurologist, Dr. Axon, who did an infusion treatment with her. This seemed to work well in the beginning and allowed Paisley to go back to work. However, Paisley was never the same.

    Paisley provided very little information about her childhood and family to her fellow officers. She felt some personal aspects of her life were not any of their damn business. Remaining private preserved her culture and prevented being teased by her police brethren. Charlie was the only one besides her family that knew she still secretly listened to the great country legends, liked a fried bologna sandwich, roamed the park with her shoes off, and had MS. Her supervisor was only informed that Paisley had an unspecified medical issue that required her to be off work for an unknown period. Most of the detectives in her homicide unit thought she had cancer, and others speculated that she was trying to get some type of compensation. Charlie had known Paisley for over twenty years, and he knew that she was an up-and-up person who loved her job. He constantly defended her, and Paisley knew it. Anyhow, Charlie was her best friend.

After a year of sitting at a desk, Paisley knew it was time to hang it up. Besides, she was stressed just thinking about the scum that she wasn't catching that she read about; the stress was not good for her. Paisley's job now mainly consisted of consulting, which was difficult for her to adjust to. After two teens who attended her daughter's school were killed in a school shooting, she was convinced she needed a change. So, she retired and moved back to her home state to the county where she swore she would never return.

Paisley's daughter Kansas was very understanding and supported her mother. It's not always common for a 15-year-old teenager to do this, but she and her mother had been through a lot since Kansas' father had died. Kansas liked the idea of living more rural and greener. She was one of these teenagers who wanted electric/hybrid cars over straight gas-fueled ones. She was about the environment, and maybe she could bring some of that to the people of Wolfe County. Without much hesitation, Paisley sold their home, loaded up their belongings, and bought a piece of property that once belonged to her Great Aunt Lula and Hurst Adams.

Kansas' father's parents had died over ten years ago, and there were no living relatives left in Kentucky. In fact, there were very few relatives on Paisley's side still living or worthy of being in a relationship with which only left only Gregory's family. Since moving, Paisley tried to ensure that Kanas maintained a connection with her father's family and allowed Kansas to make numerous visits back home to visit cousins in Chicago.

Settling back into country life was not as easy as Paisley thought it would be because old habits are hard to break. Within a week of moving there, Paisley started following the local crimes in the *Wolfe County Gazette* newspaper. The biggest crime her first week living there involved a stolen tomato plant taken from someone's porch and a spare tire from their garage — nothing like Chicago crime. She quickly deduced that the Gulligold boys, who lived across from the crime scene and ran a junkyard, were the culprits. It took the local police two months, and she had solved it in five minutes. She thought about calling it in, but she remembered that she was not supposed to pull herself into police work per her promise to Kansas.

She had not always been a big city detective. She grew up two miles from her new home. Her parents were farmers too. Sadly, she couldn't visit the old homestead anymore. It was made into a nature reserve to rehabilitate wild animals for the Eastern Kentucky area. Paisley had given it all up to become more worldly, protect the innocent, and solve crimes rather than figuring out the best time to plant and what to feed a cow. Despite what she did, Paisley's parents supported and loved her. They worried about her but felt that she was making a difference in this world.

Regardless of her Chicago culture exposure, Paisley was still a country girl at heart. As a teenager, she had been in the FFA and ridden horses on her daddy's cattle farm. Paisley had even raised two pigs to show off at the county fair in high school. When she moved back home, she shifted more toward poultry and goats. That experience paid off because goat milk was used as an alternative for making some of her ice cream flavors. Fresh country eggs, which were part of some of her ice cream recipes, added to the richness of her ice cream. It didn't hurt that they made the best omelets. When she got antsy and wanted some excitement to decrease the boredom on the farm, she bought an off-road vehicle to play in the mud on the backcountry roads and trails.

Something caught Paisley's interest this morning in The *Lexington Sentinel*, which was the primary state paper. There was a piece regarding missing pregnant teens across the United States. The article implied there were not enough efforts being made by law enforcement to find these young women. It further suggested that these girls' poor socioeconomic status was the primary reason for not putting resources into the investigation. It listed over one hundred pregnant teens who had been reported missing from Kentucky in the past five years. One of the state police head honchos stated that it was being looked into and that the case was a high priority. Paisley knew what that meant — we know about it, but we'll get to it at some point.

Paisley finished the article and told herself to keep her theories to herself. She was making ice cream and not solving crimes. A knock on the back porch was heard, and Paisley shuffled off to answer it. It was Gary Quaillan. He always came over at 5:30 a.m. to have coffee with her. Morning coffee and bullshit had been their established routine since she purchased the land from him. The two had immediately hit it off when they first met. When they started talking about national crime trends, growing up on farms, and losing people close to them, they realized they had a lot in common with each other.

Farm life was an everyday conversation between Gary and

Paisley, along with any unsolved crimes that were making noteworthy news. Like Paisley, Gary was a widower, and his wife Vivian had died two winters ago from a heart infection. Vivian was only sixty-seven. Neither talked very much about their deceased spouses, but both shared the mutual experience which seemed to strengthen their friendship bond. More than anything, Gary loved mystery novels, detective-based shows, and anything that involved the word "crime" in it. He thought about becoming a policeman in his early days, but his daddy's health problems required him to take over the family dairy business.

"I was reading about more of those pregnant women being kidnapped — such a shame. No leads and no one seems to care," he said, very concerned.

"Gary, you are right about that. If these girls had come from well-to-do families, it would have made the national papers and the FBI would have taken over the case. Local and state cops would have been chasing it full time," she said in some disgust about the law enforcement system's inadequacies and prejudices.

"Coffee is good this morning. Did you take my suggestion about adding a little chicory?"

"Nah, I just cleaned the Keurig. How's Doodle today?"

"Spry for a three-year-old rooster. I hadn't told him that one of his gals was headed to the pot tomorrow night. Probably upset him."

"Which one?"

"Caroline. She's chicken and dumplings."

"Sounds good. Alas, poor Caroline, she gave her life to feed your cholesterol."

"I know it. Kansas ready for school to start next week?"

"You know Kansas. When is she ever ready? She's complained

about living here since we opened shop and started taking care of critters. In the beginning, she was all for it, until she had to work."

"She'll adapt. Give her time to find some good friends and maybe a boyfriend."

"Slow down there, matchmaker. Your grandson Ephrem might like her, but she's only interested in books right now."

"I'll try to tell Ephrem to hold off on courting her. He's sixteen, got a license, and can drive a tractor."

"She's fifteen, has a second-degree blackbelt in karate, and can drive a parent crazy."

"Got the point. Needless, that boy drives me crazy. When his daddy and mama died — I thought I was done raising kids. Ephrem is kin, though. I couldn't abandon him, and I love him as much as Doodle."

"Loving kids like a rooster. That's a new one."

"You opening at ten o'clock today?"

"Yeah, but I got to get in by six-thirty. I'm running low on Buttermilk Blackberry, Strawberry Shortcake, and Blueberry Pie Crumble ice creams, and they take time to make and freeze."

"It's Monday, so I'll be there for my usual today. Don't spare the whipped cream."

"It's free too. You made that part of the land purchase deal. Oh, don't get me started on getting my main dairy supply from your cows."

"Best milk and cream in the state. My state fair blue ribbon every year tells me that."

"Best of all — you get to have all the ice cream that you can eat as long as you live. You are quite the bargainer."

"You have to when you are dealing with greedy banks, stubborn mules, disobedient cows, and hens who can go on strike anytime and not choose to lay an egg."

Gary finished his coffee and then went back to complete his morning chores. The senior farmer had some help from his grandson and a few part-time neighbors, but he did most of the work himself. He had grown up in hard times, and his family barely had enough to scrape by growing up. They ate a lot of squirrels, opossums, and groundhogs when meat was scarce. Gary knew about hardship and the pain of losing someone, so it was easy for him to relate to Paisley. He considered himself a trusted friend, and he believed that she thought the same of him.

Paisley woke her tired daughter up from a deep slumber to help at the ice cream shop. She told her that no work meant no money for a car, which was a motivator. The red-haired, fair-skinned, freckled Kansas got up, showered in five minutes, and came down to grab a cold coffee drink. They left five minutes later after setting the home alarm and ensuring her big Australian Shepherd Duke was let out.

Paisley still carried a gun, kept a collection of firearms in the home, and maintained a security system to ensure the safety of her and her daughter. Back in Chicago, she had been part of a special forensic crime unit that worked on the most heinous and bloody crimes. She was good at her job, and she knew how psychopaths behaved and thought. Even after leaving the CPD, Paisley still worried that one of the former criminals she had tangled with would come for her or her family.

Even after her husband was killed, she continued to catch killers. It was what kept her going — that and getting justice for her husband's murder. If it weren't for her MS, she would have continued until they drug her out of the precinct. Being a detective had long hours, pulling her away from Kansas. With the MS, Paisley needed to spend more quality time with her daughter before her condition grew worse. Kansas had already lost her father, and she wanted some normalcy for Kansas as well.

The drive from the farm to the store was fifteen minutes. The city of Fester was small with four traffic lights and mostly one-way streets, and everyone was Mayberry-friendly. The ice cream store had been a former gas station that went out of business and had been abandoned for over ten years.

While Paisley turned on all the lights and worked on getting ingredients together, Kansas was sent to fetch some heavy cream from the walk-in refrigerator. Before she even opened the door, her mother texted her to bring eggs too. Then came the text from Ephrem asking Kansas what she was doing. Kansas was already aggravated; her mother and Ephrem were pushing her buttons this morning.

Kansas swung the door open and stepped into the large, freezer room while texting Ephrem. Not paying attention to her environment, she fell over something on the floor, and found her ass and cell phone brutally landing on the subzero tile. When she picked her phone back up, she noticed that she now had a crack at top right side matching the other one on the opposite side of the phone.

She muttered to herself, "Damn idiot workers. Leaving a mop or broom in the middle of —"

When she turned around and saw there was no mop or broom but something else that had caused her to go down, Kansas screeched at a deafening level. Paisley heard her daughter screaming; since old habits never die, she drew her gun from her ankle holster and made her way to the back of the store. She was just glad this was on a good day, and her MS allowed her to use her hands to grip things.

CHAPTER THREE

A body in her walk-in refrigerator — this would not be good for business. Paisley made sure that Kansas was good before she helped her up. Kansas was tough but not quite as tough as her mom. She never forgot that her mother had done for a living before coming out to *Green Acres*. Paisley looked over the crime scene and examined the victim. She was careful not to disturb anything and wore the nitrile gloves she used for working in the kitchen.

Paisley had Kansas call the local police, but she could only leave a voice mail. Feeling old habits falling back in place, she had Kansas take a seat in their office so she could check out the crime scene. After all, she had more experience with homicides than these local elected officials had in a lifetime.

The victim was young, probably not more than seventeen. She was dressed in sweats and a University of Kentucky tee shirt. She appeared to be well-fed, and there were no signs of drug use. She had most of her teeth, so meth was probably not an issue. From the marks around her neck, she appeared to have been strangled by a coarse rope.

    A pool of frozen blood had formed underneath the victim's head on the cold tile. Paisley looked closer, and she saw the source of the blood — a missing ear. The victim appeared to have defense wounds on her forearms from being struck hard by some object. There was a large abrasion on her forehead from being battered as well. The victim's ear seemed to have been removed by something sharp, such as a knife. Paisley noted several other cut marks on the victim's face, hands, and arms. Paisley thought the perpetrator might have accidentally slashed the ear off. She estimated that the teen had died around four to six hours ago. Paisley further noted that the victim's stomach protruded to some extent. She thought that maybe the stomach bloating was gas filling up the intestines because she was starting to decompose, but that couldn't be too much of a factor when she was in the walk-in freezer. Then she realized that the girl had been recently pregnant. Could she be one of the young girls that were being abducted?

    Paisley stopped theorizing and trying to piece the crime together when Fester Sheriff Gerald Stone and his deputies, Zeke Guffey and Jasper Hock, walked into her shop.

    "Okay, which one of you called this in?" Sheriff Stone said, looking at Paisley and her daughter.

    "I did," said Kansas.

    "I'm —" Paisley tried to explain who she was but was cut off by the sheriff.

    "We'll get to that. You all are new to this county, aren't you?"

    "Yes and no. Not that it matters now, given the current situation," Paisley sarcastically said.

    "Well, in my position, you hear things. Nice shop. Too bad it's a crime scene. We'll need to question both of you at the station while we do our CSI thing here," Sheriff Stone said in the utmost confidence of his department's competence.

"Can't. We didn't get that equipment request. I just hadn't told you," explained an embarrassed Deputy Hock.

"Well, now I got to call the damn state police to do the crime scene. Call them, Jasper," Sheriff Stone said with disgust and frustration in his command.

"I could help if you like," Paisley responded.

"Now, what would an ice cream shop owner know about crime?" the Sheriff Stone sarcastically asked.

"My mom was a detective in Chicago for twenty-four years, for your information. How long have you been walking the beat?" Kansas said, annoyed by the obnoxious sheriff's attitude.

"Oh, I see you are a backtalking one. You'd better get her under control. I doubt a "woman" police detective would move to good old Wolfe County, let alone Fester, especially after living in Chicago. Sorry, mam. But if you are a detective, then I am a brain surgeon." The sheriff said, smirking, satisfied with his zinger.

"Wow. I'd love to be as clever as you think you are. If you'd quit talking and get investigating, you might have a chance to catch the killer," Paisley retorted.

Deputy Guffey, who had been quiet, snorted and covered his mouth when the sheriff glanced at him.

"Mam, I'm going to have to ask you to watch what you say. Disrespecting an officer of the law —"

"Officer. You're an elected stool pigeon. Half the town says it. I'd be —" Paisley added.

Noticing her gun partially sticking out from her pants, Sheriff Stone drew his firearm and pointed it at Paisley. "Deputy Guffey, please remove the firearm from the owner of this establishment."

"What are you doing? I have a right to carry a concealed weapon in this state. Are you crazy? The victim in the cooler has not been shot," responded Paisley to the threat.

"I'll be the judge of that," Sheriff Stone said in response. Deputy Guffey took Paisley's handgun and put it in his jacket pocket. "Deputies, please escort these two ladies in handcuffs to the station for questioning. If they open their mouths, charge them with obstructing justice and disrespecting an officer."

Each deputy pulled out a set of handcuffs and had the ice cream makers put their hands behind their backs. All Paisley could think of was "Welcome to Deliverance." They were both escorted out of the shop to the police car. Twenty or more people watched the show from across the street. Paisley wanted advertising for her store; she got it — just not in the manner that she expected.

CHAPTER FOUR

The little jail cell was fairly clean — cleaner than any cells in that she had ever seen in Chicago. In this *Twilight Zone* version of Mayberry, this town's Andy Taylor was either a pathological megalomaniac or working on being the best asshole he could be. Deputy Zeke Guffey locked Paisley and Kansas in their cell and walked off to finish his chocolate iced Krispy Kreme doughnut and coffee while listening to the morning Trading Post on the radio. The Trading Show was a radio call-in segment of WRJK 59.9 AM that allowed people to trade and sell things five days a week. It had been around since Paisley was a little girl. She recalled her grandparents buying and selling items through it all the time — some things in small towns never change.

"Well ... Do you think we will get to call our attorney or someone?" asked Kansas.

"I'm wondering that myself," Paisley responded while testing the bunk to ensure it supported her weight. "Wasn't sure if this thing was sturdy enough to support a fly. I certainly didn't want to bust my rear."

A phone rang at the deputy's desk, and a few minutes later, he walked back with a portable phone. He placed it in a tray and slid it through the meal slot in the cell bars.

"Make your one call. Then put it back on the tray and push it through to the other side, tough lady," the deputy commanded while keeping one hand on his pistol.

"Sure," Paisley responded politely.

"Mom, who are you going to call?"

"Well, we don't have any relatives left living here, but I have this family friend. I believe he can help us. The problem is I don't have his number memorized."

"Now what?" asked her concerned daughter.

"Hey! Mr. Deputy. The number I need is in my contacts on my cell phone. I know I can't have it, but could you look up the number. I got memory problems. What do you expect — I'm originally from here?"

Deputy Guffey was ready to deny her request before she finished her sentence, but then he looked at Kansas and felt some sympathy for the teenage girl. He knew about those young girls disappearing around the state, and his heart melted a little. He also remembered from his trauma training that being exposed to someone killed could be traumatizing, and he should be offering some support — no matter the circumstances.

"Okay, I'll let you use your phone, but you gotta give it right back. Don't need to be making the news with some crazy-ass video about jails and abuse of women. Not that that has happened here or anything. I mean, that lawsuit was thrown out against the last sheriff."

The portable phone was traded for the cellular. Kansas was not informed who her mother was calling. She thought that she'd probably call Gary since he knew everyone in the town. After a few seconds of pleasantries with the party on the other end of the phone, Paisley simply explained the situation to the person and promised to make them dinner and catch up with them real soon.

After her cell phone was reclaimed and bagged in the personal property envelope, Deputy Guffey went back to his desk to finish the last few minutes of the Trading Show. He had so hoped that someone would be selling a small boat for fishing over at Cave Run Lake. However, his enjoyment was cut short after a few minutes when the sheriff came into the office. He was red-faced, and he appeared as if someone had kicked him in the gonads. He chewed Zeke out and began a tirade about why no one tells him anything. Paisley knew what had happened and was just smirking the entire time. Kansas was perplexed by her mother's behavior and finally had to ask.

"Who did you call?"

"Just, wait for it. 5 — 4 — 3 — 2 — 1."

Sheriff Stone was now profusely sweating, taking the cell keys, and turning them in the lock. "Well, I guess you are special after all. Better get home. Still got your ice cream place taped off for an investigation. State police are there right now."

"Thank you," Paisley smugly replied.

"Zeke, give them a ride back to their car. I wouldn't want them to have any problems. Oh, make sure they get all their belongings back," Sheriff Stone added.

"That's very nice of you, Sheriff," Kansas commented.

"Please, my apologies. Sometimes —" Sheriff Stone tried to

finish his sentence before Paisley cut him off.

"Forgiven. We just want to get back to making ice cream. Little frail women like us — that's all we are meant to do."

On the ride back to the Ice Cream Shack, Kansas still wanted to know what had happened to get them released so quickly. Seeing her daughter was impatient, Paisley spilled the beans.

"Uncle Sturgill, also known as Frank Sturgill Prescott, III, was a mentor to me growing up. He helped guide me and ultimately led me to be a police officer. He was one of my daddy's personal friends and my godparent. It doesn't hurt that he's also the district judge here."

"That explains a lot. You think he set the sheriff straight?"

"At least for a short time. Men like Stone — male chauvinist — hard to keep them in their place very long."

Deputy Guffey pulled into the parking lot of their ice cream shop. Even with the circumstances, Paisley still thanked the deputy. The deputy did not return the gratitude with "You're Welcome" but grunted and drove off.

"Looks like the Kentucky State Police are still gathering evidence. The coroner has probably already come and taken the victim to the state for an autopsy. That's standard procedure," Paisley noted while looking at the crime investigation going on at her shop.

"Mom, this is kind of creepy, you know. I'm a cop's — former cop's daughter, but it doesn't mean that I like talking about crime anymore."

"I forget. Your newest thing is to travel the world and learn romance languages."

"You're one to talk about changing gears in life. You're a former cop selling ice cream in the small town that she grew up in."

"Can't knock that. Go ahead and start the car and get it cooling off. I see someone that I want to talk to."

CHAPTER FIVE

Paisley made her way over to a middle-aged man with thick black hair with slight graying at the temples, sporting a goatee and mustache. He was at least six-two and weighed 200 pounds. He was muscular and looked like he had a washboard for an abdomen. He was just getting off his phone when he heard a whistle, and someone yell out to him. He turned around and squinted his eyes to see who was making all the noise.

"Yo, Stretchie! You got this case covered?" Paisley inquired in a serious tone catching the man off guard.

"Paisley. Is that you? What the hell? It's been eighteen years since I last saw you. It was at that police convention in Chicago. You were a promising cop on a fast track to detective. How are you doing?"

"Wondering how much longer you are going to be keeping me from making money?"

"What?"

"This is my ice cream shop."

"Oh, I didn't know. Are you living here now?"

"Yep, retired for medical and sanity reasons."

"I didn't know. I work most of the homicides in this area. Been a detective for the past ten years. Got tired of traveling roads and found solving murder cases was what I really liked."

"I miss it, but not the stress. It just exacerbated my medical issue. How's your wife? Gina — right?"

"Was Gina — now it's me, myself — Oh, less I forget there's I. My first marriage ended five years ago. Complained that living with a cop was lonely, and she was always scared I would be killed. Have a son from the marriage who's now sixteen. His name is Luke. He lives with his mom in North Dakota. If I remember right, you got a kid. She would be around —"

"Be fifteen, going on thirty. Her name is Kansas. She's out in the car. We just got out of jail."

"What?"

"We called the police about this mess you are investigating, and when the sheriff arrived — it went downhill from there. You see — I have a gun because I was once a cop, and you don't leave home without it. Then Sheriff Taylor and Barney arrested us and made me use my "Get Out of Jail Free" card. That's the short of it."

"I see you've met Sheriff Stone and his elite, competent law enforcement force. I'm betting the "Get Out of Jail Free" card was Uncle Sturgill. Stone means well, but he's more worried about the next election coming up more than listening to folks. Sorry about that. You know elected officials are voted in. Most are not former professionals with training. Stone is not likable for the most part, but he's honest. Never known to take a bribe, just a drink now and then. He does have a problem with women. I'm sure you've encountered that already."

"First-hand. Glad to report that he's still a male chauvinist pig."

"Somethings will never change. You look good. I heard about your husband from Sturgill, by the way. I hated to hear that."

"We still don't have any answers. It's a cold case that's frozen solid these days. I still keep looking for clues, but everything has dried up."

"I've heard how good you were. You caught a lot of the bad guys. I think you will eventually catch him, her, or them. Where are you living?"

"Bought a piece of land next to old man Quaillan along with part of his farm. Gary and I have coffee together every morning. Older men make better lovers," she said, smiling while trying not to think of her geriatric neighbor of being naked.

"In his case, older men make better corpses at the funeral home. He has got a heart condition. The local barber at Campbell's tells me about everyone when I sometimes stop in for a haircut. It could be gossip, but whether it's the truth or not — you know how this town is."

"Life in a small town."

"Do you miss the work?"

"Sometimes. Like right now, I'm thinking that there's a connection between the missing pregnant girls identified in the newspaper and this one."

"I've thought of that. If you have time to discuss the case, I could make it official and get you on as a consultant. I don't want to aggravate your medical issues, but I've known you since first grade, and there's nothing you couldn't figure out."

"Let me think about it. I've got some white chocolate, butter pecan, and vanilla ice cream to make. I still might be able to salvage the day with afternoon sales if you all clear out.

"Okay, Pastey. Here's my card. Give me a call when you are ready."

"Pastey? Really? You're going with that. My nickname was a more acute event. Yours is a life-long attribute and more suited."

"You should not have eaten the homemade paste in class," he said smiling.

Surveying the scene, Paisley scoffed. "Hurry up and clear out. I'd had this secured, bagged and tagged, and cleared out an hour ago. Chop, chop, detective. I got ice cream to make and bloodstains to clean up. I'd appreciate it, Stretchie."

"Yes, mam. Just as bossy as you were in high school."

"And then some," she said in a superior manner.

CHAPTER SIX

The entire day had not been a total waste. Paisley had reconnected with a former school buddy and a fellow police officer. She had also sold over fifty ice cream cones — thanks to the free advertisement of the police pulling in nosey patrons. She was also offered a consulting position.

When she returned home, she found Gary sitting in a rocking chair on her front porch reading a cooking magazine. For some reason, she was not surprised that he was there. She believed that Gary genuinely cared about her and her daughter.

Kansas ran ahead of her to get the first shower. Kansas only yelled out, "How's it going, Mr. Gary?" and sprinted into the house before Gary could answer. Paisley walked up to Gary and greeted him with a warm hello and full smile before heading upstairs for a less warm shower. Gary nodded in return and continued to read his magazine, which was upside down. He patiently waited for Paisley to come back to shoot the bull. Knowing Gary, Paisley guessed he probably already knew what had happened and would interrogate her.

From the bathroom window, Paisley noticed Ephrem in the distance driving the tractor around the field, cutting grass, and shaking his head to whatever music he was piping into his head. She realized that she needed to get some farm work, including her livestock, but she was not up to the job today. Perhaps, she could get Kansas to help her. She might even offer Ephrem some cash to take care of a few things.

After a quick shower to wash off the germs from the jail cell and crud from work, she grabbed a cup of coffee and sat in the rocker next to Gary.

"In the slammer. What are the neighbors going to say about you?" Gary said in a serious tone while continuing to look at his Kentucky Farm Foods magazine's recipe for a prime rib roast, which had now been turned right side up.

"You're the only neighbor for miles. I suppose that I'm going to hear about it right now," she responded in an annoyed manner.

"Margaret Gardner at the local IGA told me all about it while I was trying to pick out a head of lettuce. Nosey, old lady. So, glad I didn't marry that one. So, what happened? Thought I'd just get it from the horse's mouth."

"Just like any typical day. Got up. I went to make ice cream. Dead body found in the back area of the store. I called the local sheriff. He shows up. Sees that I carry a gun. He doesn't ask questions. He arrests me."

"I suppose that you just happened to bail yourself out."

"Nope. That'd be Uncle Sturgill."

"You got powerful friends. Knowing Sturgill, he probably

chewed on both sides of Stone's ass. Did you notice if Stone had any left when you got out of the hoosegow?"

"He still had some but very little left to hold both his pants and ego in place at the same time."

"So, what's the story about the dead body? It's time to chat about the crime. I just listened to the latest *Rural Crime* podcast. They say killings are blooming in small towns."

"This is Fester in the middle of nowhere in a county that everyone forgets. The only thing blooming here on most days is ragweed. By the way, I ran into an old friend who's a big Kentucky State Police Detective now. You remember me talking about Stretchie?"

"Stretchie. That's Janet Knight's boy — Bishop Knight. Used to help on the farm when he was younger. Worked hard — a little lazy on mucking out stalls — didn't like putting down new straw. So, is he working the case? Did he give you any insight? Tell me about the victim. Do you have any thoughts of a motive for murdering someone in an ice cream shop?"

"Slow down there, Sherlock. These are the facts. I entered the store at 7:55 a.m. this morning. While I was getting things ready in the front, Kansas went back to get some ingredients. There was a scream, and I ran back, and there was the victim. She was no more than seventeen, maybe eighteen. It was difficult to tell her age because she was covered in dirt and mud as if she'd been through a pigpen."

"What'd she look like?"

"She was probably around five-four, dirty-blonde hair — cut in a pixie style — her eyes were blue or maybe blue-green. She appeared to be wearing clothes that were twice her size. Even her shoes appeared to be too large. She also looked like she had been recently pregnant. She had numerous lacerations and abrasions, too — like from defending herself. She also had an ear missing, probably from a knife attack. Pretty sure she was strangled to finish her off."

"Damn savage attack. I know what you're thinking — she's one of those girls that might have been kidnapped like all those others that have been missing."

"It's too coincidental not to be. That's my gut feeling," Paisley said while rubbing her hand and arm roughly.

"Is it happening?"

"The numbness and tingling are manifesting their ugly little heads again. I'm afraid that a relapse might be coming on."

"Remember — no stress — just relax. Do you feel like talking more?" Gary concerned asked.

"I do. Something about talking about it seems normal to me. Too many years in the ditches — I guess."

"What did Stretchie say about it?"

"Not much. He just had the facts, and the body was sent off for an autopsy. He did ask me to be a consultant for them."

"What did you say?"

"I haven't talked to Kansas yet. She's fairly protective of me. If she even gets wind that I might be having a relapse —"

"Hell hath no fury like the scorn of a daughter."

"Sage one, I don't think that's the way that goes."

"Works for me. I only raised boys."

"I'll call my specialist tomorrow. I'm overdue for a check-in anyway."

"I can help if you need me to."

"I'll let you know. When am I going to get some of that

wonderful smoked butt again," Paisley asked while her stomach growled to signal that she needed to eat something soon.

"Come on. You think all I do is sit around all day smoking meat for you to eat. This isn't a BBQ joint, you know. I got a farm to run."

"You run it about as well as your mouth, Gary. Now get. I got chores of my own to do. I'll get Kansas on it or call for Ephrem to help if it gets too hard. I know he'll do whatever Kansas says anyway."

"He's whipped and doesn't even know it."

Gary left, and Paisley ate a snack. She'd heat up something from the freezer later for dinner. Feeling a little more energized, she went to her barn. She mucked out her two horses' stalls, fed and watered them, and made sure the chickens were up for the night in their coop and the tool room in the barn was secured. She took another shower to get rid of the sweat and animal stench, but she needed something to help cover up the smell of death left on her earlier today. After the shower, she added a bath with some Epsom salts scented in lavender which seemed to do the trick.

Supper was a frozen pizza and a premade salad that only required croutons, cheese, and store-bought dressing. Kansas picked at her salad for a good reason. There were some brown pieces and some parts that were starting to liquify. The salad was not out of date, but it was not fresh. The pizza was slightly overcooked, but it was eaten, and not much was said about it.

"Kansas, you remember that I said I would always be transparent with you about things. So, there are a few things you need to know. One — I've been asked to consult on the homicide regarding the girl found in our store. Two — I am starting to show signs that my MS is coming back. I can tell by my energy level and some of the physical issues that

I'm experiencing."

"Great, mom. Just great. This has been a shitty day already, you know. Consulting will just stress you out, and who do you plan on going to see for this? We aren't in Chicago anymore."

"Language, young lady. First, I think that the consulting will be a lot less stressful. I'm not in the field, and I won't be arresting or chasing criminals. Consider it as a researcher position. Second, I was referred to a specialist in Kentucky by Dr. Applegate, who lives about sixty minutes from us in Lexington — Dr. Anna Davis. From what I have been told, she's a little quirky, but she's considered one of the best. Worked several years at John Hopkins and Vanderbilt. I'm calling her tomorrow."

"Okay, but it's just you and me now. Who am I supposed to go to when I need someone, and you are incapacitated?"

"Listen, I'm going to be alright. You are making a mountain out of a molehill. We take one day at a time, preparing for what we can. Remember everything you learned in the MS family support group and don't forget we made a plan just in case this happened again."

"I know, but that doesn't make any of this easier. Kansas, I think we should talk about what happened at the shop. It's normal to be in shock after seeing a dead body and don't forget you did get thrown in the slammer."

A perturbed Kansas responded, "No, mom. I'm fine. I've seen your case files lying around for years and —"

"Why are you looking at my cases?"

"I've see all the pictures of victims and between rated R movies and other things on TV, I've been desensitized over the years. I'm okay."

"I'm just saying. These things have way of —"

"Drop it, please. If I need to get my head shrunk, you'll be the first to know."

Paisley blew out a deep breath and nodded in agreement. Kansas left, and Paisley knew her daughter was upset, but it was best to give her the space and time. Paisley took another long bath in some Epsom salts, hoping she might get some relief from aching joints and stress. Her aching joints were not from MS but related to arthritis. She had double trouble, and she did not want to tell her daughter about another medical condition.

The numbness and tingling in her extremities had subsided some, but she knew an MS episode was around the corner because hot water only tended to make her muscles and body feel worse, but it helped with her arthritis — damn if you do, damn if you don't scenario for sure. Then there it was — the feeling of electric current going down her body but then stopping part of the way and feeling like she was getting a little shock. She hated that feeling. Worst of all was the MS hugs that hit without warning.

Paisley dried off, almost losing her balance but caught herself on the sink. She did not need a concussion. She made it to her bedroom, took some ibuprofen, and laid down. While trying to read the news on her phone, she noticed that her vision seemed worst in her left eye. Things were indeed speeding up.

She fell asleep within fifteen minutes. She was thankful for that. If she had to restart infusions and meds again, she wouldn't be getting much rest due to the side effects. It would also rob her of her stamina, and energy for a couple of weeks — a luxury she could not afford at this time.

CHAPTER SEVEN

Paisley contacted Dr. Davis' office, and an appointment was scheduled for the following week. The nurse reviewed her symptoms and their severity over the phone and determined that she did not need to immediately see the doctor. Paisley hated waiting, but she could be a very patient person when she needed to be. Being patient is what helped her catch many killers. The adrenaline, the rush of solving the crime, the chase of the guilty (or highly suspected), and bringing the killer to justice is what gave her purpose in her job — she hated giving up being a cop.

Paisley's cell phone rang. The number was an unidentified 606 area code. She figured it was just another marketing jerk trying to sell her a warranty on her car or house. She declined the call and proceeded to work on her morning crossword puzzle. Then her phone rang again — the same number. Paisley realized this was a persistent salesperson, and she needed to mess with their mind.

"Is that you, President Truman?" Paisley asked while pretending to be a senile older woman.

"No. I was calling for Paisley Hunter, mam. Maybe I have the wrong number."

"Are you asking for me to vote for Ford again? I didn't like him as vice-president, so why would I put him in over Carter. Who did you say this was again?"

"I didn't. This is Bishop — Bishop Knight."

Changing back to her normal voice, Paisley surprised her old friend. "Stretchie, I'm sorry."

"Pastey. You've grown young and lucid. What was that all about?"

"Too many scams and marketing salespeople who are unwanted calling me."

"You had me fooled."

"How did you get my number? I remember taking your card but not giving you my number."

"I have access to so many things, including the sheriff's police report that has the info."

"I thought that you were waiting on me to call?"

"About that — the rushed autopsy came back. This girl's name is Pamela Pearson from Pikeville. She's been missing for over five months. She lived in a trailer court with her grandmother and twenty-two-year-old brother. She had given birth in the last few days. Anyway, the soil sample and the contents in her blood indicate she was living here in Wolfe County for a while. Those cases of missing pregnant girls across the state — I think they may be connected now."

"Interesting. Question is — what is the motive? Are these girls willing in the beginning, and then it changes? What is the reason for their abduction? Are we talking about a baby black market? What happens to the girls after the babies are delivered? Is this some macabre serial killer with a fetish for killing pregnant women? Lots and lots of questions."

"You're on a roll. Listen, I'm short on resources right now. Much of our resources are being directed toward protecting the governor while he's traveling through the state on his campaign. Not a popular man right now among those who are running drugs who'd take him out if they could."

"I need to see my doctor next week to give you a solid commitment — but — I guess it wouldn't hurt to browse a little. Where are you?"

"Look out your front door."

Paisley pulled back the curtains on her window, and Stretchie was standing there looking through the glass like a hungry dog waiting to be fed.

"What the hell? Can't cops knock? Get in here now," Paisley demanded in a joking manner.

"You know me. Always have a backup plan in case they won't answer the phone. Anyway, being in person makes it less likely you'll say no. Here's a copy of the autopsy report and the facts gathered on this case and all those others across the state. State of the art encrypted flash drive."

"Thanks, but I'm thinking that you just have too much information on me."

"The perks of being a cop. Beats the old days of thick papers, or you'd have a forest of papers to read through," he proudly said. The password is Stretch2890 — all together.

"Cup of coffee. No donuts. I know that's a bummer for a cop," Paisley offered, hoping he'd stay around a little longer.

"Coffee is fine, but I prefer green tea. I also like a bagel and plain cream cheese over a donut," he replied while patting his gut.

"I can do both. Just give me a few minutes."

The two old friends sat down for the next two hours and just caught up with each other. He talked about Luke, and she spoke about Kansas. They discussed his ex, and she talked about her frustrations over the stalemate of Gregory's investigation. Memories of high school and who they dated dominated the last part of their conversation. They had dated for about a year in high school and broke up on amicable terms.

Stretchie had always been an excellent friend to Paisley since they had shared a box of crayons in kindergarten. They had lost touch with each other after high school. There were the occasional social media "likes" and running into each other, but nothing to amount to anything. She had never thought of dating him outside of high school, but now, she was older and missing someone in her life. At forty-four, she would not get any younger, and if she found love again, she knew Gregory would understand. However, Kansas most likely would have an issue with it.

CHAPTER EIGHT

Lexa Reed had been in two residential group homes and three foster homes in the past three years. She knew she had mental health issues and didn't want to address them. She liked feeling the energy when she had a manic episode. However, her reckless decision to have sex with the older man giving her a ride was a mistake because she was now seven months pregnant and stuck in Nonesuch, Kentucky, with no food or money. At sixteen, she was street smart, but she had poor common sense regarding thinking before acting.

While in Nonesuch, she met another runaway, Douggie Grappler. Douggie was around her age. He told her that he had run from home because his parents didn't understand about him being gay. His parents were threatening to send him to a conversion camp ran through their church, and that's when he ran. Douggie's residence was under the same bridge with several other homeless youths. He had moved to a new place whenever he felt the urge to follow his instincts. For shelter, he lived in a small four-person tent that was battered and patched several times. He appeared to be respected and have some clout with the other youth. This made Lexa feel that she could trust him.

Douggie thought he could help her. He told Lexa about a woman who helped take care of girls and wasn't part of the system. He had offered to share his shelter and some of his Ramen noodles with her. He had her phone number and offered his cell phone for her to call. Lexa was slightly hesitant, but with a little bit more of his smooth rhetoric, Douggie convinced Lexa to trust him.

Lexa liked what she heard when she called. The woman who identified herself as Della said she would help Lexa deliver the baby and get her money. Lexa had no second thoughts about getting rid of her baby. After all, she would be a singing sensation, and a child would just drag her career down.

Lexa was an ideal victim. She had no family — they had died years ago in a house fire that her brother Lincoln had ignited. Lincoln killed himself a year later, and no other family was left to tend to her. Suicide and cancer had taken most of her remaining family out. She bounced around in the system until she just decided to go out on her own.

Unknown to Lexa, Douggie was a plant that got paid to recruit pregnant girls. He was over twenty and not sixteen. Douggie's main job was to identify desperate and needy girls who were pregnant. He had primarily been working in Kentucky, Illinois, and Ohio, but the person in charge said they had all kinds of operations in the United States and Canada, including the Virgin Islands. Douggie looked forward to a promotion and being away from this hellish job. As a reward, he was paid $500 for each pregnant girl he recruited and received one week a month in a nice hotel with new clothes and prepaid hotel food. He had heard about others who moved up that made more money, got their own homes, and a flashy new car. This was his goal.

A gray van with no identifying marks pulled up within an hour of calling. A grandmotherly woman introduced herself as Connie and the other pregnant girl in the van as Bonita. She had Lexa grab a seat in the back.

Connie promised to take care of her. She offered both the girls water. She handed them each their own personal pizza that she had purchased from Mama LaRisotta's Pizza Emporium. She informed Lexa that they would be traveling a bit and asked both girls to get some sleep after they had eaten.

Lexa noted that the other young pregnant girl was no more than thirteen or fourteen sitting there. She didn't acknowledge Lexa, and Lexa didn't care. She wasn't there to make a friend anyhow.

Both the girls were hungry. Neither had eaten much of anything in days. Within five minutes of eating, both felt light-headed and dizzy. Soon they both blacked out. Sometime later, they awoke in a small bedroom that looked like it had been converted to a prison cell. The windows had bars on them. There was a sink and toilet combination like they had in prison cells. A shower was built into the room and had shampoos and soaps like hotels provided. It was evident that these were stolen because one said Hilton Hotels. There was also a small dresser containing four sets of sweats, t-shirts, and flip-flops — none of which were their sizes. There was no television in the room, only books about nutrition and pregnancy.

Still foggy, Lexa was starting to get some of her senses back. That's when she noticed that she had a shackle around her right leg and was chained to the floor. She screamed out, and no one answered. The other girl who had ridden with her was still passed out. They were prisoners. For what purposes and for how long was a question. Whether she lived or not — that was something only her captives knew. For the first time in her life, she was concerned about her unborn child over her own life.

CHAPTER NINE

At 11:30 p.m., Kansas was up watching a documentary on Jim Morrison. She liked old music, and the Doors fascinated her — something she had inherited from her father. Although she was a devoted Beatles fan, she wanted to hear music from groups that experienced tragedies and then seemed to fade away. She often wondered who was the heart of the group that kept it afloat. Jim Morrison had definitely been the one who made the Doors memorable.

On the other side of the house, Paisley was unable to sleep. Although Paisley had taken a low dose sedative to help with some of her numbness and tingling, the medication wasn't strong enough to keep the sensations from keeping her awake. She would eventually sleep, but not so deep that she would allow a burglar to break into the house. She had an early warning system in case there was a break-in. Duke and their two corgis, Olive Oil and Popeye, would make sure to alert the entire house. No criminal, stranger, or piece of food would escape their keen senses.

Something hit Kansas' window. She thought it might be a bird but thought it was too late for a bird to be active. Then there was another hit to the window. It was weird that the dogs were not barking. Normally, the dogs were throwing a fit to get outside to investigate any noises or strangers around.

Curious, she went to check for the source of the noise. There was Ephrem. *What the hell does he want this time of night?* she thought. It certainly explained why the dogs weren't barking. They liked him more than her and her mother. Ephrem was always giving the dogs treats and playing with them.

Kansas and Ephrem had bonded as friends in such a short time. They liked a lot of the same foods, music, movies, and television shows. Obviously, he had something to say, or he would not be pestering her this late. Ephrem preferred in-person conversations instead of his cell phone to text or talk; she still preferred texting using social media to communicate. Lately, he had been showing up unplanned and ignored most of her texts to schedule a regular hang-out time.

Ephrem was a brawny, tall 17-year-old with auburn hair and brown eyes. He was handsome, and he had an attractive smile, enhanced further by his charming southern accent that Kansas could listen to all day long. Since moving to Wolfe County and hanging with Ephrem, she had noticed that her Chicago midwestern accent had been slowly changing. She caught herself picking up some of the countryside slang and was often teased for it by her Chicago friends when she FaceTimed them.

Kansas opened her bedroom window and climbed out onto her roof. Her overlook of the property allowed her to see who was coming miles down the road before they pulled onto their property. A few seconds later, Ephrem climbed up the trellis and joined her.

"You could have texted or called," Kansas said, trying to lie that she wasn't happy to see him.

"You know I like seeing you in the flesh."

"So, what's up?"

"School starts back next week. I'm a junior, and you're a sophomore which means that we've moved up the ladder."

"You didn't come to talk to me about that. Stop the crap. What's up?"

"Gramps told me about what happened. I've been meaning to come over, but I didn't want to — I didn't want to —"

"It's all right." There was a scratch at the door, and Kansas stepped back in to let her two corgis into the room. "You two are useless for protecting this house. That's why Duke gets all the treats. Alrighty — find your spots on the floor. You can sleep with me. No snoring, Olive Oil."

The two short-legged canines found their spots, spread out their short legs, showing off their bunny butts, and immediately went to sleep.

Stepping back out onto the roof, Kansas grabbed a blanket to keep the black off her bottom. She offered Ephrem a place to sit, and he moved as close as he could to her. Kansas looked at Ephrem now under the full moon. He was ripped for a sixteen-year-old. Farm life had been rewarding in that aspect.

"Getting back. Are you alright? It was a dead body."

"Eph, my mother was a detective for a long time. I used to look through her files when she wasn't around. I've seen lots of dead body pictures. This one just happened to be a real body. I screamed a little — only because it surprised me — but I didn't become hysterical. I'm fine."

"Good. You sure?"

"Yes."

"Listen, if you ever need to talk."

"I can always count on you and my roof for a conversation." Ephrem somehow managed to move a little closer, and they both sat quietly watching the stars. Kansas slid her hand into his hand. He reciprocated and wrapped his fingers around hers.

CHAPTER TEN

--- TWO YEARS AGO ---

Running as fast as she could, D.J. Pearson made her escape from the remote cabin resting in the middle of nowhere. She had used a bobby pin that she had found on the floor between the cracks to pick the locks on her shackles and the door to her room. She was known amongst adolescent thieves as "Pearson the Picker" — able to pick anything with any tool. After all, she had learned from the best — her child molesting father Larry the Locksmith. Larry the Locksmith had taught his daughter the ins and outs of burglary and how to get into a home without breaking a tumbler. She had been an expert lock picker since eight years old and used it to her advantage to escape from cop cars and juvie lockup. Now, she was about to have a baby.

They, whoever these lunatics were, had lied to her about the whole situation. As far as D.J. was concerned, she had been locked up against her will and forced to eat healthy organic crap. Darcie argued that D.J. and the others needed to be locked up for their own good because it was in their nature to run. *Just because everyone else was chained up didn't make it right*, D.J. thought.

Regardless of what was said, D.J. knew the real reason she and the others were secured was to prevent them from running off with an investment that was worth a hell of a lot more than she was getting paid. Although D.J. was promised fifty percent of $10,000 in cash before she had her baby, she had still not seen a dime. None of the other girls had been paid anything either. She was starting to feel like a fool, and that was one thing D.J. would not allow.

Like all adults she had in her life, those running the cabin constantly lied to her. D.J. knew that Darcie's empty rhetoric about this being some type of special program was utter bullshit. She knew Darcie was no therapist or doctor. She'd had enough therapy over the years to know legitimate treatment. The diplomas hanging on Darcie's wall were more than likely faked. Hell, she'd forged high school diplomas and social security cards many times to get a job long enough to build enough money to move around.

Then there was the latest lie — Darcie told D.J. that her high blood pressure indicated a high-risk pregnancy. D.J. had never shown any signs of having high blood pressure in her entire life. Yesterday, when Darcie stepped out of the medical exam room, D.J. checked her blood pressure, and it was normal. D.J. was no medical expert, but her granny had been a nurse and had taught her how to take someone's blood pressure and pulse.

The truth regarding her and the other pregnant girls' fates was revealed when D.J. witnessed Emily Fisher having her baby while trying to sneak out of the cabin. As soon as Emily had her baby, the baby was taken, and Emily was sedated again. Darcie and her goon partner wheeled an unconscious Emily into a room and left her. Another person dressed in a full hazmat suit soon entered the room and moved Emily to a metal table.

What D.J. saw next was abominable. She watched as this hazmat killer gutted her roommate and started slicing Emily into pieces and inserting them into freezer bags. D.J. held her vomit and watched until she couldn't watch anymore. This would be her if she did not escape. Now, she just needed the right moment to run and never look back.

When the person in the hazmat suit opened the cabin door, D.J. ran past the mad Butcher and escaped into the woods. She was able to find her way to the creek, where she spotted a canoe. She had remembered the basics of canoeing from 4-H camp to her good fortune and hoped she remembered enough to get downstream. She was lucky that she was being fed well, or she'd been too weak to paddle.

The moon was full, making it easier to navigate the water. At the end of the creek, three miles up, she spotted a bridge over the water connecting to the main highway. Even though she was wanted for theft, runaway, and assault, she was going to do the right thing for once. She would go to the police and let them know about this place. She was hopeful that maybe the cops would drop her charges, given the degree of criminal activity there. For the first time in a long time, she wished she had gone to live with her Aunt Jillian.

How she wished that she had never agreed to take a ride with that sweet little older woman in New Jersey. She brought her here to this hell. This was no damn home for wayward mothers in a serene setting like she had been told. Promises of money and a chance to change were promises for the soon-to-be dead. Just like they had been at home when her father had raped her numerous times while her drunken mother said nothing.

A cattle truck stopped and gave D.J. a ride. The driver's name was Dearborn Hollinger. He claimed to be a good Christian man and hated to see anyone left on the road. D.J. had managed to make up a story of being on a camping trip with her friends. She told Dearborn that she got into a fight with her friends, leaving them, but had no ride back. She also lied about being nineteen. She asked where Dearborn was headed, and he said he was on his way to a slaughterhouse located on the north Chicago side. She felt that she had just escaped from a slaughterhouse. Regardless, Chicago was fine with her because it put some distance between her and those psychos back in the woods.

Unlike most men she had known, Dearborn turned out to be a nice person and said a prayer for her before she got out of his truck. *Where to now?* That was her big question. Dearborn had been kind enough to give her a twenty-dollar bill. She needed food and shelter. The food would be easy, but her money wouldn't last long. A Big Mac, large fry, strawberry shake, and two apple pies seemed to please her unborn baby. A far cry from the tofu, green power salads, and other organic healthy crap that she had been fed for the past two months.

D.J. was due any time and worried that she wouldn't have enough strength to keep going. She had been small compared to the other young girls, but she was tough. She had used drugs before she found out that she was pregnant. At least, she was smart enough to realize that she didn't want to raise a child.

At 2:30 a.m., the street was fairly abandoned. She found a women's shelter a mile from the McDonalds and headed in that direction. As she was crossing the highway, she fainted in the middle of the road.

Luckily for her, an EMT returning an ambulance for some electrical repairs did not hit her. The EMT got out and helped D.J. into the back of the ambulance and got her to lay down on the stretcher.

The EMT started to call the hospital, but D.J. told him to hang up because the baby was coming now. Understanding the panic in her face, he hung up, pulled the ambulance over to the side of the street, and asked her to relax and let him do his job. He helped her remove her pants and gave her a sheet to put over her. He positioned her and took a look. She was a little over nine centimeters, and the baby had started to crown.

He asked her to begin pushing. Remembering her breathing, she began to push the baby out. They had told her she was having a little boy — they probably lied about that as well. Then again that may have been the only truth because moments later a beautiful baby boy was wrapped in a towel and handed to her.

The EMT insisted that she be taken to the hospital. She continued to beg him not to take her to one. Finally, he asked her if she was in trouble with the law or someone else. She was now petrified. The EMT asked her to consider the police because maybe the police could do something if she was scared of someone or something right now. D.J. looked at her newborn son and felt something that she had never felt before — love. Love for the thing that had given her heartburn, backache and caused so many problems. It didn't matter who the father was. She never had to tell her child who it was. Her baby was innocent. She would protect him. She would keep him and raise him differently than she had been raised. He looked like a Derrick. Derrick would be his name if she got out of this.

"Yes, please. Let me talk to the cops," D.J. replied.

"Okay, let's get you to the hospital first to get you guys a good check over. I know a cop who'd —" the EMT tried to say before the backdoor of the ambulance was jerked open.

Two men wearing masks pointed their guns with silencers at both of them and demanded that they be quiet and give them any cell phones. The EMT complied. D.J. just remained calm and held her baby tight. The taller of the two men got into the driver's seat and drove them around to an alley off the street, and then he returned to the back of the van.

"Who are you? What do you want? There are no drugs in this van," said a now angry EMT.

"We're here for the baby and that girl," said the smaller of the two men.

"You can't have my baby," cried D.J.

"That's not the deal," said the taller one, now pushing his gun into her head.

"How did you even find me?" D.J. asked.

"You're worth money, honey. There's a GPS tracker injected under your skin when you're first brought in. We do it while you are still out. None of you ever know it's there," said the short, plump assailant.

"What's this about?" demanded the EMT.

"Nothing, and that's all you need to know," the taller one shot back.

"You'll not be taking this baby or her any —" said the EMT as he stood up and tried to lunge at the shorter man.

The taller of the two thugs squeezed his gun's trigger twice. Both bullets went through the frontal lobe of the EMT's head and exited out the back of his skull, splattering the EMT's brains all over the back of the ambulance.

"She's not going to come willingly, and if anything happens to the baby —" the shorter man sputtered out before being interrupted by his partner.

"I'm not dealing with a "Taker," and you know I'd almost bet we'd be on the Butcher's block if we don't come back with the baby alive," commented the taller one.

"Well, I guess — the baby it is then. We just dump the body into the river," said the shorter of the two as he aimed his gun toward the girl.

"No. No. You can't. He's mine. I won't —" said a desperate D.J. fearful of her life.

Before she could finish her words, two bullets were squeezed from the short assailant's gun, striking D.J. in the head, and killing her. The baby lay in her arms with blood splatter on the towel and left cheek of the newly born infant. The taller assailant then took the baby and went on to their car.

Wrapping the dead mother in a sheet, the shorter of the two men finished cleaning up the scene. He needed to find a place to dump the girl's body away from the scene. The river was the best choice because most DNA washes out in the water.

Before they left, he decided to go through the EMT's wallet for some cash and viable credit cards. There was a VISA and an American Express. He might be able to sell the cards. There was very little cash — nothing but five tens, but that would buy three or four lunches. He tossed the wallet toward the front of the ambulance, and the following driver's license fell out:

Gregory Hunter
1597 Wick wood Lane, Apt. 2322
Chicago, Illinois 60602
Driver's License #: H555-4499-0001

The killers didn't flinch about leaving the abandoned ambulance and dead EMT. There was no need to worry about the dead EMT. EMTs get killed for drugs and robbed all the time. The shorter killer threw the dead girl into the back of the other car and drove off to find deep water. When D.J. was tossed into the water, an infant cried at the loss of his mother.

CHAPTER ELEVEN

The drive to Lexington was quiet and uneventful. Paisley wanted to make the trip a little fun and less serious for Kansas who was accompanying her. She thought they could go to the Fayette Mall and shop after her doctor's appointment. She hadn't bought Kansas anything new for the school year yet, and this was her chance to get on her good side. Although Kansas liked to shop, she felt her mother was more important than the newest fashions coming out. Kansas told her mother, no less than five times during the trip to Lexington, that she would make sure her mother followed the doctor's orders.

Physician's Drive was just off New Circle Road in a newly developed area for businesses. It was close to many suburban homes and was easily accessible off the main interstate. The wait time for Dr. Davis was only about thirty minutes. This was nothing compared to when Paisley's first saw her Chicago neurologist — a two-hour wait just to get an exam room.

To save time, Paisley had already completed her paperwork

online and was able to have her medical records transferred to Dr. Davis' office before her appointment. In her mid-fifties, Dr. Davis was a petite woman who liked to dress casually and for fun. She greeted Paisley with a friendly handshake and smile that made Paisley feel everything would be fine.

"Mrs. Hunter. Glad you could make it. I've reviewed your records, and I know you are anxious to get down to business. So, you think you are having a flare-up?"

"Yep. Seems to be some of the same signs that I had right before they diagnosed me with this."

"Well, let me do a quick review of your latest MRI, and then we'll get to some preliminary testing.

Dr. Davis reviewed the MRI images that were taken twelve months ago. She did a lot of noise making that doctors do when they are in deep thought or examining documents. She looked at the last notes written by Paisley's old neurologist Dr. Axon. Kansas tried to act uninterested, but her attempts to fake texting caught her mother's attention, who gave her daughter a stern motherly look and some advice.

"Kansas. It's okay to be part of the discussion. It's what you do when you become an adult."

"Let's get another MRI and go from there. We have our own machine. Just much more convenient. I'll get to see the images by tomorrow morning. In the meantime, let's do some basics. Any problem with your vision?"

"Nothing that remains constant."

"Problems with strength in your hands, legs, or fingers?"

"Hands seem weaker, and I'm feeling a little off balance when I walk."

"Numbness and tingling in your extremities?"

"Yes."

"How about incontinence or numbness in the saddle area?"

"No accidents but starting to feel numbness there."

To assess Paisley's walking speed and gait, Dr. Davis led her to the hall and had Paisley walk back and forth the hall's length. Dr. Davis then assessed Paisley's arms, legs, and hands for strength and sensitivity. Finally, Paisley was asked to follow the doctor's finger to evaluate her vision.

"I can see some things are slightly regressing based on the notes from your last visit with Dr. Axon. The amount seems minimal, but the MRI will tell us more.

"I see you are not on anything right now. Let's start a dose of steroids. I think we want to look at some options. I'll wait on your results, and then I'll contact you tomorrow afternoon. I see your insurance is one that generally cooperates with doctor's orders. That'll be helpful. You're also a retired police officer. Good to see a woman in a male-dominated world making a mark."

"She was a detective too. Solved all kinds of homicides," Kansas proudly bragged.

"I feel safer already. I bet you are her cheerleader and her mother when she needs it," commented Dr. Davis.

"Whenever and however, she needs me to be there, I take the most befitting role," Kansas stated.

"Paisley, it looks like I don't have to worry about home support. I've sent a script to the pharmacy next door. Just pick it up on your way out. Call me if anything happens before I call you with your test results. Brian will take you down for the MRI in a few minutes."

They left the doctor's office as soon as the MRI was completed. It was not as unpleasant as Paisley had thought it would be. She was glad to have someone who seemed cool and made her feel at ease. Having Kansas there was a great asset as well.

"Mother."

"Okay, let me have it."

"Mother, you have to promise me that you'll keep your appointments, take your medicine, and keep your stress level – very low. Before you begin to object, let me remind you that I'm in this with you and have been since the diagnosis."

"Okay. I get the picture. I promise." All the while, she was thinking *I promise that I will keep myself occupied with low-stress cases — maybe.*

The trip to the mall was a reward for both of them. Kansas found more clothes on sale than she had anticipated, and Paisley found a new pair of boots for stomping around the farm in style. As an added bonus to their outing, a text from the screen printing company located in the mall indicated their new t-shirts had come in. Now ice cream patrons could pay the fair price of twenty dollars for a comfy cotton shirt that promoted their ice cream wherever the purchaser traveled.

Paisley sometimes forgot how she had decided to be an ice cream artist. But it was in her blood, just like being a cop was. On her mother's side, her grandfather owned an ice cream shop in Lebanon, Ohio. She spent two months working there and learning to make ice cream every summer. She liked making ice cream as much as she liked putting away bad people. It was relaxing, and it gave her a sense of purpose, especially when she saw little kids make a mess and smile.

Three cups of coffee and four hours later, Paisley began intensely reviewing case-related documents after rising and doing chores. Sally Hemmings, the manager of her ice cream shop, was in charge for the next week so Paisley could focus on the case. Part of that was Paisley's doing, and the other was Kansas' to reduce her mother's stress. Sally was dependable, loyal, and strict, but she was not always customer friendly. She was a local girl who graduated high school last year and didn't have an interest in college and wasn't stepping foot outside the town. She applied for the position and was hired without hesitation. From the get-go, Sally showed a knack for making sweets. She had even come up with some flavor combinations like blackberry and peach cobbler with pie crust ice cream and lavender and lemon sorbet.

 As Paisley read through the documentation, she was astounded by the number of missing pregnant teens. There were over 153 cases of missing teens suspected of being pregnant just in Kentucky in the past two years alone. This did not take into account those that went unreported or runaways who fled from Kentucky. Some of the reports indicated that several other states had shown an increase in the number of female youth suspected of being pregnant and missing too.

 Paisley continued reviewing every case that Stretchie had provided to her. Her ice cream shop victim, Pamela Pearson, had been an unfortunate casualty of neglectful parents and a child welfare system extremely short of resources. Pamela was originally from Pikeville and had been reported missing for a while. She had hidden her pregnancy from others because no one interviewed at the time of her disappearance seemed aware that she was pregnant. Her second cousin, Rachel Fluker, finally came forward and spilled the beans. Rachel informed social services that Pamela was pregnant and that the father was most likely her adult half-brother Sidney because he was known to rape girls in the family.

Additional interviews conducted by the police reported that Pamela had been spotted in Hazard, Kentucky, before she was declared missing. Pamela had a cousin, Martha Deary, living there, and it was suspected that she had hidden out there for a while. The cousin was not initially forthcoming with the truth because her cousin was on parole but came clean after being threatened with a parole violation. One of Martha's neighbors reported seeing Pamela talking to a male in downtown Hazard several times where a homeless youth hung out. The only description given regarding the male was that he appeared to be an older adolescent, had a shaved head, displayed a wizard's wand tattoo on the left side of his neck, and was about five-eleven.

Drawing from her profiling skills, Paisley began a list of common traits of the missing girls:

- Pregnant
- Under eighteen
- Little to no family support
- Domestic violence likely in their homes
- History of runaway behaviors
- Promiscuous, possible prostitution or sex trafficking involvement
- Most likely experienced moderate to severe trauma
- Attachment issues, possibly reactive

Although not all of the victims shared the same issues, many had the following:

- Removal from their biological homes
- Psychiatric/psychological issues
- Substance abuse
- Anger issues
- Victims of rape/incest

Paisley began to write down Kentucky as a common factor, however, after she got done, she concluded there might be similar backgrounds with other victims in surrounding states, and perhaps the whole United States. The questions then became: Who is benefiting from this situation? Is this a centralized operation? Who are all the players because this would involve medical personnel, criminals, and maybe suppression of local and state law enforcement? She had one person connected to the FBI that she wanted to talk about this case — her old partner Charlie Yocum who joined the FBI after she left the Chicago Police Department.

The next day came quickly. It came quicker than Paisley wanted it to. She knew that Doctor Davis would be calling her back with her MRI results. At least Paisley had managed to make a ton of notes on the case. She'd already promised Stretchie that she would call him with her impressions. Right now, she had chickens to feed, a manager to tell which ice cream needed to be made, and an elderly neighbor sitting in her kitchen reading the local paper and drinking coffee who was eager for their regular morning chat.

"Looks like Slick Millworth's gas station was burglarized last night, according to the paper. Surprised it made it into this week's edition," Gary said as he clucked his tongue.

"What would anyone want from that dump? It's ancient and still has 1977 windshield wipers in the display case," Paisley added.

"Who knows? I see another worse crime."

"What?"

"Tomatoes are being sold for $4.59 a pound at the IGA. Highway robbery if you ask me."

"Next, you'll be telling me about arti — chokes three for $5.99 is a crime," she joked.

"No, that would be reasonable. So, what have you figured up about these gals missing? I saw you taking notes sitting at the kitchen table when I was taking my nightly constitutional to put the chickens up."

"Convenient viewing for that constitutional. I think this goes well beyond the borders of Kentucky and maybe expands to the whole United States. Who's in charge, who's profiting, who do they already own and control, and where's the central location of whoever is running this enterprise — those are just a few of the questions that need to be answered. I got a friend in the FBI that I'm going to pump for information, though."

"I think you'll figure it out. You're a smart one. Where's Olive Oil and Popeye at? They are usually here to lick my hands or try to take my bagel."

"I let them out this morning to do their rounds. Let them find any predators and any weaknesses around the hen house. Duke told me he was tired of doing all the work. Time to earn their keep. You know I use your cream and my eggs for this ice cream. I have to protect my interest. It's unlikely many predators around here bother dairy cows."

"Not unless they are human. The pups will keep you informed."

"If they want to be fed, they damn well better. We still on for dominos tomorrow morning?"

"You challenged your elder, so be prepared to pay the price of humiliation," Gary strongly stated.

"Well, it's only a peanut butter milkshake at Dairy Queen at stake, but it's worth it. I expect not one micro-ounce of it to have melted before you get home with it," Paisley demanded.

"I expect the same courtesy. Weird you own an ice cream shop and want your prize from an inferior ice cream place."

"I don't have to make it, and it's comfort —"

Paisley's phone rang, and she looked at the caller. "Sorry, we have to call it a short morning. It's my FBI connection. Let yourself out. I'll see you tomorrow."

Gary waved goodbye and left, taking his coffee cup with him. He'd return it tomorrow. It was a fairly common practice.

"Hey, Charlie. Big FBI guy. Thanks for calling me back.

"Paisley, you sound like you have a little country accent, or are you reverting to your natural state?" kidded her former partner.

"You got me. I've turned into a country bumpkin again. So, now that you've had your smart-ass moment, how are you? I haven't heard from you in over four months."

"Keeping busy with everything you can think of. Working on some political corruption in Cooke County. Nothing new there. How's your love life?"

"Who'd want an old broken-down cop making ice cream and

living in *Green Acres*?"

"Loving yourself there, partner."

"This is more than a catchup call. I'm doing consulting for a state police detective."

"You retired. Kansas will have your hide if you are adding stress —"

"She's already all over me. Anyway, I need to know if you have any national data on missing pregnant teens."

"Not my department or case normally, but I can see what I can do. Does this have to do with those pregnant missing girls?"

"Yes. I suspect that a lot is going on, and this is an organized crime racket. I need some data to figure out if I can find a pattern or any more connections."

"Give me some time, and I'll get back to you. Maybe, I'll make a trip down to see how my old partner is doing and see Kansas."

"Just give me a heads up, and I'll make sure I'm not working in the shop. I'll also need to clear the chickens out of the guest bedroom."

"You're kidding me."

"I'll leave that up to you to figure out. Thanks, Charlie."

"Bye."

Paisley hung up the phone and noticed the jolt of electricity running from her back to her left leg. She was now worried that she might be going down for the count.

Before Dr. Davis called in the afternoon, Kansas had made her mother promise that she would abide by whatever the doctor said. Paisley promised while keeping her fingers crossed behind her back. While waiting for a prognosis, the two of them worked on a new recipe. It was for a cherry cobbler ice cream that both had tried at another ice cream store. They believed they could replicate and improve upon the recipe. They bought tons of cherries from a local farmer and had stored lots of them in their freezer. Their first attempt resulted in the flavor being too sugary and the cobbler being way too soggy. The second attempt was too much vanilla. The third attempt was just right. They ate half the batch before writing the recipe down to prove it was the best recipe.

At a little after four o'clock, Dr. Davis called. The news was not as grim as Paisley had thought. There was some inflammation of the spinal cord but no new lesions. Dr. Davis emphasized taking the steroids and asked Paisley to schedule an appointment next month. Dr. Davis would determine if she needed an infusion at that time. In the meantime, she asked Paisley to keep her stress levels low. Paisley informed the doctor that she had already increased her yoga to twice a day and planned on doing yoga with their pigmy goats. Dr. Davis smiled and considered it an interesting method, but she knew people paid good money to do that with animals.

After asking a few more questions to Dr. Davis and hearing the doctor actually indicate that consulting would be fine at this time, Kansas gave her mother permission to continue consulting. To lessen her mother's responsibilities, Kansas also offered to take over the afternoon feedings of the barn critters to help out. Unbeknownst to her mother, Kansas had an alternative reason for feeding the animals — Ephrem had promised to meet her in the barn to help out. She and Ephrem hadn't kissed yet, but it seemed like a romantically rustic place to share one.

CHAPTER TWELVE

Gwendolyn's ribs were succulent. The ribs had been in the smoker all day, cooking low and slow. The pecan wood chips provided the best flavoring of all the woods. Brining the ribs before cooking made them tastier and more tender. Sea salt, bourbon, water, and select seasonings were the secret to a perfect twelve-hour brining from their experience.

The Butcher loved the smell of human meat smoking in the morning. The Butcher's little cabin near the water was a favorite place to have a meal in peace. It was away from the world and social etiquettes. The Butcher remembered when they had carved Gwendolyn up six months ago. She had been fed well, and the amount of fat in her was just right. Soon they would be killing two new young tender girls to add to their freezer. With the new girls, the Butcher was thinking of salt curing them and making jerky from their buttocks and breast meat. They drooled as they thought of filleting them and chewing on their mouthwatering flesh.

The Butcher was not always a serial killer for hire. In fact, they probably considered themselves more of a hunter. The Butcher's craving for flesh started when they were a toddler and only grew as they aged. Their paternal grandfather had been a cannibal as well. It had been a way — secret from others — that had remained in the family for over three generations.

The Butcher learned while staying with their grandfather the thrill of traveling out of Wolfe County to larger cities and hunting the forgotten homeless. They had always preferred someone older than thirteen and younger than twenty. This was about having the leanest meat with the slightest impurities. The Butcher's grandfather had died at the ripe old age of 91 from eating like this. Maybe it was a genetic predisposition to want human flesh. For the past twelve years, the Butcher discovered that post-partum young girls with heightened hormone levels who needed to increase calories had been the best tasting meat.

The Butcher had discovered the Red River Gorge baby racquet by error while hunting for young meat. They noticed that some of the pregnant girls were being taken away from their hunting areas. A middle-aged woman pulled up in a van most of the time, and two or three girls left with them. There also seemed to be an inside person helping set up the pickup because it was so well coordinated.

Feeling this might be someone that could jeopardize or expose their own hunting grounds, the Butcher followed one of the unmarked vans. The van drove over two hundred miles and ended up in the stretch of the woods that backed up to the Red River Gorge, close to the Butcher's home area. A female driver helped unload a pregnant teen who was taken downstream by canoe. Where she was taken to and for what purpose was the next thing the Butcher wanted to figure out.

    The following week, the Butcher was prepared. They drove to the site a few days before the van would make the drop and hid a canoe in the woods behind some brush. Rather than drive back to homeless hangouts, he waited for the van to come to him. Just like clockwork on Friday, a van showed up and unloaded another girl. As soon as the canoe launched with the driver and teen, the Butcher launched their canoe and followed the two into the darkness while staying as far back as they could behind them.

    The Butcher followed their canoe for about four miles downstream. The canoe finally pulled off onto a bank. They were met by a large man who tossed the girl over his shoulder like a fifty-pound sack of feed. An off-road vehicle was waiting for them a few feet up the shore. The man strapped her into the passenger side of the vehicle. He drove the vehicle up a steep trail leading to an unknown place in the woods.

    The Butcher followed the trail, making sure to follow the fresh tracks since the trail split off at times into other directions. After several miles of walking, they came upon a cabin in the woods. The Butcher looked through the living room window and saw the recently transported girl being led into bedroom and then shackled to the floor. As soon as the bedroom door was shut, he heard a noise coming from the other side of the cabin. A man and a woman sat in a kitchen with the window open, drinking coffee and having an unpleasant conversation.

    "We've already got too many here, and I can't handle more than a few of these pregnant brats at a time. You need to take her back, Monk," said an overweight, middle-aged woman dressed in scrubs and wearing a stethoscope.

"Your haircut looks like shit, Darcie," said the tall, muscular man who was balding on the top of his head and hadn't shaven for days.

"Shut the hell up, Monk. I didn't ask you to provide an opinion ... You ogre."

"Now the niceties are out of the way — let's talk about deliveries," Monk said in a business-like manner.

"I got two ready to go anytime, and I'm not inducing any quicker than I have to. Not good for the baby — not good for me."

"Okay, I get it. The uppers have orders."

"We are only one of two hundred places they operate. Can't they pull from them?" Darcie asked.

"Short on supply and all of them we can get counts. Desperate rich people want brats in good health. Don't even care if the babes have disabilities. Political parents use that as leverage when running."

"I'll let you know when I can. I only take care of them while they are pregnant. You take care of the transport of the infants. I've told them I'm not going to kill any more of the girls. I've got enough on my plate. They aren't paying me enough anyway. I'm still a million short for that house and living expenses in the Caribbean," a frustrated Darcie shot back.

"Poor, poor Darcie. Tanning concerns or are you afraid that you won't attract the right person," taunted Monk, trying to push his coworker.

"It won't be you. I like my women, younger, dumber, and scared of me."

"You would. You scare me. Here are the papers on this one. She needs a good exam. Not too bright. She'll be fairly compliant, according to our baby scout."

"Let's get back to what I was saying. I ain't killing anymore," Darcie declared.

"You know the uppers won't care, and you will be the next to die. We leave no witnesses, no one to claim the children, and no bodies that can be tied to us."

"I've been careful. We have deep shafts off these coal mining operations that lead to certain death or starvation. But I'm not doing it."

The Butcher shoved open the cabin door, wearing a hunting suit with a full face covering and waving a 12-gauge shotgun. "Hands up, you sick shits!"

"Who the hell are you?" demanded Monk.

"Your cheap partner. Your answer to your problem," responded the Butcher.

"What?" Darcie asked.

"If you want me to kill them, I'll do it for nothing. Just don't question me," replied the Butcher.

"I'll have to clear it with the uppers. So put up your damn shotgun," Darcie added.

"Call now and get it approved, or I'll kill you both and all those girls here. Just know that I will kill you also if they say "no." So, make me sound like a fucking savior," the Butcher threatened.

"Okay! Okay! Just relax." Darcie dialed a number and waited for someone to answer. "It's me. Got a solution for our disposal problem that you know I don't like. I don't know, but he looks like he will fit in. He's holding a gun on me right now and says he'll kill Monk and me if he can't kill for us. How much? He says for nothing. I think he'll be discreet. Most killers have to be. Trial run. Okay."

The Butcher interjected themselves into the phone conversation.

"Tell them that I will make sure their bodies don't go to waste, and no one will find their remains."

Darcie started to explain, but the individuals on the other end of the phone had already heard the Butcher. Their answer was a trial run, and they would evaluate their work.

Months later, the Butcher was still on duty, proving their value. Their partnership with Darcie and Monk was unusual, to say the least. Although the Butcher received payment for their work, they often gave the money to Darcie, which only reinforced Darcie's dependence on the Butcher. The Butcher did not need the money, saying that what they allowed them to do fulfilled their desire to kill and eat. There was no love between the two regarding the Butcher's relationship with Monk. The Butcher intensely disliked Monk, considering him a festering puss-filled sack of flesh; Monk felt the Butcher was a psychopath that would kill everyone at some point. Regardless of what anyone thought about them, the Butcher would have succulent young meat at their fingertips — convenient as a grocery store.

CHAPTER THIRTEEN

--- November 1995 ---

Bishop Knight just finished a brutal, nail-biting game against Breathitt County High School. He was praying that a scout would spot him. The coach had said there would be one sitting in the upper bleachers looking for raw talent to mold for the Kentucky Wildcats. Bishop wasn't the best point guard in the state, but he was in the top fifty. He was so hoping for a scholarship to play basketball for the University of Kentucky, but at this point, he'd settle for any school that would take him.

Bishop was just one day over 18 years old, and he was ready to leave home and do something. He wanted something that served the public, but he wasn't sure what. He'd thought about the military, but he wanted a chance to experience college life and not four in the morning runs on Paris Island. Although a persistent, convincing Marine recruiter had been calling his house every other day trying to get him to commit, Bishop was still on the fence. What had caught his interest recently was seeing the state police working a crime scene at a convenience store robbery. If he decided to travel the "thin grey line," he would be the first in his family of lawbreakers to travel such a path.

Fester High School barely escaped defeat — 65 to 66. Bishop was so glad they had won. He didn't sink the winning shot, but it has to look better when your team wins.

His favorite cheerleader Paisley motioned him over after the game. She had cheered him on whether he missed or hit a shot. He was heavily sweating and didn't want her to smell his funk. He waved at her and hit the showers. After a long shower, body spray, and excessive deodorant use, he found her gossiping with some of the other cheerleaders.

Paisley and Bishop shared the same birthday and a lot of other interests. They had been dating for less than two weeks but had known each other since elementary school. To him, Paisley was pretty — no, she was beautiful. Her blonde hair, big ocean-blue eyes, cute button nose, and long, athletic legs made her desirable, but her looks came in second to how intelligent she was. She was also tough and didn't pull punches.

"Good game, boyfriend. How about a reward?" Paisley said as she stood on her toes to kiss his lips while the coach and principal gave them the evil eye. "You played above par, and I think you've impressed the scout. I saw him take notes on you more than any of the others. By the way, did you drink something orange and have garlic today?"

"Damn. I forgot to brush my teeth, but I'll take what I can get," he replied with a smirk the size of Texas.

Pulling her hair back behind her ear, Paisley exclaimed, "Damn, my earring is missing. Shit. Can you help me find it?"

They searched, and just as the coach was ready to turn the lights off and make them leave, Bishop found it underneath the bleachers. He got down on his stomach and stretched his long arms to their fullest extension, and wrestled with the earring with his long, skinny fingers to recover it.

"Here you go," Bishop said with a sense of pride.

"Thank you, Stretchie."

"How cute — a nickname. I'll let you call me that."

"I don't think you have an option."

"I guess I can call you Pastey. I remember when you ate half of a jar of paste in elementary school, and everyone called you that for months. Confused the hell out of your teachers who thought your name had been Paisley."

She kissed him and bit the edge of his chin.

"Do I taste any better?"

"About the same. If you only tasted like paste — I'd even settle for glue," she responded.

Stretchie licked her neck back and slightly bit her lip, causing it to bleed.

"You taste good. I could eat you up."

"I'm not sushi. Why don't you try cooking me before trying to eat my face off?" she responded while licking the blood from her lips.

"I might just try that sometime."

"I think that I love you, Stretchie."

"No thinking. I do love you, Pastey."

CHAPTER FOURTEEN

Two Philadelphia girls recently reported missing were on their way to the cabin near the Red River Gorge. Neither girl knew the other, but they both came from Philadelphia, were pregnant, and scared. The two girls were different from many of the other girls — they came from money, loving and supportive homes, and were generally well behaved. They were the newest items for sale for interested clientele considering premium orders.

Their transporter Margie Duncan could have cared less what happened to them — after all, she was paid well enough not to feel any guilt. She was a protected asset of the organization that employed her. The Delphine Frederickson Orphanage Foundation (DFOF) kept her out of trouble with her parole officer and out of prison. The non-profit organization was well connected, legally and illegally, across the globe.

This was Margie's first shipment to Kentucky from out of state. She'd worked all across the United States and Canada. She knew every highway and backroad to keep the cops off her tail. She kept a scanner on, and the operation had enough police operatives to let any Taker know when something was coming.

Margie knew Kentucky well. She'd grown up not far from Butcher Holler near Jenny Wiley State Park. Margie hated Kentucky and asked for extra money to return to the place she called hell. In fact, she had spent sixteen years in hell before she got out. Her father sexually abused her, and her mother beat her and forced her to sleep with men for drug money. The news of her parent's death never caused her to bat an eye when the guard informed her. She just continued playing Gin Rummy for extra cigarettes. Her four siblings left home as soon as they could. When her mother and father died, she was in prison for running a prostitution ring and dealing heroin in New Jersey. None of her relatives on either side cared enough about her to take her in or check on her. Besides, most were either in jail or running from the law. Returning to Kentucky would be traumatic, but she was in control this time.

Margie was briefed about the Kentucky operatives and knew what to expect. The operation in Kentucky had proven successful; now, it was time to accept more girls from other states. However, the two girls Margie was transporting were special because they possessed traits that two buyers specifically requested. One client wanted an albino with white hair. Another client wanted a young girl with green eyes and red hair because he was fixated on Irish women. It didn't matter what these sick millionaire/billionaire bastards wanted because she made money from it. She didn't care what happened to these girls. As far as she was concerned, she had been through a similar experience, which only made her stronger.

The Black Market Syndicate (BMS) was also behind the innocent-looking Delphine Frederickson Children Orphanage

Foundation. The orphanage was named after a fictitious woman who never existed a day in the real world. The internet was flooded with fake stories about her rise from an orphanage to become a savior to the innocent and abused. They even had someone hack into a government database to fake records and forge books to make them appear old to provide evidence of Delphine Frederickson's existence. After all, what law enforcement agency looks at an orphanage that, on the surface, helps kids?

The fictitious story regarding the patron and benefactor of the orphanage went as follows:

Born and raised in eastern Oklahoma, Delphine Frederickson, formerly known as Josephine Redd, was orphaned by her parents at the turn of the twentieth century. She was adopted by a local butcher and his wife, a seamstress. In the beginning, life was good, however, when finances ran low and the butcher's shop closed, things changed. Her adoptive parents beat her and made her eat scraps of raw meat. Her adoptive mother stuck her with needles or sewed her clothes to her body.

Eventually, Josephine escaped to New York and stowed away on a boat going to France at fourteen. Shortly after arriving, she was taken in by Mademoiselle Dubois, a wealthy widow, who found Josephine staying in her horse stable. She connected with Josephine, who became like a sister to her. Mademoiselle Dubois helped Josephine obtain a formal education and connect with the right people. She was the catalyst that turned Josephine into a proper young lady.

Josephine decided to change her name as she was no longer the little girl who had been abused. She decided to be a champion for children who were abused and oppressed. She chose Delphine as her first name as it had been Mademoiselle Dubois' mother's name. Her last name was taken from a wealthy aristocratic family in the United States that was well respected.

When Mademoiselle Dubois died of scarlet fever, she left all her possessions and money to Delphine. Delphine felt sad remaining in the home where her benefactor had died. She decided to move back to the United States and open an orphanage in Philadelphia to help other children. She used her wealth and influence to encourage adoption among the well-to-do and helped establish laws to protect neglected and abused children. Of course, the story was nothing but utter bullshit as Delphine never existed. Some truths were sprinkled within the story, such as money and abuse of children.

The BMS was a special type of criminal organization mixed with influential people united to ensure a business venture that earned money while those in charge remained anonymous. This allowed them to do as they pleased and operate in the shadows. Hiding under a charitable organization was just another smoke and mirror protective scam to laundry money and run illegal operations.

The BMS did not care about any of their associates' and operatives' opinions as long as they were loyal and compliant. Margie just wanted to do her job and be left alone. Margie had no intentions of being disloyal because of the BMS' power and connections. The BMS had extensive resources and could find and kill anyone because of this. She had heard they had someone in every county of every state who had some type of political or legal ties. She had even heard their connections went as high as governors and senators.

The BMS had been initiated over twenty years ago. No one knew who started it, but Margie knew the council of fifty-nine members made all the decisions. One person was the president of the syndicate, who called most of the shots, even if that was with a gun, muscle, or financial penalties. Each BMS council member represented their state, including American Samoa, Guam, Northern Mariana Islands, Puerto Rico, and the U.S. Virgin Islands. Canada and Mexico representatives were added five years ago. Indeed, it was a very profitable and well-organized underworld group.

Like a large organization, they shared the profits and losses. Bonuses were paid to each council member who distributed a percentage to their lieutenants and flunkies each quarter. All council members and BMS management associates signed a contract for five years of their life. There were only two ways to be discharged from their contract — by death or fulfilling five years. If a council member or management associate made it five years, they were set for life. A rotation every five years of members made it difficult to track them. There were also opportunities available to move up the ranks within that time frame given the nature of their business. After leaving, all council members and associates were provided with a million dollar a year retirement.

However, loyalty and being quiet was a life-long part of the contract. To break any silence with the BMS was a breach of contract, meaning a death sentence, including all immediate family members and close friends. An action like this had been taken in two incidents, one in Rhone Island and another in Florida. Two generations of families were erased in one night because two former BMS associates decided to meet with the FBI. In both cases, the investigating FBI agents were killed in what appeared to be bizarre automobile accidents. Any case records were doctored or deleted, removing any evidence that would allow pursuing future leads. No one crossed the BMS or messed with their profit margins.

The BMS's income came from selling babies, human slavery (sex and labor), drugs of all kinds, extortion, robbery, and legitimate businesses. They had even expanded to breeding infants with specific genetic traits for prospective adoptive parents and for special clients with desires and needs being fulfilled. It wasn't just pregnant teens that supplied the BMS with babies and people for sex and labor trafficking. DNA cloning, surrogate mothers, and test-tube babies were all part of the business for-profit venture as well. No one cared how the money was made as long as it was made. It was their answer to a diversified portfolio driven by greed.

Although no one outside the BMS knew it, the organization owned the Big Reggie's Barbeque chain, Harry's Gourmet Burgers, and Pascollini's Pizza chains with the franchise rights. There was one in every state, and all made profits in the black every year since they had been in operation. In addition, they operated three financial institutes tied to Wall Street and two major news media outlets online and on television. Indeed, they were well connected and influenced the public through the media and market.

The BMS used the best accountants who were kept isolated on remote islands with limited contact with others. Most of the accountants were loners, and they were given large homes with expensive cars and fringe benefits as long as they remained loyal and did good work. Accountants were the only ones that could not leave the organization after five years. It was lifetime employment — until death do you depart. This ensured that their accountants would never squeal on legitimate or illegitimate operations. For certain, it was a tight run organization.

The two Philadelphia girls arrived groggily and still drugged when Monk carried them out of the van. The two teens were just as pretty as the rest of their other girls, except the albino freaked Monk out since he had never seen one before. He checked the girls for any phones or personal items. It appeared that Margie had done an excellent job frisking them.

Before the two girls became fully conscious, they were chained in their rooms to await their infant's acquisition and delivery. These girls were also different from the other cabin captives. They were not from trailer trash homes or poor socioeconomic conditions. The oldest of the two with the red hair, De'Jane Primgood, was the daughter of a prominent banker. The albino, Revlon Danderguard, was the daughter of a research scientist at a food processing plant.

BMS had top people to investigate and research for them. To find girls with these specific traits, profile information was fed into a database that the BMS had built, allowing them to enter any demographic variables they wanted. The extensive database network was also secretly connected to all levels of law enforcement and other government offices such as the Bureau of Vital Statistics. This is the primary reason the BMS stayed three steps ahead of everyone and was so successful. As far as the members of the BMS were concerned, their organization would live on for centuries, and no one would be the wiser.

CHAPTER FIFTEEN

The rain fell hard. Between the rain and the heavy fog rising, Charlie's vision was significantly impaired. He continued his drive from Chicago toward Fester, Kentucky, listening to Duran Duran's *Hungry Like the Wolf.* He was hungry like a wolf right now but stops along the way were only convenient stores. What he wouldn't give for a double-decker club sandwich from Earl's Sandwich Shop. He'd have to wait. The drive was a little over six and a half hours with no stops, and he still had three hours to go.

He had left at 3:38 a.m. from his apartment. It was nothing new to him to be up early. He'd stayed up so many times from stakeouts that his nights and days ran together — but that's sometimes what it takes to catch the criminal. He liked working for the FBI but missed the pace of a city detective. These days, he was in many meetings, had more paperwork and briefings, and he traveled out of state. This trip would be a welcome break.

Since Paisley moved away and he took the job with the bureau, their relationship had been like the weather outside — damp and muddy. He hadn't seen his old partner in a while. They texted occasionally and liked each other's stuff on Facebook but had not genuinely kept in touch. He had meant to stay in touch but had immersed himself in his work. However, he was concerned about her being involved in police work again. He didn't mind looking into the pregnant girls' disappearances, but he knew how the multiple sclerosis impacted his old partner's work that last year.

He had known her husband Gregory before he was partnered with Paisley. Charlie and Gregory had served together in the same army platoon while on a two-year tour in Germany. Neither saw any action, and both enjoyed hanging out with each other. They got into a few harmless misadventures in Berlin that included skipping out on bar tabs and getting lost for three days while on furlough.

Charlie was hurt as much as Paisley when Gregory was found dead. He became involved with the case from the beginning. He remembered all the details surrounding the case. He knew that Gregory's ambulance had been found in an alley off one of the more questionable neighborhoods. Gregory had been shot twice in the head — execution-style, but it was hard to tell if it was a professional hit or just a druggie that had a flare for theatrics. Some of the cops on the force thought that Gregory might have been dealing drugs, but Charlie shut those rumors down before they got back to Paisley.

There was no information about the motive as much as a guess that someone thought he had some drugs. The truth was the ambulance had been cleared of all medications and most of its equipment so maintenance could be performed. He lost a friend, Paisley lost a husband, Kansas lost her father, and Chicago lost a great EMT who had saved countless lives, including Charlie's.

Perhaps Gregory was just in the wrong place at the wrong time, but his murder weighed heavy on Charlie's mind. He knew Paisley had Gregory's unsolved case on her mind all the time — just like he knew that she would have given her life to save her husband, and she might still put her life on the line to put away his killer. Charlie needed to check on her anyhow. Gregory would have wanted that. He owed it to the man who kept the pressure on his abdomen from a shotgun wound that he got from a carjacker.

Charlie had no children, and he was practically like an uncle to Kansas. He was as excited to see her as he was Paisley. Trying to create a good entrance back into the lives of Paisley and her daughter, Charlie brought a fresh Chicago-style pizza from Palazo's Pizza in a cooler, expressly prepared for Kansas. Palazo's was Kansas' favorite, and he wanted to surprise her.

Charlie looked at his GPS, and he was less than five miles from his next turnoff. He was still hours away. He had packed a small bag for the weekend with the plan to stay with Paisley. After all, Paisley had an extra room, and he'd staked out with her for days at a time, keeping things platonic throughout their professional career. He had thought of dating her at one point after Gregory died and then decided that he didn't want to spoil a good friendship.

Charlie had been raised a city boy, but his grandparents had lived in rural Illinois, and he had visited them on their small orchard growing up. He wasn't a person who wanted the farm life, but he liked visiting it. He found it hard to believe that his tough-as-nails partner was now feeding animals, churning ice cream, and living a carefree life. This was a 180-degree flip — after all, she had lived for the hunt.

He looked into his rearview mirror and didn't see anyone behind him. Old habits never die when you are a cop, and you make enemies with criminals who have no morality. The small scar under his left eye where a drug dealer had tried to carve his initials was a reminder of how things can go sideways. He saw the bags under his eyes that had followed him from his years with the CPD that were getting accented by his time working for the FBI. He was aging quick. He was getting ready to be forty-eight and felt sixty-eight. His jet-black hair was streaked with grey-like lightening. His mustache was peppered, and he noticed yellowing with his teeth, except a white molar because it was a porcelain crown. He still looked respectful, but he realized that his looks were beginning to fade. Marriage and children were things not on his life's list. He was married to law enforcement.

The information he had gathered for Paisley was more significant than anticipated. It indicated that some big-time, black-marketing criminals might be involved, some of which were tied to a couple of drug cartels and mafias. It was a big moneymaker for those that wanted children for various reasons. No one knew who ran the organization, but it ran from Canada to Mexico — all through North America — and might even include some U.S. territories. Kentucky was just one small potato in the sadistic and cruel abduction of young girls and babies. None of the girls had ever been located. There were stories of these girls having their babies sold off, being sold as sex slaves, or forced into labor.

Feeling a little lucky, he decided to test his luck playing the lottery. It was a habit to stop in each state with a lottery and buy a ticket.

He secretly hoped he would win so he could buy that boat and beach house on the Gulf of Mexico in Florida. He was hoping to have a new life outside of law enforcement. Besides the lottery, he liked the track and casino. Gambling was his vice, and he had been fortunate enough at this point not to lose his apartment or car.

Clemons Grocery Store off Highway 11 looked like it was out of the way enough to be one of those lucky get rich places. That was part of his approach to buying scratch-off tickets — it had to be a small store in the middle of nowhere because those are the ones that get sold the least and would hopefully yield a big winner. He pulled in and gassed up. The store was a small mom-and-pop operation. There was even a barrel with a checkboard sitting on it. He felt that he was in one of those episodes of *Green Acres*. All he needed now was Mr. Drucker to come out or spot someone climbing a telephone pole to make a phone call.

He bought one of the $30 Thoroughbred Race scratch-off lotto tickets. It promised twenty-five chances to win and a grand prize of one million dollars. He scratched the ticket off one box at a time. Five minutes later, two horseshoes, one bottle of bourbon, two barns, two harnesses, one jockey, two haystacks, two horse heads, two bags of horse feed, one racetrack, two bourbon distilleries, two horse trailers, two piles of manure, two mint juleps, and two roses — a big loser. He threw the card in the trash and bought his weekly Power Ball ticket. He always played his mother's, father's, and his birthday as part of his numbers every week. He'd never won over $10 since he was old enough to play Power Ball, but it wasn't for the lack of trying.

He arrived in the big city of Fester a little after ten o'clock and decided to go by the ice cream shop and surprise Paisley. He liked ice cream 24/7 and preferred it over alcohol. (In fact, if anyone looked in his freezer, they would find no less than three gallons of ice cream.) According to the store's sign, the store was not open until 11:00 a.m., and not a single car was parked in the lot. He thought he'd just sit and wait on her in the back near the employee parking. Feeling a little tired from the drive, he took a nap.

At 10: 41 a.m., someone tapping on the glass of his window awakened him from a reasonably good nap. A tall, overweight, full-bearded man with a sheriff's badge was staring at him. Charlie rolled his window down.

"Hello. Can I help you?" Charlie responded by stretching his arms out and yawning.

"This was a recent crime scene, and you are not parked in the front like a customer. May I ask what your business is here?"

"It's a surprise for an old friend."

"Uh-huh. Well, I don't ... Freeze. Keep your hands where I can see them. Don't move at all, or you'll be splattered."

"Now, deputy —"

"That's Sheriff Stone. Open the door and get out of the vehicle. Real slow."

That's when Charlie realized why he was being targeted by the local law — his shoulder holster was just dangling in view with his weapon, and he was parked at a former crime scene. He thought that the sheriff must be thinking that the criminal always returns to the scene of the crime.

"Listen — Sheriff — Stone. I am a —"

"I don't care who you are. I need your hands on the roof of the vehicle."

"If you let me explain. I'm Charles Yocum with the FBI."

"Really. Hanging out at the back of an ice cream shop. Show me your I.D., Mr. Bigtime FBI man."

At that moment, Charlie realized that he had left his FBI identification back on his nightstand at home because this was supposed to be a vacation.

"They are at home."

"Okay. You've got Illinois plates, and all my database can tell me is that it's registered to Charles Yocum, 287 Grandwater Drive, Apartment 34, Chicago, Illinois. Nothing about an occupation."

"If you'd —"

"Hands behind your back. You're going with me for questioning."

"But —"

"No butts, unless you are sitting on them in the back of the patrol car. Watch your head."

Now Charlie was living in Mayberry hell. He had one call, and he knew who it would be."

"Welcome to Fester," said the jailer who slid Charlie into his cell next to another man who resembled Otis from *The Andy Griffith Show*. One call was allowed. Sheriff Stone said that if someone could vouch for Charlie that he would release him. If not, he'd start questioning and investigating him like he was a member of the mafia.

Charlie called Paisley's cell phone, and it went straight to voicemail. He left a calm but yet urgent message:

"Hey, Paise. Charlie here. I'm in the Fester jail. The sheriff has me on suspicion of looking suspicious. Left my credentials at home. Please bail me out. I'll owe you one."

Deciding to conserve his energy, he decided to finish his nap out. It was relatively peaceful and quiet with the occasional grunting of his cellmate, who either burped or farted every time he shifted position in his bed. Three hours later, the jailer released Charlie from his cell and took him to the front reception area where Paisley was waiting.

"Took you long enough," Charlie said while taking his personal items back from the jailer.

"I don't get voicemails or calls sometimes for hours out here. It's a perk of living in a rural area. Sorry about that," she laughed. "If it's any consolation, I've been where you have been — recently at that."

"Well, it's good to see you at any rate," Charlie replied while checking his wallet for any missing cash or credit cards. "What did you tell them?"

"I told them that you were my former partner and an FBI agent."

"How'd that go over?"

"They don't like me much anyway, but they are still letting you out of jail."

"You ... Jailer ... Where's my service weapon?" asked a surly Charlie.

"Sheriff says he's keeping it until you show some FBI ID," answered the skinny, older gentleman sipping coffee.

"Really. Have him call the FBI headquarters in Chicago and ask for Agent Dreama Garfield. She can set the record straight. I expect it done by tomorrow before noon when I return to retrieve it."

"I don't know if he — "

"If not, she will send a team down here to look at how you work with the federal government. Could be a nasty investigation. I would hate to see elected officials go under such scrutiny and embarrassment. Would be in prominent newspapers across the whole country. I can see the byline: COUNTY LOCALS JAIL FBI AGENT WITH PREJUDICE.

A nervous jailer replied, "I'll be sure to tell him that. We kind of like keeping to ourselves here and not bringing attention to —"

"I think you got the picture. See you tomorrow. Shall we goeth to you ice cream shop, your majesty," Charlie said playfully to his old partner.

The former Texaco gas station that had been converted to an ice cream parlor by Paisley still held vigil over his 2015 Honda Civic. Paisley had bought the place at a steal and found decent contractors to remodel the building. She used to come here when she was much younger with her parents to get gas or cigarettes for her father; she had always thought it would make a superb place for a restaurant or something one day.

Wolfe County had only recently gone wet, but bars were still not a thing yet, only liquor stores. When she was looking for something to do, ice cream made good sense as a business. Since Paisley could ship ice cream using dried ice pretty much anywhere, she was not limited to the community. She had thought about an ice cream truck, but there weren't enough kids to buy ice cream consistently to make it worth it. However, she did have a few contracts with the state parks and several diners in the surrounding counties. This helped keep things afloat during the winter months when sales were down in Fester.

"I really like what you've done here. How about ice cream?"

"I think they might have some here. Might be good enough for an FBI agent."

"You think so. I have some files if you'd like to look as we lick."

"Let's just chit chat a bit. We can talk about what you've got when we get back to the house. Come on in. I know the owner. I think she'll comp the ice cream for law enforcement."

CHAPTER SIXTEEN

Charlie and Paisley talked late into the afternoon before Paisley headed out to do her farm chores. Paisley offered Charlie the opportunity to help with the chores, but Charlie informed her that his time would be better served in reviewing documents rather than mucking stalls. He took a seat in the large walnut rocker on the porch and looked out onto his old partner's farmland. She had indeed become something more than a cop.

Charlie had never really sat in a rocking chair before. He had always thought that rocking chairs were for the elderly who retired. Just sitting in it made him feel twenty years older. It was not the most comfortable chair, but the rocking motion seemed to calm him. Whether it was the rocker or something else, he needed a distraction to soothe his nerves after he began reviewing reports on the missing teens. The thought of what probably happened to these young girls and their babies just made him nauseated.

The roaring sound of a loud truck with dual exhausts was heard coming toward the farm traveling down the gravel road. Seconds later, a hefty red F-150 pulled in front of the barn across from the house. Charlie watched as Kansas was dropped off by some good-looking adolescent. Then the biggest surprise came when little Kansas proved to be bigger than the state that she was named after when she French kissed her driver.

Wow. They grow up too fast in the country, thought Charlie.

Seeing a familiar face on the porch, Kansas ran toward him like a kindergartener finishing their first school day to greet their parent. "Uncle Charlie!" Kansas said as she gave him a big hug.

At that point, the driver of the truck tipped his hat toward Charlie and rolled out, making sure to gas the truck so the exhaust system could be noticed. It was followed by country music being cranked up loud.

"In the flesh. How's my little Cotton Candy Girl?"

"Oh, don't call me that. I'm too old for that. Besides, cotton candy breaks me out."

"I just remembered that."

"What are you doing here?"

"Just on vacation."

"Nope, I don't believe that for one second. This has to do with that case mom is consulting on."

"You're sure that police work is not in your future?"

"No likely. You know she's having a relapse. I've already read her the riot act."

"And you know that she won't listen. Why waste your breath?" Charlie replied indifferently.

"I feel better when I bitch. Now, those look like case files. Put them aside and enjoy the farm life. I'll see you at dinner. Homework, you know."

Kansas started to walk into the house, and Charlie asked, "So, who's the guy in the deafening truck you were exchanging saliva with?"

Looking around for her mother, she lowered her voice. "He's nice. He's our neighbor's grandson. His name is Ephrem. You will leave him alone and not mention what you saw to mother, or I will not talk with you again."

"Perhaps you are more on the criminal side with blackmailing. I was young once. I'll leave it up to you to say anything or just let things happen that cause it to crash. See you later."

"Okee Dokee!"

When Kansas was about halfway up the stairs, Charlie yelled out, "Just an FYI — I brought your favorite pizza from your favorite place. It's in the frig."

That stopped Kansas in her tracks, and she ran back downstairs, grabbed the box out of the frig, and gave Charlie another quick hug.

"Finally, some culture around here. Thanks!" she exclaimed. As quickly as she had run down the stairs, Kansas was in her room with the pizza, which she planned on not sharing with anyone.

Eating on the healthy and lighter side due to her MS, Paisley had made a quiche for supper with a Strawberry salad. The quiche was vegetarian, and the custard base was mostly egg whites — she was also trying to lower her cholesterol. The crust was made of almond flour to help cut her gluten consumption. How she missed a strawberry iced donut with a Macchiato. Paisley had found some decent healthier desserts, but they were not the same. Tonight, she'd settle for a gluten-free dark chocolate brownie with a scoop of Double Dark Chocolate Chip Skinny ice cream made from goat milk with a cup of strong black coffee.

Dessert got her thinking about the recipe she'd been working on that would stereotype cops more — Boys In Blue Glazed Donut and Coffee Ice Cream. It was coffee ice cream with pieces of glazed donuts in it. She hadn't put it out yet but was close to perfecting the flavor of fresh glazed donuts dipped in coffee. She could only imagine how much flack she would have received if she'd been marketing it while on the police force.

As promised, Charlie kept his word about Ephrem, but Paisley had seen the lip lock from the top of the barn while she was getting Wilma down from a rafter for the night. (Wilma was one of those hens who did as she pleased and needed prompting.) Paisley preferred that Kansas not follow Wilma's example.

As per her natural demeanor, Paisley confronted her daughter over dessert. "Thanks for sharing the pizza. Surprise you are still hungry."

Kansas smiled back and playfully answered, "I'm a growing girl. Gotta have my Ps and Qs."

"Speaking of growing, I saw Ephrem and you playing tongue wars. You failed to mention you were seeing him," Paisley said while giving her most fearsome interrogation look, which set Kansas on edge.

Dropping her fork in mid-bite, she blew out a large breath and shot back, "Mom. Listen. Ephrem. Ephrem and I — we like each other. We want to see where this is going to go. What's wrong with that?"

"Nothing if I want to play ignorant and stupid.

"I'm almost six —"

"Sixteen, and I'm almost forty-five. Listen, he's a neighbor, a grandson of a friend. If you break up — it will make an uncomfortable situation living next door and at school."

"For you or me?"

"Both."

"I can handle it, mom. By the way, he'll be over later to play cards."

Charlie cleared his throat and interrupted. "Not my business, but I'd be happy to interrogate him."

Both simultaneously responded, "No!"

"Just trying to help," Charlie said as he threw his hands up in the air.

"Have him bring his grandfather too. He might as well be in on this. Besides, he's won too many games of Gin Rummy against me. I need to earn some of it back."

"Fine," Kansas rudely responded as she tossed her hair, cleared her plate, and went back up to her room.

"You sure you don't want a teenager?" Paisley asked her old partner.

Charlie thought for a second and shook his head. "I got two cats; they give me enough trouble. I'll pass."

Ephrem and Gary showed up to play cards at seven o'clock like clockwork. Gary and his grandson were introduced to Charlie — then it was down to business. Paige had decided to skip the rummy and go for poker when they arrived. Charlie had been a regular at her home in the windy city playing poker with three other cops and two of Gregory's EMT friends. Kansas had watched as a little girl and had learned quite a bit from them. Gary had played poker all his life, and his grandson had poker games with his high school buddies at times.

Paisley dealt everyone five cards. She so loved playing five-card draw. The ante had been made to be ten cents. Kansas had loaned Ephrem two dollars' worth of dimes and expected to be paid back at a twenty-percent rate. After all, banks charge interest. Everyone took three cards, and the bets were made. Charlie had three eights and won the pot. No one was bluffing or manipulating the pot at this point. Then Paisley passed the deck off to Gary. Gary shuffled and asked Charlie to cut; then Paisley started in.

"Gary. These two kids have started seeing each other. You have any thoughts on that?"

"Like I said — one day this week or maybe it was last — be a good thing if they started seeing each other."

"So, you have no concerns since they live next door or that this will cause problems if they break up?" Paisley said in a profoundly concerned voice.

"Mom. We just started. You act like we've been in a rocky marriage waiting to go over a cliff," Kansas responded.

"Can I say —" Charlie attempted to say something before being told "No" by everyone in the room.

"Listen, Paisley. These kids are going to find love at some point. Maybe it won't work out, but like you and I did, they have to give it a try. How many did you date before you found the right one?" Gary pointed out.

"I'll give you that one, Gary. But it could impact their social life at school and our friendship if it goes south," Paisley added.

"We are big boys and girls, and don't bury our heads in the sand," Gary replied to her. "I'll go twenty cents on this hand."

Everyone said they were in. Gary took one card, Charlie took two, Kansas took three, Ephrem took one, and Paisley took three cards.

Additional bets were made, and Paisley brought everyone back on the subject. "Okay, let's set some ground rules. You both are young, and I know Kansas has not had many boyfriends — at least that I am aware of."

"What kind of ground rules?" asked a curious Ephrem who had just been sitting back listening to all the talk.

"Let's start with reasonable times together like a curfew. There are no visits after midnight on Friday or Saturday and none after 9 p.m. on Sunday through Thursday."

"Agreed," Kansas said while nodding to Ephrem.

Gary added, "No closed bedroom doors. All I need is for another kid to take care of. And you'll let us know where you are at together every time you leave the house. Don't forget that I can track your phone, grandboy."

"Two pair," Charlie added, revealing he had the highest hand.

"Damn, I think you won almost a couple of bucks in that pot," Gary exclaimed.

"Other rules continued. Charlie, hold off on dealing until we set the remaining rules," Paisley attentively demanded.

"Okay. I'll just play solitaire while you all figure this out," Charlie said, slightly annoyed.

"No sex, but if you happen to find yourselves in that situation, use protection and take responsibility. Ephrem, no hanging out at the ice cream shop while Kansas is working, and don't be all over each other in public — like my ice cream shop. People talk in this town," Paisley continued.

"Work out your fights and arguments before leaving each other," Gary piped in.

"Never ever hit or abuse each other physically, mentally, sexually, or by any other means. If that happens, I will personally make sure you spend time in the hoosegow. That goes for both of you," responded Paisley in an authoritative manner.

The room was quiet for a minute except for the cards that Charlie was lying in piles on the table for solitaire. Gary even pointed for Charlie to move a few to a different pile.

"I guess we got that settled, mom. Let's play cards. I'm here to win and not talk about rules."

For the next ninety minutes, they played cards. Paisley broke even, and the big winner for the night was Charlie. Paisley was glad that she had invited others because Charlie took their money this time. There was enough time left before curfew for Ephrem and Kansas to spend some together before Ephrem had to go. While the young couple spent time in the living room watching YouTube videos, Charlie, Gary, and Paisley played investigators.

"He's alright to talk to about this case. He and I are good at talking about these things. He actually should have been a cop with the instincts he has," Paisley said, trying to give her friend clearance for Charlie to talk about his findings.

"How could I ever say no to you? Okay, this appears to be a big organization. Maybe even a syndicate. There's talk around about them in all the 50 states, Mexico, Canada, and parts of the U.S. territories.

They just don't move drugs. They are peddlers of the flesh — babies, young girls for sexual pleasure, and forced labor. They say that each state, country, territory has a council member who is legal and legit with lots of connections. They have people under them, but it's very controlled and hush-hush. I've seen some patterns that Kentucky is a growing investment for them."

"Kentucky. Wow. I would have never thought anyone would have wanted us except for basketball, bourbon, and horses. Maybe pot one day," Gary interjected.

"Seems a little bizarre. What else?" Paisley inquired.

"None of the pregnant girls are ever found — until the dead girl in your shop. She fits the profile, and she had been missing for some time. I think she escaped from one of their local birthing and holding units close by. I'm thinking by the soil samples that we are talking some place in the Red River Gorge," Charlie reported.

"That's a lot of area to cover. I think it's like 29,000 acres. Lots of secluded places. National parks have a lot of places that they don't even go to. Could be considered an unsanctioned Body Farm like they got in Tennessee," Gary informed them.

"You are right about that. We need to figure out where these girls are coming from so we can stop them before something happens to them," Paisley offered up.

"Could be anywhere and everywhere," Gary added.

Handing an encrypted flash drive over to Paisley, Charlie said, "Here are all the cases that I have identified. There have been over 20,000 in the past five years across the U.S. It's a lot of girls. These are only the ones that were reported missing. Not everyone reports their kid is missing, let alone pregnant … Not even all schools."

"Damn. That's a lot," Paisley responded, whose mind was blown away by the number of teens missing who were pregnant.

"It's not good. I guarantee that whoever is doing something with these girls is getting rid of the bodies in a way you cannot find them or selling them off to someplace where no one will inform anyone of it," Gary commented.

"I'll get to the bottom of this. Thanks, Charlie. I owe you."

"Well, you could start by thanking me with another slice of brownie and ice cream."

"What's this about ice cream and brownies. Pay up. I'm the loser tonight, and I deserve a reward," Gary added.

"Coming up," Paisley said with a big smile.

CHAPTER SEVENTEEN

Something was different about the Butcher tonight. The Butcher had arrived early wearing apparel different from their regular garb. They typically wore a hazmat suit, but they were wearing coveralls and a welding mask tonight. They seemed slightly anxious to get to work and leave. This made Darcie somewhat nervous. She didn't like changes in routines, and she never liked anything that endangered her from retiring rich. Like most days, her fellow coworker Monk did not pay attention and cared less about the Butcher as long as the job got done.

Two girls were in labor right now, and one was expecting twins. Since their operation was upgraded by the bosses above, they now had two classes of mothers — disposable and sellable. Candice, who was having twins, was disposable and fresh meat for the Butcher. Her identical twins would bring a high value to that billionaire whose wife wanted kids but didn't want to give birth to them. The sellable girl was a dark-haired beauty with green eyes known as Emerald. She was to be sold for six million and needed to remain pretty and unbruised.

Expected delivery times for both girls were running close. Darcie knew that Monk would have to assist. They were short-handed, and they were still looking for an additional hire. Monk had been trained as a mid-husband, and there were no noted complications for Emerald. The twins were more complicated, and their births could involve calling Doc since one had become a breech.

Doc, also known as Rendell Thackery Pullet, M.D., head of obstetrics at Cumberland Valley Medical Hospital, was a real piece of shit. He had quite the gambling issue that led to his BMS employment in order to cover debt. He was one of the worst, if not most careless, doctors in the whole Cumberland Valley area. He had been moved to administrative work to avoid lawsuits due to his negligence. If it had not been for his father, who helped found the hospital, he would have lost his license and been out on his butt flipping burgers at Burger King.

Darcie did not want to call Doc. In fact, she dreaded contacting him. Doc had a short temper for a medical professional and did not like to be called unless needed. He enjoyed drinking, playing high-stakes poker, and womanizing more than working after hours. Still, the BMS paid a handsome retainer for him to be on-call. In return, the BMS took care of his debts, hooked him up with prostitutes, and kept his carcass out of the bottom of some lake.

Darcie placed the call. When his cell phone rang, Doc had just finished giving Mrs. Cagelin a personal exam in the bed of his apartment. He was getting ready to reexamine her before Darcie called, so he was not happy. A half-sober Doc informed her that he would be there in two hours. When Darcie informed him that Candace was at seven centimeters dilated, he told her to shove the brats back into the mother if they started to crown.

Doc also told her that if anything happened to the babies, he would make sure the "Money Makers" would be aware of who caused the loss of income. The Money Makers were an unforgiving lot, and Darcie knew too well what the consequences would be. Darcie was the fourth person to run this operation in the last seven years — not because they retired. The others had just disappeared without a trace. Darcie was in it for the money, which motivated her to follow the rules and keep her mouth shut. The Money Makers promised to let her retire in five years if she ran the business well. Darcie had come from a home of unscrupulous people, so it was no problem for her to bend the rules and blur any ethics.

Monk managed to handle the single birth just fine. He had been given instructions to keep the prize safe for the second sale. However, Monk forgot to mention this to the Butcher. As soon as Monk took Emerald's baby to the neonatal room, the Butcher got to work. Emerald was awake when they slit her throat like a pig at slaughter. The cut was not perfect, and the high-pressured jugular shot blood into the ceiling. The Butcher seemed to be off their mark because their cuts were sloppy. In fact, Monk noticed the Butcher was shaking with each cut they made into the body of its fresh meat.

"What the hell have you done? You dumb sombitch! You've screwed us all! She was for sale." Monk opened a drawer and searched for his gun.

The Butcher did not like being yelled at. Before Monk could pull the trigger, the Butcher took his filleting knife and shoved it into Monk's heart and then sliced down the middle of his chest, just like a person would do when dressing a deer. Monk fell to the floor. Blood flowed from the worthless body of the oaf that had threatened the hunter. All the Butcher could think of was *good riddance to bad rubbish.*

The Butcher disposed of Monk's body and finished carving up Emerald. They vacuum-packed her fresh meat and cleaned up her remains using an acid bath. No one had come back to check on him. The Butcher recalled that Darcie was busy delivering twins. It was a good night with one error; regardless, the Butcher would have more meat.

Darcie would cover for the Butcher's error, or the Butcher would kill her too. At least, that was the Butcher's thought. Anyhow, no one knew who the Butcher was, and they would be safe from retaliation if Darcie failed them. The Butcher knew Darcie had a strong distaste for Monk to their advantage. They could say that Monk ran off with the girl, saying she was meant for him. The Money Takers would not know any different because they would never be found. Darcie was also scared of the Butcher, so she would do whatever they said.

Darcie was finished less than an hour later, and the twins were delivered. The Butcher walked into the room, and Darcie was cleaning up. She was holding two infants. The mother was unconscious and appeared to have a more significant fat content than most victims. She was not very pretty on the outside, but her meat would most likely be well-marbleized like a ribeye. It would cook well. Darcie asked where Monk and the girl went.

"They have run off together. That's all you need to know, and that's all you will tell if you value your life and want me to continue giving you money."

"What have you done?"

"Never mind what I have done. Worry about what I will do?"

"How will I explain it to the aboves?"

"What's to explain? I gave you the explanation. Call now and don't make an error."

Darcie picked up the phone and called a burner cell phone. A woman with a raspy voice answered on the other end.

"What? I hope this is important," said the annoyed woman on the other end.

"We've had an incident," nervously responded Darcie.

"Go on."

"Emerald, one of the girls that was going to be sold — she — she has run off with Monk."

"I don't know who Monk is or care what your name is but explain before you are terminated with full prejudice."

"He just took her and ran. Said she was his and no one else's. We have the child, though."

"I see. That is at least something. Maybe enough to keep you from being terminated. We'll find them, and he'll be dealt with. However, the financial loss is on your unit. You will lose part of your pay for six months. I'll send one of the takers to fill in for a while. Whether you are involved or not, you will be disposed of and replaced if this happens again. If the Butcher was there too, let them know that their pay will be reduced for six months. You must not trust people that you work with. You are expected to take care of any problems."

The Butcher nodded in acceptance as he ran his fingers over his knife's edge with his gloved hand and made a motion of slitting a throat directed at Darcie.

Darcie gulped hard and agreed to the deal. Before the phone call ended, Darcie informed the woman that Doc had refused to come for a more complicated birth. The woman indicated that they were looking for a replacement already since this was the third complaint in two months. She said they would not be renewing their contract with the doctor, and then she hung up without a goodbye.

Although Darcie dreaded dealing with a new person, she was glad to get rid of Doc for good. Takers were an odd lot. Most had medical backgrounds such as former EMTs, physician assistants, nurses who had been disgraced and disowned by their own professional boards due to unscrupulous behaviors. They were willing to kidnap or manipulate a pregnant youth when money was involved. The main operation realized having someone who could address medical issues during transport to the satellite unit operations was imperative to preserve their income.

Furthermore, they were all trained killers who cleaned up for the Money Makers, which meant they would take Darcie out without blinking an eye. However, the Butcher had no fear of any of them. They would fillet them and dissolve their flesh if it came down to it.

When Darcie was informed that Ruth Ann Alderman would be coming, she almost threw up in her mouth. She knew Ruth Ann and what it would mean having her come there. She complained out loud that all was lost, and they were screwed and would be most likely killed. The Butcher watched Darcie rant and rave with only one thought in mind — *If this Ruth Ann interferes with my meat supply, I will carve her up like a Thanksgiving turkey.*

CHAPTER EIGHTEEN

Ephrem and Kansas belonged together like mayonnaise on a bologna sandwich. At least, that is what Ephrem thought now that he was dating the girl next door that he had longed to kiss since he first laid eyes on her. His Papaw Gary was the one that pushed him to meet her. After all, he had told Ephrem about the beautiful girl that had moved in next door with her mother and that if Ephrem wanted her — he'd better do something sooner than later. Otherwise, she would be taken.

Ephrem had little experience dating. He was still shy and awkward, but his grandfather had been educating him about women for years to get him ready for this moment. When Kansas first moved in, she caught his eye. He watched her from his house for several weeks until he finally worked up the nerve to go down to the ice cream shop. He would look for a spark and chemistry like his grandfather said would be there if it was meant to be. Ephrem wasn't sure what that would look like, but he imagined it would be like fireworks going off like in those cheesy television shows.

Three scoops of pecan praline and a text with his contact information started the process. Initially, Kansas had no intention of dating any incestual, backwoods, country hick who probably had been dating his cousin. It took time for Kansas to adjust to her new surroundings, but she finally came around. Ephrem worked on her every time he saw her until they became friends, and now they were an item in high school. Paisley still doubted that dating the neighborhood boy was a good thing. Gary seemed pleased as punch.

Gary had been a matchmaker for many of his own kin, and he knew when two people belonged together — at least that is what he told everyone. Gary wasn't much for finding a match for himself. When Paisley confronted him about his meddling in other people's love affairs and that he needed to focus on his own needs, Gary just dismissed that he had already been matched and the match had burned down. Gary had tried matching Paisley a few times, but he withdrew after he saw how other men interacted with Paisley. Most seemed intimidated by her. Gary thought that he and Paisley would have made a good match, but she was just too young for his taste.

School had started back, and Kansas had been getting rides to and from school from Ephrem. They were inseparable when they were together. They were also the hottest couple at Dewey Lawson High School, named after one of the best math teachers to ever pace the halls. However, the loving couple was not loved by all.

Brynlee Flatt was an old flame of Ephrem. He had dated her from the 8th grade through the first half of his sophomore year. Although he broke up with her, she had become obsessed with Ephrem. She carried a torch with an endless supply of fuel. When Ephrem returned to school this fall, she planned to claim him back.

Brynlee spent all summer working on a plan. She had it all laid out in her diary. It involved deceit and lies, but she knew that Ephrem would drop everything to be at her side when all was said and done. She would lure Ephrem to the edge of the school that backed up to the woods. She would then seduce him and become pregnant. She knew Ephrem's grandfather would make him marry her and raise their child. If he chose not to have sex with her, she would go to Barry Dickerson and have sex with him and then claim the baby she was carrying was Ephrem's.

When Brynlee saw Ephrem and Kansas holding hands and loving on each other as they entered the school, her eyes became wide as saucers, and her temper was like an exploding volcano. She went immediately to the girls' restroom, where she went into one of the stalls, locked it, and pulled her diary out. Inside the diary, the words "Ephrem and Brynlee forever" were written in every direction that one could imagine. Hearts drawn in human blood were on each page.

Feeling anxious, she pulled out a razor and sliced a half-inch-long cut on her pinkie finger. Blood freely flowed onto the book. She took her bleeding pinkie and squeezed it until a puddle was in the middle of a blank page. She wrote with fresh new blood using her uncut hand: "Kill the bitch = Ephrem is mine." Using a piece of toilet paper from the roll, she wrapped her pinkie and put pressure on it to stop the bleeding and returned to class like nothing had happened.

Two weeks into the school year, Brynlee put her plan into action. With Kansas out of town for a debate conference, she would not be returning to the school, making the timing perfect. After several more blood writings in her diary and hidden cuts under her knees and underarms, Brynlee persuaded Ephrem to look at her car because it would not start. Ephrem was initially reluctant to help her with the car, but then he remembered that Brynlee had stayed away from him like he had asked. Reluctantly, he complied, and Brynlee's carefully orchestrated plan became real.

"Looks like you've got a loose connector to your battery. A little corrosion that needs some cleaning. I can boost it but then take it on down to Ralph's; he'll probably charge you nothing."

"Here. I got you an Ale 8 for taking a look at it."

"You didn't have to —" Ephrem tried to reply.

"Thought that I'd reward you."

"Thanks!" Taking the bottle cap off with his key chain bottle opener, Ephrem took a long drink of the local ginger ale.

"Where did you meet this new girlfriend?" she snidely asked.

"Kansas. She's our neighbor. They own the ice cream shop in town."

"Never been to it. Dairy is not kind to my complexion. She seems nice though."

"Need to go. Thanks for the Ale 8."

"Wait a minute. Can't you tell me a little about her?"

With heavy eyes, he slowly responded, "She's really neat. From Chicago. Her mom's a —"

Ephrem dropped to the ground. They were on the south end of the parking lot, which backed up to the forested area as planned. No cameras, no security, and no one else there. She pulled a tarp from the trunk of her car and rolled Ephrem over onto it. She then dragged him out to the woods.

Brynlee had modified her plan. Her daddy was a pharmacist,

and she had access to all kinds of medications that she could easily take without him knowing it. She mixed a sedative with a dose of Viagra; she carefully drugged Ephrem's Ale 8 and put it back together like it had never been touched. She only hoped that he would be awake and conscious for most of the sex, but she could wait until they were married and raising little Ephrem Jr. to look into his eyes.

To maximize her chances of conceiving a child, Brynlee had figured out the best time to become pregnant based on her ovulation cycle. She had abandoned her alternate plan to get pregnant by someone else. She really did not want to trap Ephrem into raising another man's baby. This would be his — one hundred percent. As she took advantage of her unwilling victim, she took pictures of the act for later memories and as proof of the conception.

Ephrem woke up in the parking lot, and it was already after dusk. He was not sure what had happened. He was concerned that maybe he was diabetic or had something like mono that had caused him to feel so tired that he took an involuntary nap. He was the only one left at school. He realized that no one could have seen him. He looked at his phone, which was down to a five percent charge, and noticed that he had three missed calls from his papaw, two missed calls from Kansas, and five texts from Kansas asking him where he was.

Ephrem got into his car. He was not sure if he should be driving at first, but he felt better after he drank some water. He texted his papaw and Kansas and let them know that he was on his way home. He didn't remember even looking at Brynlee's car, let alone talking to her.

Brynlee was aware of the effects of the drug and used it to her advantage. Once Gary became aware of his grandson's infidelities and recognized she was carrying his great-grandchild, Brynlee knew he would force a shotgun wedding on Ephrem. *Poor little city girl — she'd take care of her next. It wouldn't be pleasant either.*

Since taking her first drama class at the Chicago Children's Theater, Kansas had loved acting. She was glad that Dewey Lawson HS had auditions for *The Wizard of Oz*. She had always wanted to play Dorothy, but she'd settle for the Wicked Witch if she could get it. Brynlee too was an actress — or so she thought. Brynlee dreamed of becoming a big motion picture star and moving away while stay-at-home dad Ephrem raised Ephrem Jr. She would beat this Kansas out on everything. She knew Kansas' relationship with Ephrem was short-lived one way or another, especially once the DNA test proved that it was his baby. To make sure Ephrem would only be faithful to her, and only her, Brynlee felt that she might need to scare Kansas away or kill her, whichever came first.

    Kansas read for the Wicked Witch and Dorothy. She did an excellent job reading her lines and moving across the stage, presenting great emotion. Brynlee did well, but not as well. When the final announcements were made, Brynlee was given the role of Aunt Em, which she refused. Mr. Lewis gave the part immediately to Janet Dimm. Mr. Lewis had worked with Brynlee before and did not want to deal with another histrionic actress. This infuriated Brynlee so much; she felt she needed to take out Kansas then and now.

Brynlee climbed to the top of the scaffold and loosened a light above Kansas' head. She then rigged a rope that she could release before exiting out the back. The plan seemed to be foolproof. As Brynlee opened the door into the dark, she smiled and let go of the rope. She saw Kansas in the chair on stage, and then she heard a scream and then a loud crash. She couldn't help but laugh some. It would be considered an accident.

The problem was that the heavy light did not hit Kansas. Instead, it struck Xeric Davis in the shoulder, resulting in surgery and three months of homeschooling. Brynlee was not happy about missing Kansas. She knew she would have to try later. Regardless, she would have Ephrem soon. She knew that being patient was the key to getting her way — something she was getting better at.

Eight weeks after Brynlee had taken advantage of Ephrem, she drove to see his grandfather. Gary was in his barn office. Having an office in the barn allowed him to closely watch his prized possession — his dairy cows. Gary had just finished checking the quality of the cream and had logged in his results when he heard a knocking on the office door.

"Hello. Can I help ya?"

"Yes. I'm the mother of your great-grandbaby."

"Excuse me."

"Your grandson, Ephrem. He's got me knocked up."

"Who are you?"

"Brynlee Flatt. Lester Flatt's daughter."

"Yes, the pharmacist with the bluegrass musician's name that cheats customers. Pregnant. Is that so? You can prove this?"

"Yep. Here's my pregnancy test. I'm willing to do a DNA test and go to court to prove my point. Unless you want to make the papers or news, which you know my daddy has some weight here, you'll have Ephrem marry me. You just need to sign the papers for him."

"Your asshole daddy. Ephrem has a girlfriend. You don't look very pregnant. When did this happen?"

"August 28. In the woods at school."

"You're about two months then. You got any other proof?"

Brynlee whipped out her phone and pulled up the pictures of her being intimate with Ephrem.

"He doesn't even look awake. What the hell did you do to him?"

"Gave him what all men desire. Maybe he wasn't fully aware of it, but he still got off, and I got pregnant."

"I take it he knows about this?"

"Probably doesn't remember anything. I haven't said a word about the pregnancy to him or anyone else. Not even sure how good Ephrem's memory is related to the event leading up to it."

"I see. What's in it for you? I smell a scam."

"Nothing except to be raising this little bundle of joy with Ephrem. I've loved him for the longest."

"What's your daddy think about this?"

"Like I said, no one else knows. I don't think he would care as long as I got married. Since mama left, he just lets me do what I want."

"I think that I need to talk to Ephrem."

"You do that. I'll be back tomorrow, and we can have a big old talk about a wedding and raising this baby."

"Sure. Just show up."

After Brynlee left, Gary looked for Ephrem. He found him on the porch swinging with Kansas. Gary politely asked Kansas to go home for a while so he could take care of some family business with Ephrem. Gary shut the door to the house and closed all the blinds. As Kansas left, she thought she heard the sound of something breaking and then hitting the floor.

Brynlee was running late for supper with her father. It was already getting dark. Her car was losing power. She pulled off onto the side road near the Red River Gorge entrance. She figured that her tampering with her car months ago may have caused the problem. Luckily for her, a van, driven by an unsightly woman, accompanied by another adult female who was just as homely, stopped to help her.

"Looks like bad cables going to your battery. They'll need to be replaced. Won't charge the alternator unless you get it fixed," the passenger said.

"I've been meaning to get that fixed. My baby's father said the same thing."

"So, you are pregnant, honey. You can't be more than seventeen," said the driver.

"Yes, two months in the oven, and I just turned seventeen," replied a proud Brynlee.

"We could give you a ride," offered the passenger.

"I can call my daddy," Brynlee responded while nervously looking at her cell phone with no service.

"Honey, not much chance of service in this area. We'll give you a lift. If you are hungry, I have some leftover pizza. Baby's got to eat too," said the driver.

"Okay. I was just going about five miles out toward Pineridge," Brynlee answered.

"What's your name?" asked the driver.

"It's Brynlee."

"Nice to meet you. I'm Valerie, and this here is my sister Kitty," the driver responded back.

Brynlee never made it to supper and never returned to Gary's. A missing person's report was filed the next day by Brynlee's father, which was taken lightly by Sheriff Stone. Less than a day since Brynlee disappeared, gossip began around the school that she had run away from home to California.

CHAPTER NINETEEN

Leg pain that felt like thick gauged needles pricking her awakened Paisley from a deep sleep. Paisley sat up in bed, grabbed a couple of ibuprofen, and chased them with a sip of her Fuji water. She prayed that the OTC meds would make some difference since her legs were really bothering her now. She knew this was not a good sign. She figured that the MRI had not clearly picked up on a new lesion, or there was more deterioration that couldn't be seen. She wanted to be transparent with Kansas, but her gut told her that she needed to be part of this case. Somehow there was something about it that was personal. Maybe it was because her daughter was the age of many of these girls or something else. She didn't want to call the neurologist. The doctor would probably push for the infusion, which would take Paisley down for a week.

Given everything going on, Paisley decided to take a night off from her diet to have some comfort food. Gary and Ephrem were invited over to feast on the chicken and dumplings that Paisley had made in the crockpot. During supper, Kansas talked about the Flatt girl that had disappeared. Kansas said that drama students were gossiping that Brynlee had allegedly run away and that she was a cutter. Ephrem seemed a little sad and revealed that he dated her and hadn't talked to her at school for some time since they broke up. He was worried about her safety and wished her no harm. This seemed to satisfy Kansas.

Gary further added that Brynlee had a reputation of being a troublemaker and a little loose with the boys. He further indicated that her father was not the most honest person, and you needed to count your pills in your bottles to make sure you weren't cheated. Paisley took everything in and processed it. She looked at Gary, and he knew, like himself, that she might be a victim of the Black Market Syndicate.

After the teens disappeared into the living room to watch the *Avengers* on Disney +, Gary filled his bowl with a generous helping of cherry cobbler and added a scoop of vanilla ice cream. Because of Brynlee stopping by to visit him just before she disappeared, Gary was a little nervous. He tried to appear comfortable and proceeded to ask questions about Paisley's case.

"So, I know that you think that this girl is a possible victim. Any forward movement on the case?" asked Gary.

"None. I believe I will have to start following some leads and doing some door-knocking. You know — old-fashioned detective work. Kansas may not like it. She'll worry about my stress and MS, and she'll not like covering for me at the shop."

"I know you have some more symptoms. I can tell that you seem more easily tired. I suspect your legs."

"You're good," she said, complimenting him.

"My cousin had MS. She talked about all her symptoms and

issues. Bless her heart, she passed fifteen years ago. It wasn't MS that got her. Driving a tractor after one in the morning while drinking some bad shine — that took her out," Gary added.

"I'll keep that in mind and avoid tractors and shine. Back to the case. If this girl was promiscuous, she might have become pregnant, making her a possible victim. Socioeconomically, she doesn't fit the other girls' backgrounds. However, she may have lied, disguised her situation, or been at the wrong place. I'm thinking of going to Chicago to see Charlie. There's a connection between the girl in my freezer and a body that was found on the outskirts of Chicago about two years ago who had just given birth."

"Well, that's a coincidence. What's the connection?"

"They were sisters."

"How did —"

"Shared the same mother. Birth records were pulled on both and compared."

"There's something that I need to tell you."

"Did one of your cows commit a cow-napping?"

"No. Ephrem doesn't know this, but Brynlee came to see me before she went missing. She told me that Ephrem got her pregnant. I didn't believe her. She showed me pics of him, and her engaged in the act. From what I can tell, she doped him. Ephrem did not remember anything after waking up in the parking lot lying near the woods. He just thought he had mono or something. He knows I'd kick his ass if he cheated on Kansas. She said that I'd get Ephrem to marry her or else. She left after telling me. Said she'd be back to hear when the wedding would occur. That was the end of it. A day later, she was reported missing."

"You know you could have come to me. Why hide something like this? Why do you believe he wouldn't have had sex with her? Not to insult you or him, but he's a guy."

"He hadn't seen her for a while, and he was adamant that he didn't want anything to do with her."

"Some things offered to boys are hard to resist."

Gary looked Paisley directly in the eyes and provided the best defense he could offer for his grandson. "I know Ephrem. He's a good boy, and he's in love with Kansas."

"Why haven't you gone to the police with this information?"

"No one has returned my call from the sheriff's office."

"Stone!"

"You think he's sitting on this."

"He's as qualified as a turnip to conduct an investigation. You should have contacted the state police. I'm calling Stretchie."

Paisley called Stretchie and informed him of what Gary told her and that Sheriff Stone had been informed already but had done nothing thus far. Less than thirty minutes after getting off the phone with Paisley, Stretchie called back and said he set Sheriff Stone straight. Paisley didn't mind that Stretchie tore into Stone, but she knew it would only complicate things for her in the future working with local law enforcement.

"Gary, we need to question Ephrem. Stretchie will be over soon. He's doing a lie detector test to be sure that you and Ephrem have no involvement in Brynlee's disappearance."

"I know that both of us will pass with flying colors," Gary proclaimed.

"I guess that we'd better brief the two before he gets here,"

Paisley informed him.

The conversation with Ephrem and Kansas went about as well as predicted. Ephrem denied any cheating or sex with his ex, and Kansas questioned him like he was in an interrogation. Ephrem still had no recollection of talking with Brynlee, and Kansas barely remembered her at the play audition.

Stretchie showed up and went straight to business. Gary volunteered to go first to decrease any anxiety Ephrem might have about doing the test.

"Okay, Gary. Let's start with some basics," Stretchie said. "What is your full name?"

"Gary Wayne Quaillan."

"What is your current age?" the detective continued.

"73."

"Let's try a simple lie to make sure there's no issue with the machine. How many times have you been married?" Stretchie asked.

"Twenty."

The needle went to the far side of the polygraph machine.

"That's good. It knows you are lying and telling the truth. Tell me about Brynlee's visit with you."

"I was in my barn office. I'd just finished logging in some data on my cream samples, and there was a knock on the office door. She was just staring at me. Then she starts in about being knocked up by Ephrem. I told her that I didn't believe her. She said she'd be back with more proof the next day. She had pictures but Ephrem appeared to be drugged. I questioned Ephrem, and he swears he hasn't talked to her in some time. He doesn't recall being with her either. I believe him."

Paisley watched the needle, and it tended to remain unwavering.

"Gary, did she give you an idea about where she was going or if she was meeting someone?" continued Stretchie.

"She mentioned an aunt, but that's it."

"In your conversation with her, did you threaten her?"

"No. I think I called her dad a cheat, or did I just say that to myself. I can't remember."

"Okay. Seems your story is pretty intact. Ephrem, you're up next," said Stretchie while pointing for Ephrem to take a seat at the table.

Ephrem pulled his pants up and took his hat off. Stretchie hooked him up. To decrease additional distress for Ephrem, Paisley asked for Kansas to go to her room. Kansas was reluctant at first and then left.

"Ephrem, let's start with the last time you saw Brynlee?"

"It was in May of this year at a school baseball game. Just said "hi" as we passed each other. We broke up last fall. We'd been going back and forth trying to remain friends, but it wasn't working. She was being — obsessive and caught in the past. Liked to cling to me too much. Felt smothered," Ephrem replied with some nervousness in his voice. However, the polygraph still indicated he was telling what he thought was true.

"How did you get along?" Stretchie inquired.

"Early on — very well. Afterward, not so great. Argued a lot."

"Did you ever have sex?"

The room grew quiet. Ephrem began tapping his foot.

"We talked about it."

"That's not the question. Please answer."

"No."

The polygraph indicated he was lying.

"Let's try this again. Did you have sex?"

"Yes and no."

"Ephrem. It's either you did or didn't," pushed Stretchie.

"She gave me — she gave me — a handjob."

"When did that happen?" followed up Stretchie.

"About a month after we started dating," Ephrem replied.

"Did you have intercourse?"

"She said she wanted to screw me. I was willing to, but then she started talking about having babies, and there was no need for protection. It kind of turned me off. I ain't someone wanting to raise no kid at my age. To answer your question, we talked about it, but we never did it."

The polygraph was calm, and Ephrem appeared to be honest about the issue.

"Ephrem, you are excused. Don't skip town," Stretchie warned.

Gary asked Ephrem to go home, and he would meet him there.

Ephrem asked before leaving, "Can you tell Kansas that I didn't do anything? I don't want her to be mad at me."

Paisley replied, "Sure." Paisley immediately texted Kansas: *Appearing innocent at this time. Be nice to him.*

Ephrem exited. Gary, Stretchie, and Paisley sat around the table while Stretchie wrote a few more notes. While Stretchie packed up the polygraph, they talked.

"You and Ephrem were the only possible witnesses that might have seen her before she disappeared. She never came back to see you, and she never talked to Ephrem. Sounds like she may have raped your grandson after drugging him. Her motivation seems to be her obsession with Ephrem. She might face charges once she is found for that. Right now, being pregnant at her age — that makes her a risk of being kidnapped these days," stated Stretchie.

"Where do we go from here?" asked Gary.

"No, we in this. This is an official police investigation. You'll need to keep your sleuthing to theories," Paisley interjected.

"Okay. I get when I am not needed," Gary added.

"We need to take a road trip to Chicago to see Charlie and look into my freezer victim's sister who was found in a lake two years ago," commented Paisley to draw attention to the case that coincided close to the time her husband was killed.

While Paisley and Stretchie began planning their trip, Brynlee's cell phone's memory and cloud storage were being erased. Afterward, a man in a hoodie threw Brynlee's phone into the floorboard of her car. He then dropped her car into the scrap yard's compacter using a giant magnet. No one else was at the old, abandoned salvage yard to care. It had been marked closed and with no trespassing sign for over ten years. The salvage yard's sole purpose was to destroy evidence and sometimes bodies for the BMS. Looking into the car's window, the man smiled as the vehicle was made into a cube of scrap. Unbeknownst to the unnamed man, it wasn't just a cellphone and a car that he had destroyed. There was also a bloody diary resting under the car seat, evidencing Brynlee's obsession for Ephrem, along with questions to ask her aunt about how to prove paternity. There were even notes indicating what she did to

Ephrem and which day she raped him. However, no one would ever know because the cube was dropped into a giant vat of acid which instantaneously turned it into slush.

CHAPTER TWENTY

Paisley awoke with hands that would barely open. From the way she was feeling last night, she knew that it would be one of those days. She had taken the liberty of putting the paraffin warmer on a timer the night before so it would be ready when she got up. She immersed her hands into the hot, liquid wax and pulled them out. This would help some, but she would have to stretch them out more to get them to work right. She still hadn't told her daughter that her symptoms were accelerating. There was some tingling in her saddle area, but it was minor compared to when she first got the diagnosis. When she had the major incident that put her in the hospital, she swore she'd die before wearing a Depends and getting catheterized. That's why she worked so hard to retrain her bladder and bowels by going to the bathroom on a schedule.

She took another dose of ibuprofen and made herself a cup of strong coffee. For some reason, coffee seemed to help with some of her MS symptoms. The jury was still out on whether coffee psychologically or medically helped — she just knew she felt better after a couple of cups. Based on the time on the cuckoo clock, Kansas would be down soon, and Paisley wanted to pretend that nothing was wrong. As she was pushing down on the Keurig, Gary showed up with his paper and favorite mug for their morning ritual. She liked Gary a lot, but there were days like today when she didn't want to see him. Gary was very perceptive of situations and might say something to cause Kansas to investigate her condition more. Paisley didn't need any more complications, especially since she also planned on telling Kansas that she was going to Chicago to follow up on her case.

"What flavor of coffee today?" asked her wanna-be crime-solving neighbor.

"Hazelnut, but I have regular if you like."

"I'm a little nutty, so give me the Hazel. You got any new hunches on this case?"

"Not a lot at this point. No idea who's running things in this state and where the girls are disappearing. I'm starting in Chicago, where the freezer girl's sister was drug out of a lake. She was pregnant too."

"Coincidence or just planned killing?"

"Not hundred percent sure. I think this "Black Market Syndicate" is behind it, and the girls and their babies are part of it. I suspect there is a local operation around here going on. I wouldn't be surprised if Sheriff Stonehead was involved. Seems some crooked law enforcement is always involved."

"You going with Stretchie?"

"Yes. Before you start on matching —"

"Matching who?" said a wide-awake Kansas who stumbled into

the kitchen in search of caffeine.

"Gary and his obsession to match couples. Never mind him. Are ya off to school?" Paisley inquired while making a to go cup for Kansas.

"Waiting on Ephrem to take me. He's been through a lot. It wasn't great that you questioned him like a serial killer last night."

"Proved him innocent — didn't it?" commented Paisley.

"We texted till after midnight, and he was so upset. He was worried that he would have to stop seeing me or I'd break up with him."

"I don't think that's going to happen. That boy deeply cares about you," said a reassuring Gary.

A horn blew outside the door, and Kansas started to walk out, but her mother interrupted her departure. "Honey, I love you. I need you to stay with Jolene Grossman for a few days. I need to take a trip back to Chicago."

Kansas stopped from opening the screen door. "Mom, does this have to do with the case?"

"Yes. It's a lead, and I need to see Charlie. Stretchie is going up with me."

"An investigation or a romantic getaway?" Kansas asked.

"That's what I've been wondering," added Gary with a shit-eating grin across his face.

"Both of you stop. This is strictly a case-based trip," blasted Paisley, who was hiding her left pinkie that was starting to shake and involuntarily flex.

"Okay, Mom. But staying with Ms. Grossman requires extra capital. She might be your childhood friend, but she's a big bore. I'll need some money to buy a milkshake and go to a movie tomorrow night.

Please tell her it's okay."

"I will if you are back to her house by ten o'clock. I'm assuming that you are going with Ephrem?"

"Yeah."

"Gary, you okay with this?"

"Ephrem will be a perfect gentleman, or he'll get more chores than he's had in his years of living."

"We'll work out the details this afternoon. I still need to pack."

"Love ya," replied Kansas, who blew her mother a hurried kiss, as she rushed out the wooden screen door, causing it to slam loud against the frame.

As soon as Kansas was out of sight and earshot, Gary said, "Good job hiding that evil little pinkie misbehaving. She'll eventually catch on."

"Shut up, Gary."

The rain fell hard and heavy onto the car window. Stretchie and Paisley had chosen to drive over flying because of budgetary expenses; besides, they wanted some scenery and conversation along the way. It had been a while since Paisley had been with a man that she liked, let alone, once loved. Stretchie still had that same boyish charm that he had in high school. He could still flash a smile that made you feel comfortable and aroused at the same time.

Breakfast in Indianapolis seemed like a good stopping point for the two. They were still around three hours out. They had left at four o'clock in the morning, and both were wide awake, thanks to the strong coffee that Paisley had brewed for them. Business was part of their breakfast, and both pulled out their note pads and went over their observations and theories.

"The Black Market Syndicate is the key to all this. Find a break in their chain and exploit their weakness," said Stretchie with a loaded fork full of hash browns, dripping ketchup on the table.

"I concur, detective. I believe we've got our own local hive of hornets that we need to stir sitting somewhere in or around the Red River Gorge."

"I hope your gut is correct about this. Otherwise, we're wasting time stirring the nest."

"Have I ever led you astray?" she naughtily asked.

"Come to think of it — about five times. Would you like me to start with the swimming hole at the lake when you told me that grapevine would hold me, and I fell on my ass before I got two feet from where I started. It didn't help that some animal had crapped in the spot I dropped."

"As far as I was concerned, you were on target."

"So, what's our angle when we get to Chicago?"

"We are going to meet Charlie at his apartment. He can access all the files we need from there, and we can take a field trip to the crime scene."

"I'll leave it in your capable hands. Here let me get the tab. Kentucky State Police are obliged to cover this as part of your consulting contract."

"Thanks. Can't call it a date for certain now."

Charlie hadn't been up very long when the two arrived. He had been on a stake-out for a supposed terrorist who turned out to be a harmless, innocent student at a community college. Evidently, some racist students had tried to set him up. Good thing for the alleged terrorist that the students setting him up were caught in the act and melted like butter on a hot griddle when put under pressure. Now, they would be the ones in jail facing charges.

The autopsy report of the young girl found in the lake indicated that she had given birth shortly before her death. The baby was never located. The delivery was natural. Few clues pointed to a person of interest. However, there was a Cooke County EMT services sheet wrapped around the girl's body. It was suspected that she was killed before being dumped into the water. She had no identification on her. Two years ago, she had been arrested in Winchester, Kentucky, at a Walmart for shoplifting. If she had not been arrested, she would have remained a Jane Doe.

"Her sister was strangled at my store. Different methods for sure. Makes me think the BMS uses different hired killers to take care of their problems. Probably contractors. There was no evidence of anyone else entering. Definitely prompted me to beef up security. I'm still trying to figure out why my shop? What made her choose my shop?" Paisley said, puzzled.

"Easy access. When we checked your back door, it appeared she had picked the lock," answered Stretchie.

"I've upgraded to a heavy-duty door and lock with a video

surveillance system. Trying to keep crime down in Fester. Ice cream is a hot commodity," Paisley added to lessen the serious tone of the conversation.

"At first, we thought she might be a druggie, prostitute, or someone who happened to be in the wrong place at the wrong time. Proved us wrong," Stretchie added.

"We both believe that she escaped from the Black Market Syndicate holding station in Kentucky. The soil samples they found in her hair, between her toes, and her nails indicated she had been somewhere in the Red River Gorge recently. We think she broke loose and got the hell out of dodge and was hunted down and killed like a deer," Paisley stated as she rubbed her pinkie on her left hand, which was twitching again.

Both astute detectives noticed the agitated baby finger immediately.

"If this case is getting too stressful —" Charlie blurted out.

"If you are having some problems, we can back off —" interjected Stretchie.

"Both of you can keep your opinions and concerns to yourself. It just so happens that working a case keeps me calmer than sitting at home worrying about if I will be in a wheelchair in five years or that I need to just do nothing and let this disease take over. Keep your concerns for when I need them. Now, let's get back to the case."

"Yes, mam," both responded.

"Says she has family from the Chicago area. I'm guessing she was abducted here and taken to Kentucky for ripening. Let's start with the crime scene. I want to know where she got that sheet, and I want to talk to their mother and anyone else that can tell us something," Paisley spewed out.

"Their mother is in prison, some half-siblings sprinkled throughout several states, and her daddy was killed when a heist went bad at a pawn shop a year ago," replied Charlie.

"Let's go. We can work out the interviews later. We only have a limited time to get clues and eat decent pizza. I want Louie's tonight," requested Paisley.

"You got it," Charlie responded.

The drive to Maple Lake was uneventful. Paisley made them stop at Joe's Donuts for old-time sake for pitiful black coffee and sugary donuts. It reminded her of the old days working for CPD.

No one was out at the former crime scene. The victim had only been a few days deceased when her body was discovered by a young couple whose dog had jumped into the water to retrieve a frisbee. Charlie indicated that they were not even sure where the body had been initially tossed into the water with 8000 feet of shoreline.

It seemed like the girl may have been moved from the original crime scene, and the body dumped to disconnect. Other than being a sheet with the Chicago EMT service stamped on it, it held nothing to indicate how she had gotten it. If the girl had been killed two nights from the day she was discovered, she would have been killed around the same time Paisley's husband was killed. He worked for the Chicago EMT. *Could there be a connection between both of their deaths?* Paisley wondered.

Paisley decided to keep her suspicions to herself. She would review her husband's case tonight at the hotel. She had digitized all of the documents related to his case to access the information from the cloud anytime she needed it.

A trip out to the Logan Correctional Institute would hopefully provide additional answers. Charlie remained in the car to deal with some new developments on other cases he was working. With Charlie's clout, Stretchie and Paisley were easily granted access to the prison and permitted a courtesy interview.

Lyndie Pearson was brought to an interrogation room and handcuffed to a table. She was serving a fifteen-year sentence for selling and manufacturing meth near a school. She was probably once a gorgeous woman, but now she had an excessive loss of hair and teeth, and her skin looked like it was part elephant.

"Listen, I don't know what ya want, but I'm already doing time," replied the convict with a tattoo of Gene Simmons in KISS makeup on her left arm.

"I'm Paisley Hunter, and this is Bishop Knight. Lyndie, we want to talk about your daughters. I'm sorry for your losses," Paisley

"If I cared, I guess I'd say something like thank you. The truth is those two gave me hell. Didn't let me keep a man or make any money. They were always running off as soon as they could get a chance."

"I take it that you weren't close?" asked Stretchie.

"Who is? Listen, I ain't seen them in a long time, and it wasn't a reunion to remember. Both getting knocked up — at least it wasn't at the same time. Maybe they thought someone would play house with them. They're dead now. I'm doing my time, and then I'll make something of myself this time when I get out."

"When did you last talk with either of them?" Paisley pushed.

"D.J. — about two or so years ago. She was trying to hook up with somebody who gave new pregnant teens big money. Sounded too good to be true. Heard she was shot and found in a lake or something. Bad way to go. My cousin was shot when he was five. He lived but then drowned later that year. Weird."

"What about your youngest?"

"Pamela ... I didn't raise her. You could ask my skank sister who kept her but she's dead. I ain't seen her forever. She always thought her older sister had the answer to everything. I got word that she got knocked up too. I never heard how she died. Not that I'm interested."

"Pamela was killed in Kentucky. She was abducted. We believe she was killed for her baby as well."

"So, I got two dumb shits for daughters. I sure didn't need to be a grandparent. They're dead now, so ... No reason to worry about stupid shit anymore," she said while tearing up.

"Do you know anything about where D.J. met these people offering money for her baby?" asked Stretchie.

"The word here is they got an operation somewhere near the Clybourn Bridge. That's all I got."

"Think of anything else?" Paisley asked.

"Yeah, go to hell. I have television privileges in five, so I'm going. Guard, we are through."

It wasn't a lost cause to talk to Lyndie because they left the prison with a new lead. It sounded like they needed to investigate whatever was happening at Clybourn Bridge. Paisley and Stretchie discussed it with Charlie. They all planned to go down after nine o'clock tonight when the less respectable Chicago citizens came out.

Charlie dropped Paisley and Stretchie off at their hotel. Paisley took a shower. There was something about being in prison next to the scum that made her feel like dirt. As soon as she showered, she grabbed her Mac Notebook and loaded her husband's investigation files. In less than five minutes, she found what she was looking for. Although there were no drugs in the EMT vehicle her husband was driving on the night he was killed, the inventory showed only one item missing from the van — a white Chicago EMT sheet. Her hunch had been correct. Her husband's death was somehow linked to D.J.'s death. She then pulled up the blood sample from the EMT vehicle. Besides her husband's blood, there was blood from another person — identified as female. Some remnants of amniotic fluid were found on the floor, suspected of being there from a former birth but never confirmed who had given birth in the van.

Paisley now believed that her husband had been an innocent victim. He must have stopped to help and was killed in the process. The girl was probably tracked or had a tracking device and was killed after giving birth. The tracker was probably overlooked. Paisley was now excited that she was on her way to solving her husband's death. At the same time, she was angry that she hadn't seen this connection before. It took the death of this girl's sister in her shop to put the two together. Perhaps it was coincidence, fate, or Gregory pointing her in the right direction.

CHAPTER TWENTY-ONE

Damn, the traffic was loud above Douggie Grappler's tent. He had recently rotated from a spot in New Jersey and was tired of moving and living like the homeless. Last week it was Arkansas and the week before it was Kentucky. He was becoming more and more impatient with the BMS. Sentiments of anger and disgruntlement summed up how he felt about his predicament. Douggie had played his part for nearly three years, and he was promised that he would quickly move up, but he had been lied to by his BMS handler over and over. Penelope Gold, who started a year later than him, had already moved up to one of the local council seats. He knew that he could continue as a lowly pregnant mama recruiter for now. Still, he'd be kidding himself if the BMS would keep him around much longer in his current role. He was already approaching twenty-three, and he couldn't pass for someone under eighteen for much longer.

Douggie thought about quitting but quitting the BMS was not that easy. Regardless, he had nothing else to do and nowhere to go. Douggie's old man had kicked him out of the house five years ago, and his mother was dead by the time he hit grade school. He had no idea what had happened to any of his sisters. They had left years before he did. Any other relatives were a myth or some whore his father brought home who he was told to call "aunt" or "stepmom."

Tonight, looked like it would be a good night. Two new young, pregnant girls had made their way to Clybourn Tent City. Both made a straight line to the fire, trying to warm up. They looked hungry, tired, and vulnerable — just how he liked them. Douggie pulled out his acting chops and began his facade. He started out being friendly and sympathetic; then, he built some trust to get them on board. In reality, Douggie had no idea what became of the girls once they left, nor did he really care. He just figured they were better off than how they started — he certainly was. He had no idea that these not-so-innocent bitches were just pieces of meat to be sold to others for deplorable sexual fantasies or worse. For Douggie, each one he convinced to sell their baby meant time away from this shit hole and more money in his pocket.

The first mark was a black girl no more than fourteen. She was small for her age and was shy. She looked as if she hadn't had a bath in weeks. She went by the name LaTisha. The other girl was at least a couple of years older, with black hair and blue eyes. She appeared to like food, given she was slightly heavyset even before her pregnancy. Her favorite food right now was a big bag of Doritos and any orange, cheap, sugary soda. Her name was Martina, but everyone called her Marti.

Douggie offered them one of his extra tents for shelter, indicating the two could share it. He gave them the spill about him being the "go-to" person at the camp. He explained that his job was to make sure newbies were kept safe and didn't starve. He tried to make them feel at ease by telling them that he'd been where they were at, and no one had cared about him, and he was surviving. He also told them all about how he had sworn if he survived his first year on the streets that he would help others. He called it "paying it back to the streets." Like so many other pregnant teens, both girls believed him.

After stealing a couple of boxes of chicken and potato wedges for the two girls from the local convenience store, Douggie began asking them about what life had been like for them.

LaTisha said she was orphaned because her parents "went and overdosed," and she was going to be forced to live with her bitch of an aunt. She didn't want to be in the system and instead took her chances on the streets. She'd ran and got knocked up with some dude whom she met at a shelter. That was three months ago, and she didn't even know his name.

Marti was from a family that had spoiled her for the most part. She got whatever she wanted, but her parents only paid attention to her older sister. When she got pregnant, her parents wanted her to have an abortion or give the baby to her childless cousin to raise as her own. Marti told them to go fuck themselves and ran off. Her baby's father was some older dude who came to a party at her parents who worked with her dad. At that point, Douggie knew that Marti may not be the best target because parents with money don't like to lose their valuables, even if it is not to their liking all the time. He focused more on helping LaTisha in his conversations, but it seemed that Marti and LaTisha had bonded. Wherever LaTisha went, Marti wanted to go as well.

Around 9:15 p.m., three homeless adults ascended upon the Clybourn Bridge. The bridge was located in the middle of Chicago with a full view of traffic, trash, pollution, and the homeless that people ignore. Paisley was quite pleased with her clothing choices — a Christmas sweatshirt that read "Grandma Rocking in the Season," torn granny jeans, and holy boots. She had even blacked out a couple teeth to give the impression of poor oral hygiene. Charlie made a perfect-looking bum, but he looked like he modeled himself after Charlie Chaplin's *Little Tramp*. Stretchie looked the most ridiculous of the trio, wearing a jogging suit at least forty years old, a Yukon hat made of beaver, and pushing a shopping cart with one wheel that wouldn't turn. Regardless of what Charlie and Paisley thought, Stretchie received a compliment for his attire from Harry, a former down-on-his-luck banker, who offered him a couple of cans of tuna for the sweats.

Each of them had entered from different directions. No one at Clybourn Tent City paid them particular attention. Homeless people moved in and out all the time here. As far as most were concerned, Stretchie, Paisley, and Charlie were just more unknowns passing through. The majority of the temporary residents were friendly. Most new guests were invited to stand around the burning barrels to talk, and those thirsty were offered bottled libation. None of the trio partook from the shared bottle. However, to make others more at ease, they pulled out their own bottles in brown bags, which they had previously filled with tea, to keep up appearances.

Their tip that a young recruiter hung out at the bridge paid off within the first hour. They noticed Douggie standing over talking with two young teens who appeared pregnant. However, they wanted to observe him before bringing him for questioning. Paisley offered to go over and pry. She thought since being a female would be less intimidating and wouldn't suggest cop (or ex-cop) right away, she could infiltrate without much suspicion.

Cautiously, Paisley made her way over while taking large swigs of the fake liquor. Her MS, which naturally made her off balance, made it appear that she had been drinking as she worked less to control her gait issues. Immediately, Paisley's presence made Douggie anxious and annoyed as he trusted no one.

"What's up?" Paisley said while slurring her words.

"Talking. This is kind of a private conversation if you don't mind," responded Douggie.

"Free world, public land ... Last time I checked. What you say, ladies?" Paisley responded as obnoxiously as she could.

"Oh, let her stay. Ain't too many of us women here anyway?" piped up LaTisha.

"You want a drink?" Paisley said as she took a swig and spit back into the bottle simultaneously.

"Nah. We'd better not. Besides, we are pregnant. Got babies to take care of," added Marti.

"Me too. You see that guy with the cart. He and I did it — in that cart. Now, I'm knocked up. No money, honey."

"Sorry about your predicament. Nothing we can do to help. Again, old hag, this is a private conversation," responded a ticked off Douggie.

"Douggie, you just told us that someone was going to be by later that could help us. Was that bullshit?" LaTisha pointed out.

"No. They usually just help younger mothers. Not crones," he replied.

"Crone. I'll have you know that I'm not a day over thirty-four," Paisley replied, feeling a little angry at having her age made fun of by some two-bit punk.

"Listen, lady. Just go back to your cart and have a baby in it. It's natural," Douggie said.

"Fine. Nice meeting you, ladies. I can't say the same to you, Douchie," Paisley said as she moved slowly away. She was able to catch some of their talk before being out of earshot. She heard "van," "11:30," and "be ready to go."

Paisley went back to socialize with her pseudo-homeless friends and informed them of the situation. They would wait until twenty-five after eleven and move into place; then Paisley would cover Douggie and Stretchie, and Charlie would cover the van and the girls.

The van pulled near the homeless camp right on time. An older woman smoking a Camel was blowing smoke out of the window, flipping her wrists as she talked to someone on her phone.

"There she is? She won't wait long, so you need to go now," Douggie informed them.

LaTisha and Marti grabbed their few belongings and headed toward the van. Before the girls could get a couple of yards from Douggie, Paisley tackled him. Feeling scared, LaTisha and Marti speedily ran toward the van. Charlie and Stretchie, expecting the van to pull to the other side, began to run toward the girls.

The woman driving the van noticed the girls running and hit the sliding van door button. The two girls jumped inside. All Charlie and Stretchie could do was watch the van squeal out and head to the main street. Unfortunately, the license plate was covered with mud. Only the number "5" was visible. The van's model and color were also difficult to determine because of the poor lighting.

Paisley flipped Douggie to the ground, and she put his arms behind his back. She gladfully handcuffed him and turned him over while his face wallowed in the mud.

"I got mine. Where's yours?" Paisley asked her partners.

"Well, we just happened to be on the wrong side when the van pulled in," Stetchie said while trying to catch his breath.

"You bagged the slime bucket recruiter," Charlie noted.

"Who are you shits?" Douggie said while spitting out mud.

"We are your interrogators. You going to sing like a bird by the time we get done with you."

Paisley and Charlie pulled Douggie up. Douggie spat at them.

"Just like old times, Charlie," Paisley responded.

CHAPTER TWENTY-TWO

Smoke blew from the van's window like an industrial chimney spewing pollutants. The chain smoking woman driving had hardly said a word to the two girls after their escape. Marti nor LaTisha were not in the mood for conversation anyhow. Marti had thrown up in the back of her throat as soon as the van sped off, and LaTisha had managed to pee on herself some. Both girls had chosen to be quiet to further analyze their predicament. They had begun to realize that some criminal elements were involved in whatever they had gotten themselves into. Now, they were rethinking if they wanted to be part of that.

After putting some distance from the Clybourn Bridge, their driver Valerie offered them a bag of Big Bruno's Bad Burgers with some fries. The fries were soggy, and the burgers were cold. Even though they hadn't had a decent meal in weeks, they had lost their appetites, and Valerie had lost her first attempt to sedate them. Valerie would try later when their appetites were driven by a baby's need to be fed.

Both girls asked for a pit stop shortly after leaving the Chicago city limits. The old van seats were uncomfortable, and LaTisha's hemorrhoids bothered her. Valerie told them it was her job to ensure their safety, so she had to go wherever they did. Marti was no fan of Valerie, who smelled like a greasy, rancid pile of human flesh that had been deep-fried in cigarette ashes. Marti's instincts were good for the most part when it came to people — Valerie was up to no good.

Marti was the first to push an escape plan. Using her lipstick, Marti wrote the word "Run" on a square of toilet tissue and passed it to LaTisha under the stall. LaTisha was immediately on board with the plan since they were most likely being chased back at the bridge by cops. For the next few minutes, Marti continued to write notes on toilet paper and pass them to LaTisha with her plan — stealing the van and leaving Valerie stranded. Both felt stealing the van would be a piece of cake since both had extensive experience stealing vehicles. The plan's success hinged on getting away from Valerie, who carried a gun and watched them like a hawk.

Feeling the need to go to the bathroom before they got on the road, Valerie asked the two girls to remain in the bathroom with her, indicating to the teens that they would all leave at the same time. In return for the girls' cooperation, she promised them a candy bar and a soda of their choice. Both complacently agreed, seeing an opportunity to put their plan in action. As soon as Valerie sat on the pot, both girls reached under the stall, and each girl grabbed one of Valerie's legs. They pulled hard and fast. Valerie's head hit the back of the toilet bowl with a loud thud, and then Valerie slid down onto the urine-ridden tile and went unconscious.

The teens rummaged through her pockets and took her ID, keys, her cell phone. She had no cash or credit cards on her. Then they shoved her back further into the stall. Both exited the small bathroom, which had an exterior lock that LaTisha managed to lock from the outside using her hairclip. This bought them some more time.

Turning up the music and tossing out Valerie's cigs and lighter, they drove off and headed west to Nevada. They figured they both could pass for twenty-one and might find work somewhere on the Las Vegas strip. Hours later, they discovered a nice stack of cash in the glove compartment. LaTisha counted the money twice and both times it totaled twenty grand. With their new, unexpected windfall, they changed direction and decided to go to Los Angeles to be discovered and become rich and famous.

Almost fifteen minutes later, Valerie pulled herself up from the floor and washed the pile of blood off the back of her head. There was nothing she could do about the urine-soaked clothes. She checked her pockets for what had been taken. Everything was gone. She knew the BMS would definitely frown upon this incident, and she would be punished. Luckily, her uglier twin sister could help track where the girls had went, and she would make the little bitches pay.

Valerie banged on the door until someone from the gas station unlocked it. She then asked to borrow a phone, informing the employee that she had been robbed. The store associate offered to call the police for her. Wanting to keep the cops out of the situation, Valerie lied and said the two girls were her daughter and niece who took it, and she preferred to take care of them herself. A quick and angry call to her sister Kitty was made. Dependable Kitty arrived, and Valerie was fit to be tied. While Valerie bitched and laid out her punishment for the teenage miscreants, Kitty worried about their situation. She knew they had to retrieve both teens, or she and Valerie would die an unpleasant death.

Douggie was not scared. At least, that was what he was showing on the outside. Inside, he was terrified that he'd be sent to prison and become someone's little bitch or be killed by the BMS. He knew he couldn't give anyone up, and if he did, it might end poorly for him. *What did they have on him anyway?* he thought.

"Douggie Jeremiah Grappler. Good name. Looks like a few problems with petty theft from a few years ago. You went to juvie, and you've been clean for a bit. Now, you seem to be involved with the Black Market Syndicate. Organized crime — not a good thing," Paisley said to get the conversation started.

"I have no idea what you are talking about," Douggie smugly replied.

"I'll tell you what, Buttercup — these people you've aligned yourself with — they'll drop you like a turd in a toilet. They don't care. Either fess up or let them take you out. We can protect you. You know a trip to the Feds is equal to a trip to the coroner in their eyes," Charlie shot back.

"I ain't saying nothing. Anyhow, people know that I don't talk," Douggie continued to proclaim.

Wiping the crumbs off his shirt, Stretchie took another bite of his doughnut and commented, "We know that, but the guy watching you come out of the FBI building — he doesn't know what you said or didn't say. It's just being here makes you a liability. Especially, a little nobody like you that wouldn't be missed."

"You got nothing," Douggie proclaimed.

"We have a witness who said you were with one of the young girls when she was murdered," Paisley lied to manipulate and pressure the young hoodlum. "Serving time in prison for black market baby-selling and an accessory to murder .... If the cons don't kill you inside, one of the Black Market bastards will," Paisley pointed out.

Douggie was now looking pale and unsettled. He took a sip of his water. "What's in it for me if I give you some information."

"Protection. I'm with the FBI, and we have a pretty good record," Charlie assured him.

"I don't know you or them. You could be testing me. They got people everywhere, in every state, and in every important law enforcement, business, or political place. I'm a small potato that's expendable," Douggie resonated.

"Even small potatoes can make great fries. So, a deal or no deal? I can set you free and let them take care of you, I can hold you for suspicion of murder ... I got all kinds of options," Charlie informed him.

"We can start with what happens where you recruit. Start with the small things to break the bigger things open. We need to know about the babies and girls. We need to know where they go, what happens to them, and which people are involved," Paisley pushed him.

"Do it. Do something right in your life," Stetchie implored him.

Hours later, they had a lead on the woman driving the van. Her name was Valerie Cappiconio. She was a native Chicagoan who had worked with Douggie for a few years. She was what was called a "Taker." Valerie lived with her paternal twin sister Kitty Krunchie who owned a little jewelry shop under their shared apartment. Kitty had been married, but her husband was an alcoholic and wife-beater who disappeared five years ago and was never found. That's when Valerie moved in. Neither women had a history of prior arrests.

Charlie pulled their pictures up from the DMV. They were both ugly women, but Kitty was certainly uglier than her sister. In the photos, both had died blonde hair; their faces had more wrinkles than a Shar Pei, and they had matching unibrows. Both women smiled in their photos, displaying decaying teeth that only added to the level of disgust. All of them wondered if the two women had gotten even uglier than their pictures taken two years ago.

Two FBI agents were sent courtesy to the women's address. No one answered the door, and no vehicles were parked at their residence. Charlie suggested tracking their cell phones. The FBI director signed off on it, and they located Valerie's phone in Prophetstown, Illinois, but Kitty's phone was about 30 minutes out of the Chicago city limits. The trio packed up, and the two additional FBI agents traveled to assist. A BOLO was issued, and law enforcement was asked to be on the lookout for the van and the two sisters and two teens who might be traveling together. Paisley felt they would soon have some much needed answers.

Valerie was fit to be tied. She knew it would be a rough night. Kitty had always been the more rational and the calmer of the two; she knew how to calm her sister down. Kitty knew Camel cigarettes, and decaf green tea were the key to getting her sister focused. Since she had picked Valerie up, Valerie had already smoked six cigarettes, lighting one after another. Kitty smoked too but not as much.

Valerie had been doing this job for ten years and was good at it.

She wasn't bright or good-looking enough to move up to a higher position in the syndicate, but she had done what she was told to do and was well paid. Valerie needed to be well paid. She basically helped keep her sister's store afloat. She loved her sister, but the jewelry she made was uglier than she was. With her husband Neesom's death, Kitty lost most of her income. It was sad that Valerie had to kill the bastard, but no one was allowed to hurt her sister.

Valerie had also pinged her cell phone somewhere in Prophetstown. Whatever these two pregnant bitches were planning — they had stopped in the same place for some time. Kitty pulled out two handguns and made sure they were loaded. She then took a couple tasers and checked the charges. While pulling out two packs of peanut butter crackers, she retrieved an aerosol can of chloroform spray and shook it. They were ready to retrieve the packages.

LaTisha and Marti were glad to be away from Valerie and Chicago. They had twenty big ones, and they were going to relax — relax as much as two pregnant people can. They had found a hotel off the main highway and paid cash for their room. Before going to their room, they had driven through a fast food joint and picked up some candy at the local Walmart. Even after junking out on candy and fried food, Marti was still hungry and decided to walk to the drug store next door and get some more food while LaTisha hit the shower. LaTisha had just gotten out of the shower when there was a knock on room 305's door.

"Who is it?" shouted out LaTisha.

"Housekeeping. I'm here with your extra towels," said the voice on the other side of the door.

Being naïve, Latisha opened up the door. Brandishing a gun, Kitty shoved the door hard and entered the room, causing LaTisha to fall on her ass. Valerie followed behind her sister and closed the door.

"Don't damage the merchandise, Val. Damaged goods will get us killed," Kitty said to reel her sister in some.

"What do you want?" asked a scared LaTisha.

"You and your little friend. Where's she at?" demanded Valerie.

"She went to get food," she responded.

"We'll wait on her," Kitty said.

While they waited for Marti to return, LaTisha dressed and gathered her items. Valerie asked about the money. She knew they had probably discovered it. LaTisha pointed to the dresser drawer. Valerie counted it.

"There's $165 missing. I expect you'll be paying me back one way or another, including gas used in my van," Valerie angrily commented.

"Don't forget the twenty we had to slip the night clerk to give us the information," Kitty added.

"How are we supposed to pay you back? We ain't got no money," LaTisha responded.

"You'll either turn some tricks on the way to where you are going, or you have to do me. I like young ladies, you know," Valerie propositioned.

LaTisha appeared disgusted and didn't say a word.

Kitty watched from the window for the van to return to the room's parking spot. Finally, Marti returned, carrying several large bags of snacks and sodas. A key was heard going into the lock of the door.

"Hey, I can't get this turned. Got too much stuff in my hands. Can you open this up, Tish?" asked Marti who was now getting frustrated trying to turn a key while holding several bags of food.

Realizing that they would not harm her, LaTisha screamed for Marti to run. Marti threw the food in front of the door and ran as fast as possible. Kitty went after her while Valerie grabbed LaTisha's arm and held her. Marti was fast but being pregnant had slowed her down some. Kitty quickly caught up with her target. She shoved Marti to the ground and grabbed her by the hair of her head and pulled her back toward the hotel. It was past two in the morning, and no one was up; if anyone was up, they didn't care.

Charlie, Stretchie, and Paisley were alert and hyped while in pursuit. They had been driving speeds up to 100 mph to catch up to the suspects. They noticed the van just seconds after they pulled into the hotel's parking lot. They already knew that the hotel clerk had identified two girls and the two older women they were looking for. They headed to the hotel room with their guns drawn. The extra agents covered any back entrances just in case there was an escape.

Charlie knocked on the door of the hotel room. "FBI. I need you to open the door slowly. If you have any weapons, kick them out the door when you open it. We have this building covered."

"Go to hell. I got a hostage, and if you don't get the fuck out of here and let us go, I'll kill her and take as many of you bastards with me along the way," said an extremely irritated Valerie.

"Who am I speaking to?" asked Charlie.

"You're fucking grandmother. Does it matter? Clear the area and let us leave." Squeezing LaTisha's arm, Valerie directed her to speak up to show them that she meant business.

"She's got me. I'm scared. Do as she says. She crazy," said a frightened LaTisha.

"Okay. We don't want anyone hurt. Who else is with you?"

"Just me and the girl. Ain't nobody else."

Paisley shook her head. Something was off. Two girls should be with her. Where was the other sister and pregnant teen?

In the grass to the side of the hotel, Kitty used zip ties to secure her prey. She turned Marti onto her back, and Marti spat on her. Kitty wiped the spit off and then slapped Marti across the face with enough force to cause her nose to bleed.

Marti looked at Kitty in repugnance. "You're an ugly one. Where did they dig you up?"

"Keep your damn mouth shut, or I'll give you another smack."

"Smack all you like. I'll still won't cooperate."

"Have it your way." Kitty pulled out the chloroform and sprayed Marti, making Marti go unconscious. She then picked Marti up like a fifty pound bag of dog food and tossed her across her shoulder. Although Kitty was scrawny looking, she was strong as an ox.

On her way back to the hotel room, Kitty noticed three people in front of the hotel, and the van was being blocked by a car. From the looks of it, it was some type of government car. She initiated the backup plan. She threw Marti into the van and started it. The noise caught the attention of Stretchie, who turned around just in time to see the van pushing his car away, making dents and tearing headlights off along the way. Charlie radioed for the two agents to come around and pursue the van, trying to escape. The two agents, Detwilder and Cunningworth, pulled around, and the van T boned the driver's side and pushed the car into the hotel's entrance. With the agents' car out of commission, the van continued to make its escape; that's when Charlie decided to try a different approach.

"Listen, Kitty ... Valerie. Whichever sister you are. Please note your sister just ran with the other girl. That leaves you without a ride or a sister. You're all by yourself. Come on ... I'm sure you realize that the Black Market uppers won't like you losing any of their merchandise. I can only imagine what will happen to you and probably your sister if they come for you. You know how they are if the law becomes involved. Give yourself up. We can protect you if you cooperate. You are all alone now," Charlie informed her.

"I'm not one to rat out anyone," yelled Valerie.

Seeing an opportunity to get out of harm's way, LaTisha grabbed a chair and hit Valerie in the head, knocking her down. LaTisha then ran to the bathroom and locked herself in. Valerie pulled herself off the ground. She now had a knot the size of a golf ball on the back of her head to match the one she got from the bathroom incident. Valerie was now madder than a wet cat.

Valerie squeezed off two shots aimed at the metal bathroom door. One shot made a dent and a small hole. Another shot ricocheted off, almost hitting her. Hearing the shots from outside, Paisley, Charlie, and Stretchie returned fire, believing that the perpetrator was trying to shoot her way out. They fired through the window since the metal door was too thick to penetrate. They tried to aim low to avoid hitting someone in the chest or head. Valerie returned fire, but when she sat down on the floor to reload, she was hit by a bullet through her left temporal lobe, silencing the gunfight.

"Are you surrendering?" asked Stretchie. There was still no answer, and he yelled. "Are you injured?"

There was no answer again. Charlie nodded at Paisley, and she removed the passkey from her pocket and approached the door.

"We are coming in. Please kick any weapons away from you and lay on your stomach with your hands behind your back," yelled Stetchie.

Paisley opened the door with a passkey. Charlie went first. There was Valerie halfway laying down against a bed on the floor. She appeared dead. She was still holding a .25 in her hand. Stretchie kicked the gun from her hand and then pushed on her leg to see if she moved and then checked her pulse. She was indeed dead. They determined the dead sister was Valerie, but the main question was — where was her hostage?

Paisley went to the bathroom and knocked on the door. "FBI and Chicago PD out here. Are you okay in there?"

The door opened slowly, and a young black girl slowly emerged. She had been crying, and her face was puffy.

"It's okay. I'm Paisley, and these two are Charlie and Stretchie. We are here now."

"Marti. Where's Marti?" asked LaTisha.

"I'm afraid this one's sister took her, and they got away," Paisley said with a note of irritability in her voice.

"Please help her," LaTisha disappointedly pleaded.

"We'll do everything we can," Charlie answered.

Shortly after LaTisha was rescued, the coroner and crime scene investigation team arrived to collect evidence. LaTisha was taken back to the Chicago FBI office and allowed to shower before being questioned more. She was given a change of clothes and peanut butter crackers and a chocolate milk. LaTisha now seemed more at ease and was willing to talk. She indicated that her friend Marti was more like a sister, and she was concerned about her, and that was the only reason she was cooperating.

LaTisha was questioned for over an hour at the FBI headquarters. She informed them that she had no idea where she and Marti were being taken. LaTisha indicated that Douggie had been the one who had set them up. She reported that she and Marti were supposed to be paid $10,000 each, $5,000 upfront upon arrival to their unknown destination. Regarding the large amount of money discovered in the hotel, LaTisha informed them that they found the $20,000 in the glove compartment and she and Marti planned on using it to live on for a while.

After the interview, LaTisha was taken to a shelter for pregnant youth and connected with social services. She was considered an AWOL risk, so they kept her closely supervised. A CPD patrol car was stationed at the shelter just in case LaTisha did manage to get out of the building or someone showed up to abduct her.

Regardless of all the things that had transpired in the last day, Paisley was glad they had rescued one of the girls and Douggie was willing to testify against the Black Market Syndicate. Just when things were beginning to go in a positive direction, that's when Paisley and her crew got the news.

CHAPTER TWENTY-THREE

The chloroform was wearing off, and Marti had a headache. On top of it all, her body aches matched the intensity of her headache. With her hands zip tied, she could not massage her temples to relieve some of her pain which only annoyed her more. Her legs were asleep from being strapped down to her seat with a bicycle cable lock. How she wished that she had not been so stupid to believe someone would take care of her. No one cared about her at home, and no one cared about her in the real world.

Marti regretted that she had slept with De'Quill Montigue. He was a slick operator who knew how to sweet talk women into sleeping with him. He had that bad boy reputation that was so attractive that it made Marti lose her senses. So, when he said the condom broke, she didn't think anything of it until she found out she was pregnant. He denied being the father, left town, and left Marti high and dry. Now, Marti felt like finding him and cutting his manhood off. Even though she was a minor and he worked for her dad, her parents had refused to press charges so there would not be a scandal tied to her family. It was always about the fucking family's reputation.

Kitty had improvised with the bike lock to keep Marti from getting out of her seat and causing any mischief or injury. She didn't care if it cut off Marti's circulation as long as Marti and the baby were alive when she did the drop off. It had been an angry and tortured drive for Kitty. Kitty managed her stress by smoking one Camel after another like her sister. She was sure that something terrible had happened to Valerie. Still, she knew the consequences if the delivery was not made. After two packs of cigarettes were burned through, they finally arrived at the RRG pickup point three hours later.

No one was there to greet them. When that was the case, Kitty knew she had to paddle the newbies up to the cabin and walk them up. This only fueled her ogreish anger because it meant she had to get the little bitch down the river by canoe and then tote her to the cabin. She was just glad that she remembered where to go.

Marti was still partly out of it, so Kitty had to carry her and put her into the canoe. It was the same thing when they got to the trail going up to the cabin. However, Kitty would not complain because they had lost the other girl. She continued to try to come to terms that she had lost her sister to prison or the BMS ... or worse.

Darcie greeted her at the door. "One. I was fucking told two. What the hell happened? And where's your just as fugly sister?"

"Cops or Feds got her. Not sure. They probably got our scout and recruiter Grappler too," she responded.

"Oh, really. Aren't you a fuckup? Now, let me tell you this — the Money Makers aren't going to like this. It's an exposure risk. I have orders when these things happen."

"But —" Kitty tried to answer, but she heard footsteps behind her.

The Butcher stood there holding a sharp knife in his hand. They had moved up to inspecting the meat. They put their victims into three categories: those who needed to be fed well and slaughtered, those to be sold unharmed, or meat that needed to be disposed of. Taking care of those that needed to be disposed of was just one of those necessities in the business.

"Who the hell is he?" Kitty asked, pulling her gun from her pocket. Before she could get an answer or point the weapon, the Butcher slashed her throat from ear to ear. Her blood gushed out onto the tiled floor.

"Why the hell did you do that here? You clean this up!" Darcie angrily said. The Butcher stepped closer to her, and she backed off. "Okay, I'll take care of the mess. You take care of the disposal."

The Butcher nodded with satisfaction and walked over to examine Marti, who was still trying to get grips with her situation but was internally freaked out about just witnessing a murder. She had no energy to fight and did not want to end up like Kitty. She felt that remaining quiet was the best thing for now.

The Butcher opened her mouth and looked at her teeth. Then they felt the fat content in her body and smiled. They knew that she would be good eating. They already had some recipes in mind for this delectable morsel.

"Listen, I don't know what you got planned for her, but since we lost one, they may want to sell her to someone after the baby comes," said Darcie.

The Butcher nodded, but Darcie could tell he was not happy. The two had worked out their business differences and had an understanding since the one incident where Monk and the girl were killed. The main thing she didn't want to do was piss the Butcher off.

The Butcher removed Kitty and disposed of her while Darcie started Marti's orientation. Marti had no roommate because LaTisha had remained behind. Marti was more alert, and she was scared for the first time in her life. She had always been bold and brave and jumped into situations without thinking of the danger involved. Now, something was different. Was it the baby? Was she actually caring about someone else? Darcie got Marti a clean set of clothes and told her to shower. She gave her five minutes to comply or else. To get her initiated and immersed into the cabin's culture, Marti was made to attend the pregnant mothers' group to learn the house rules and meet the rest of the girls.

Darcie ran the special therapy group for pregnant mothers which met two times a week. She had kept them oppressed and downtrodden, so they would not fight back because most had lost hope. Darcie passed herself off as a therapist to build trust, but none of the pregnant teens trusted her. All of them were scared of her, but not as much as they feared the Butcher. They feared he would rape or kill them. The Butcher made their presence known on session days which terrified the young pregnant girls.

Six girls met for group, including Lexa, Brynlee, Bonita, Marti, Carolyn, and Tristine. There had been two additional girls just last week, but De'Jane and Revlon had been sold to a buyer with a special interest in young pregnant girls with certain physical attributes. For those girls who had been at the cabin the longest, this was the first they knew of anyone leaving before giving birth. Most of the young cabin residents just assumed De'Jane and Revlon decided to give up their money and leave.

As per group rules, no one was allowed to talk until Darcie said so. Marti suspiciously studied the group of fellow pregnant teens — analyzing weaknesses and looking for cohorts. Deciding to play the part of an innocent little girl, Marti played it cool and listened to what Darcie said, looking for a weakness and opportunities to escape.

Darcie started off the meeting with introductions and announcements. She reported that Carolyn and Tristine were the next two girls expected to deliver. Both were from Arizona and had been recruited in Chicago as well. Marti learned that residents who had come off high security (assigned leg irons) were given shock collars. The shock collars required a special key to be removed, and any attempts to pick them resulted in a painful shock. Darcie reminded them it was in their best interest and safety to either be chained or wear a collar because of their nomadic nature. Darcie explained that the last incident had prompted more secure measures to ensure easier tracking and punishment to those that tried to leave. She further reminded them that each had a transdermal satellite tracker implanted that would identify their location no matter where they fled and trigger their shock collars if they attempted to remove them.

Lexa provided a testimonial of how much shock collars hurt when she tried to remove hers using a nail she had found on the floor. Lexa said she was getting used to the situation and knew Ms. Darcie cared for her. Her roommate Bonita frowned and spoke something negative under her breath when Lexa spoke. It was evident that Bonita had a strong dislike toward Lexa. From what Marti could tell, Bonita was not mentally stable and possibly prone to violence.

Brynlee was another case. She was angry and pissed at everyone. She continued to proclaim being abducted and that her father had connections. It took a couple of smacks across the face by Darcie to shut her down so the group session could continue. Darcie's action also dropped the energy to a depressed level among everyone attending. Darcie told Brynlee that she did not fit into the program, and Brynlee would be shipped to another location in Canada next week. Besides, the Butcher intensely disliked her and said her meat was tainted.

There were plans to sell her to a Russian diplomat after the baby was born. Maxim Ivanov liked his lovers young, spirited, and dark-haired, and she fit the bill at 14.5 million dollars.

Marti was finally recovering from the effects of the chloroform. Although her mind was a little clouded, she was still capable of absorbing the information she had heard. Marti kept thinking about how she had made a mess of things. How she wished she had not left her comfortable suburban home with a pool. Marti slumped in her chair, feeling like she was in group therapy from hell. She'd had enough therapy in her life to hang up her own shingle and tell all these therapists to go fuck themselves.

In her most therapeutic voice, Darcie addressed the group of young mothers. "All you sows are healthy, and I don't expect any complications. We have weekly ultrasounds tomorrow, so I expect cooperation and a shower before I have to smell you. Some of you are complaining about the collars, be glad I don't hobble you like in the movie *Misery*, but that would be no good for the baby. Don't run and don't think about it, if you want your money. Besides, escape is a risk to your safety. Some girls meet unfortunate accidents."

"What money?" Brynlee pointed out. "No one has talked to me

about anything."

"You're a special case. They'll talk with you about that when you get to Canada."

"The fuck they will. If they are getting money, I want the same if I have to give up little Ephrem," Brynlee demanded.

"Raising your voice at me is one of the top five rules of things not to do," responded Darcie, who clicked a button on a remote that sent a shock through Brynlee, who screamed out in pain. That's when Marti noticed that Brynlee was not only wearing a shock collar, but she was still in leg irons.

"Remember that rule. Got it," Darcie pointed out to her wards. "Let's talk about the importance of nutrition."

There was a knock on the door. The Butcher, who had offered to fill in for Monk until a replacement could be found, opened the door. Ruth Ann Alderman walked into the cabin. She pushed herself past the Butcher and into the room where Darcie was conducting group. Darcie started to stand but paused when Ruth Ann gestured for her to remain seated. Darcie knew Ruth Ann. They had started together simultaneously, but Ruth Ann had quickly moved up the chain. There was a reason she was handpicked by the Money Makers. Darcie was not sure if she wanted to know.

"Don't get up. We have decided to change arrangements and oversight of this location. I've been given the role of statewide manager over all operations, and you are no longer in charge of your own hub. You are nothing more than a worm that I tell when to crawl. If you or … Whatever that thing is have a problem — I've got two men armed and ready to clean you out. Besides, I don't much like you. I'd rather let Sheila take your place. She's a street-level pissant from Chicago, ready to move up to a management level position. She'd kill you for it — if I let her."

Darcie didn't say a word. Knowing she knew she was outgunned, she suppressed her anger. The Butcher looked out the window and saw the hired muscle — one at each of the exits of the house. They were bigger and taller than the Butcher and appeared to be carrying quite a bit of fire power. The Butcher figured they could take them, but they might lose valuable meat.

"You are expected to pick up the slack. There will be no additional help. This thing working with you will remain for protection. Dr. Zinkoff has now been hired, and he will be on call and come at a moment's notice. I doubt he is qualified to do anything but his job, which means you better not make errors. He is reputable in his country for carrying out tasks without question. He needs Visa help anyway."

Darcie started to speak, but then Ruth Ann had that crazed look in her eyes that dared Darcie to cross her so she could end her. On the other hand, the Butcher felt the edge of their filet knife to reassure it would slice Ruth Ann's carotid arteries in a single slash. Darcie just looked down at the floor and stood in silence. Marti and Brynlee smiled to watch their oppressor become oppressed.

"Questions? No. Good. Let's start with inventory. I want every record, and I want to talk to each girl separately," demanded Ruth Ann, who sat at Darcie's desk like she was now queen of England.

"Yes, mam," was all Darcie could muster.

The call came moments after Paisley, Stretchie, and Charlie ordered at

Al's Diner — Douggie and two agents had been blown up from an explosion in the safe house. A bomb had been attached to the natural gas tank that supplied fuel to the furnace and cooking stove. It had been well hidden and had not been detected by an assigned FBI K-9 Explosive Unit which regularly completed random sweeps.

Charlie, Stretchie, and Paisley sat at the table looking as depressed as someone who had lost everything. Words were few, and actions were repetitive and reflected their feelings about losing someone who knew something about the BMS and these girls.

Stretchie continued repeatedly tearing packets of artificial sweetener open and adding them to his coffee while shaking his head. Paisley just kept spinning her spoon in her coffee cup, looking spaced out, while Charlie continued to tap his fingers on the table. It was that way for the next few minutes.

"Who's going to say it?" Paisley asked.

"What?" Charlie said.

"Someone in the CPD or FBI is working with the BMS," Stretchie accused.

"Who?" Charlie responded.

"They work with you. Who would you think?" Paisley further inquired.

"I don't know," Charlie shot back.

"What about the CPD? We did use some of their officers." Stretchie added.

"But none knew about where we took Douggie. That's FBI knowledge only," Charlie defensively replied.

"We've got a leak, and we need to plug it," Paisley said, tossing her spoon on the table, which bounced and hit the floor.

"I'd ask if you need more coffee, but maybe you all don't with the amount of tension here," said a middle-aged, red-headed waitress who was observing her customers.

"I could use a new cup. It's a little too sweet for my liking," Stetchie said, and like magic, a new cup of coffee appeared on the table.

"Without Douggie and Valerie, where do we go from here?" Stretchie inquired.

"I have a thought. We follow my husband's murder case," Paisley offered.

"What does that have to do with the BMS?" Charlie inquired.

"I believe that whoever killed him — killed the Pearson girl they found in the lake. I think Gregory was in the wrong place at the wrong time. That EMT bedsheet on the drowned victim — the blood on it matches an item missing from Gregory's ambulance supplies. There was also another person's blood and placenta found on the sheet — a baby's."

"How can that be? Wouldn't the water have ruined the evidence on the sheet?" Stretchie asked.

"Normally, but the dumb bastards wrapped her in plastic so tight it preserved areas of the sheet," Charlie informed them. "I only handled part of Gregory's murder investigation. The girl washed up later on and was assigned to a different detective back then."

"Don't beat yourself up. Can't always put the puzzle together in the beginning. Sometimes you got to outline the edges first.

Now, we pressure the BMS by hurting their operations and making the top level angry about the money flow. Let's head back to Kentucky and find where these bastards have their baby/sex trafficking hotel and shut them down, crackdown on those we take in, and send a message that we are going to take the BMS down one operation at a time. They might have powerful people in each state, but we are the law. We are justice," Paisley said while trying to rally her crew.

However, her internal motivation dropped a few levels when she felt an MS hug. She tried to hide it, but Charlie had seen it happen before. It had been a while. It was not a good time to be having an episode. Paisley did not want an infusion right now. It would take her out of commission for a week or more if she had one. She had girls and babies to save and scum to put away.

"You okay?" Stretchie asked his old flame.

"Nothing. Just a little gas. It'll stop," Paisley annoyingly replied.

Trying to take the focus off Paisley, Charlie spoke up. "Okay, let's do it. Let me make a call and ask for an assignment in Kentucky to help work the case."

"Be like old times," Paisley responded as the MS hug began to ease up.

While Charlie stepped outside to make his call, Stretchie said, "Maybe my timing is bad, but it'd be like old times if you'd go out to dinner with me as a date rather than a law enforcement partner."

"Hmmm, I don't trust a man with a gun," she jokingly responded.

"I only use it when I'm feeling threatened," he joshed with her.

"Okay, but it can't be Drakes Dairy Bar or pizza at the Shell Mart."

"Oh, we are doing this right. It'll be at Huely's Bar and Grill — one county over."

"You're on," she accepted.

"What's on?" Charlie asked.

"Just exploring an old high school romance," she answered.

"You two used to?" Charlie inquired.

"A long time ago," Stretchie responded, smiling ear to ear.

"Never knew that," Charlie said with a note of jealously in his voice that went unnoticed.

CHAPTER TWENTY-FOUR

Carolyn Jones was a quiet, keep-to-herself neighbor who was not friendly, even to her own reflection. She had never been married, and the only man that was ever interested in her was Earl Humbly, who was partially blind in both eyes, mostly deaf, and walked with a limp. He happened to die a decade ago without revealing that he loved her.

Carolyn was not an attractive senior citizen by any means. She felt washing was overrated. Her odiferous nature only made her less appealing to everyone. Her wild, white hair, disheveled appearance, hump in her back made her appear like a witch crossed with Quasimodo. In fact, she was considered a witch by many of the folks in Fester. People would even come to her to get rid of warts or to hex an unfaithful lover.

Unfortunately, the youngest of Paisley's goats, Bella, had escaped again and was thought to be on the witch's property. Bella was Kansas' favorite farm critter, and she was determined to find her before some coyote got him. Paisley had got it for Kansas when they first moved to the country to ease her into country life. In fact, their first goat milk ice cream product came from Bella and was called Bella's Simple Chocolate Pecan Turtle. It was as big of a hit as the goat was to Kansas.

Kansas knew nothing about Carolyn, but she was quickly educated by Ephrem, who filled her in on the elderly spinster who also had allegedly poisoned her father Dowland twenty years ago. The story was that Carolyn had inherited a $100,000 life insurance policy upon his passing. She allegedly stuffed a mattress full of the insurance money because she never trusted banks. It was never proven that she poisoned her father. Still, according to a plumber who saw Carolina's mattress while repairing bathroom pipes, told people that Carolyn did have an unusually thick mattress — some gossip never dies.

The walk to Carolyn's land required crossing a small stream that boarded Gary's and Paisley's properties at the far end of their fields. Kansas and Ephrem crossed it without incident. From there, you took a wooded path that slightly ran parallel to the Red River Gorge National property line. The trees were old and tall and created an isolated sense from the world. The sounds of squirrels and chipmunks scurrying and moving throughout the trees occasionally caused the young couple to stop and listen. Sometimes, when they stopped, it caused them to lock lips and kiss, allowing the curiosity, driven by hormones, to explore parts of each other that they had not touched before.

About five hundred feet from the clearing of the forest, Kansas spotted her goat. Bella was grazing with some other goats near Carolyn's barn. No one seemed to be around. Sprinting across the clearing, Ephrem and Kansas tried to reach Bella before Bella spotted them, but it was too late. The expeditious goat maneuvered around them. Neither teen was very agile, and the goat's maneuvers did not reflect well on their physical skills. Ephrem's face barely missed a pile of goat manure by less than two inches, and Kansas fell flat on her ass.

Seeking a hiding spot, Bella ran into the barn. Kansas and Ephrem pulled themselves up and pursued their target. Bella was nowhere to be seen in the lower level of the barn. They heard a bleat and looked up. Staring down from them from the loft was Bella, and she almost seemed to be laughing at them. Kansas climbed up the ladder, and Ephrem took the low ground where the goat had ascended on a stack of hay bales.

The impertinent ungulate came running toward Kansas, and she grabbed her. Kansas managed to get the collar and leash on Bella. Kansas noticed something in one of the stalls sticking out of the corner from the top of the barn. It was white and green. She asked Ephrem to hold Bella while she went over to the stall to investigate. While Ephrem held onto Bella, Kansas pulled out a green tote with a white top. Inside the tote were several pairs of tennis shoes and jewelry. There were also three IDs — Revlon Danderguard, Gwendolyn Muskeel, and Brynlee Flatt!

"Oh, my God! Ephrem. We got to get out of here. This is Brynlee's driver's license. I think the old witch is somehow involved in all those missing pregnant girls. I don't know who these others are, but I'm betting they were pregnant and missing too."

"What the hell did you say?" Ephrem asked.

A shotgun fired into the bale of hay near the stall they were in. Both fell to the ground, looking for cover.

"Who the hell are you two? What are you doing in my barn?" said a rough, raspy, and callous voice from the entrance of the barn.

Kansas and Ephrem both panicked. It didn't relieve their anxiety when they heard the woman pump the shotgun for another repeated blast.

Kansas grabbed some courage and yelled out, "We came to get my goat, Bella."

"A likely story. You are thieves looking to steal stuff and my goats."

"I can prove it. I have pictures of her and me and ownership papers. She ran off over to your property. I just came to reclaim her."

"You're trespassing," Carolyn harshly replied.

"We are neighbors. My papaw is Gary Quaillan, and her mother is the Hunter woman that bought the farm next to us. They own the ice cream shop in town," yelled out Ephrem.

"Come out then with your hands in the air," demanded Carolyn.

"Ephrem, take a picture of the stuff and shove it back. I need to tell mom about this," she said, whispering to her boyfriend.

He did as he was told, and they emerged with their hands up shortly afterward.

"That's a damn ugly goat you got there. Wouldn't make a sandwich. Next time you have something like this happen, come to the main house, and let me know. Cause next time you might be leaking after you take a drink of something."

"Yes, mam!" both said while shaking.

"Get!" Carolyn commanded.

Both ran as fast as they could and tried not to look back for fear of turning to a stone statue while looking at Medusa [Carolyn].

"You're right. She does look like a witch," commented Kansas.

"Mean as one too," Ephrem said, short of breath while trying to talk and keep up with Kansas and Bella.

"You're sure about this," said a perplexed Paisley.

"See. Look at these pictures that we took," said a very serious Kansas.

"I'm just glad you two didn't get shot," Paisley responded.

"Damn it, boy. I've told you not to go over to that crazy woman's place. She killed her father — at least they say she did. It was never proven, but I'm convinced," said an irritated Gary.

"Send me the pictures. I'm contacting Stretchie. Do not go over there again and keep that stupid goat of yours in the fenced-in area," Paisley insisted.

Paisley texted the pictures to Stretchie, and he called within fifteen minutes. Stretchie obtained a search warrant for the property. He picked up Paisley, and they rode over to Jones farm. As soon as Carolyn saw the police cars pull up, she opened her door with her shotgun slung over her shoulder.

"I ain't done nothing, and my taxes are caught up," she yelled at them in an enraged defensive tone.

"Mrs. Jones, we have a warrant to search your property, specifically your barn. We'd like cooperation and wouldn't want to arrest you for interfering with an investigation," Stetchie yelled back at her.

"Make it fast. You're goin' to be upsetting my critters as it is."

Probably stop my hens from laying."

One of the state police officers remained with Mrs. Jones while the barn was searched. Three sets of tennis shoes, three IDs, and some personalized jewelry were found just where Kansas and Ephrem said they were. Damning evidence that somehow Mrs. Jones had some involvement with the missing pregnant girls.

"Mrs. Carolyn Jones. You have just become a major person of interest regarding three missing teens," Stretchie said as he held the bag of evidence up toward her. "Officer Trent, please help Mrs. Jones into the car. She'll be going to the post for questioning."

"Screw you. I want my lawyer. I ain't done nothing. Y'all treating me just like you did when Daddy died. I'm innocent like I was then. He killed himself. You bunch of dumb asses."

Carolyn began to resist. Paisley came over and tried to calm her down. "Mrs. Jones, you don't remember me, but my mother — you know. I'm Evelyn Hounschell Hunter's girl."

"Evelyn's girl. Your mama stood by me when I got accused of killing Daddy. She was a good woman. God rest her soul."

"Let's just go and talk. Come on. I'll make sure they treat you right," Paisley promised.

"Okay. I trusted Evelyn. I'll try to trust you."

With that, Mrs. Jones climbed into the cruiser.

"You have a way with people. Always did," Stretchie commented.

"We'll see. Something seems off, but it's not looking good for Carolyn.

CHAPTER TWENTY-FIVE

Carolyn Jones stared intensely at the small interrogation room's observation mirror within the confines of the Morehead State Police post. She'd been here before a long time ago when she'd been falsely accused of killing her perverted father that she cared for until he finally killed himself. Somehow, her father tried to make amends for his perversions by leaving her a life insurance policy. It would never compensate for the abuse she endured or what her mother put up with while she was alive. Carolyn had taken care of him out of pity and because the mother she loved had begged her to take care of the old bastard.

Carolyn refused offers of water and coffee. She told Stretchie that he probably drugged them with something, and she didn't trust him. Paisley had very little luck getting her to answer questions either. Stretchie felt they needed to search for more evidence at Carolyn's and requested a new sweep of the property, including cadaver canines. Hours later, the trio received a call from the team that they had found some very unexpected damning evidence.

"What do you think it is, Lizzie?" Stretchie asked Elizabeth Rasperando, the newly appointed head of the forensic division.

"When we went down into the basement, she had three deep freezer chests. At the bottom of two of them was some odd-looking meat. At first, we thought it might be deer meat, but the names on the bags were like ... The names on the gallon freezer bags were —" Lizzie attempted to spit out what she had seen but was clearly disturbed by what she found.

"Like what?" Stretchie asked.

"The same first names as some of those pregnant girls missing from last year that we received information from the Bureau on. Mona's Rump Roast. Sara's Scrumptious thighs. I'm thinking as in Mona Pragatto and Sara Zinger." Lizzie started to gag but took a deep breath and stopped herself.

There was a long silent pause, and then Paisley said what everyone was thinking. "Can you test for human remains?"

"I can't be one hundred percent positive unless I bring it to the lab. Looking at what's in the bags, the type of bones and the markings, coloration, and — this is human flesh. Carved, filleted, and preserved like a professional butcher would do it," Lizzie responded.

"Are we saying that Carolyn is some kind of cannibal?" asked Stretchie.

"Not sure if these are trophies or entrees, but it strongly suggests serial killer material," Lizzie answered.

"Jesus! I don't know what to say. It's not looking good for her. My mom thought she was innocent of her father's murder and now this. Is she part of the BMS — Some cannibal that takes care of the unwanted mothers of these babies?" asked an incensed Paisley.

"Lizzie get everything to the lab and determine if what you have is human and if you can get DNA or blood samples from what you've got. Then cross reference with what medical info we have on the missing pregnant teens," Stretchie requested.

"You got it," Lizzie said.

Stretchie entered the interrogation room and began a new line of questioning. "I see you keep a stock of food in the freezer. Good to keep supplied up for bad weather and buy when prices are low."

"So does half or more of the county. Am I being held too for having a stockpile of food, including the three gallons of Rocky Road?" Carolyn said, patronizing Stretchie.

"We found some interesting items in that freezer. Some meat that is a little unusual," Paisley added.

"You mean the bison or the goat. I get it cheap and sell it to my neighbors for a profit. There a crime for making a buck?" the white-haired witch replied.

"No, this was something quite different. More along the lines of intelligent type," Stretchie commented.

"What the fuck are you getting at?" the suspect replied in a prickly manner.

"We found what appear to be cuts of human meat in your freezer," Stretchie accused her.

"You're bullshitting me. There's no such thing in my freezer!" Carolyn refuted.

Stretchie pulled opened up his iPad and showed Carolyn the

pictures of her freezer's contents that Lizzie had sent him. "What do you have to say about these?" Stretchie said as he stared Carolyn down.

"Those are not from my freezer," the suspect countered.

"Let's take a look at a few facts. You have items belonging to three missing pregnant teens, and human remains with their names labeled on freezer bags. I'm trying to help you like my mother did, but I can't when it feels like you are not cooperating," Paisley offered up, trying to smooth things.

"I've been set up," Carolyn defensively responded.

"Very coincidental that you were charged with your father's murder twenty years ago, and now we find things belonging to missing pregnant girls and their remains. Did we miss something on the first go around with your father and let a killer go? Did you kill young pregnant girls because you were unable to have children, or you were trying to save them from having a child from incest?" Stretchie continued.

"I don't know what you are on, but you're crazy and wrong about me," Carolyn protested.

"I'm just saying that it did come out in your trial about you putting a child up for adoption when you were fourteen that I'm betting it was your father's," Stretchie pushed.

"Shut up. Shut the fuck up. You don't know what abuse that I put up with. The day he died ... I was liberated. I didn't have to kill him. His own guilt eventually took him out. I cried on that day because I was free from my mother's promise. You have no right to make assumptions."

"But I do. We have missing girls, human remains, and it's all on your land," Stretchie stated.

"I didn't do it. You think anyone would be that stupid to leave stuff like that around for someone to find. I read enough crime novels and listen to enough crime podcasts that I would know how to hide something like that," she shouted back.

Stretchie stuck a piece of spearmint gum in his mouth and chewed annoyingly loud. "Not convincing me. Maybe you wanted to get caught. Sometimes that's what serial nutjobs like you do."

"I tell you I didn't do anything!" Carolyn said as she put her face into her hands and began to uncontrollably sob.

"Tell us about the Black Market Syndicate's operation and what you do for them. We can offer you protection. Of course, the death penalty for murder and kidnapping of minors is certain, but with your cooperation, maybe we could have your sentence changed to life without parole," Paisley added.

"The who or what? You're damn crazy too. You are nothing like your mother. She stood beside me. I didn't do anything."

"Admit it. You like killing little girls who are pregnant. You had issues with your mommy staying with your daddy. And your father — he knocked you up. It's in the record and you have never denied it. All that anger. All those pent up emotions. It snapped you and made you a killer. Someone who craved the flesh that she so missed. You consumed your hatred by eating others. Maybe you felt you were saving these girls who might have been violated by their fathers," Stretchie said to further antagonize Carolyn.

Carolyn tried grabbing him from across the table, but she was handcuffed and only managed to knock his coffee cup over.

"Damn, I've struck a nerve," he said after getting the response he wanted. Stretchie got up, left the room, and followed Paisley to the observation room. Carolyn was left alone to cuss her interrogators out under her breath that fueled the hatred in her eyes that she had only once reserved for her father.

"She's hiding something, and it's just a matter of time before she confesses it," Stretchie said, presenting his observations.

"Yes, but it may take some doing. I think we need a psych eval. Charlie once said something to me about a guy who is really good at this. I'll get the name from him," said Paisley.

"Dr. Gerald Ramkin is our best forensic consultant. I'll give him a call and get him on this now. He'll come there for a serial killer consult. He's obsessed with how they think. He's written three books on them at this point. This has the makings of another book for him," Charlie stated.

Stretchie, who was on the group call, informed him that the Kentucky State Police would be flipping Dr. Ramkin's bill. Charlie said he would be traveling down too. This presented an opportunity for the FBI as well to interrogate the suspect. It was also the first time any evidence of the missing pregnant teens had surfaced.

Charlie made the call to Dr. Ramkin. Hours later, Charlie and Dr. Ramkin took the red-eye to Bluegrass Airport in Lexington. Michael Stern, a newly graduated trooper who had been hand-picked to be mentored by Stretchie, drove them to their hotel in Morehead. They both grabbed some sleep. The next morning, they ate the hotel breakfast buffet loaded with a cornucopia of coronary-infused food which they later regretted. The two walked into the state police post a little after nine o'clock, ready to tackle the alleged BMS serial killer.

Paisley still felt something was off. Her gut was telling her that Carolyn was innocent. *What if she was set up?* She'd be an excellent patsy who had been once accused of murder who'd fit the bill. Plus, who'd care if they fried the white-haired witch? Paisley left the interrogation and returned home soon after Charlie and Dr. Ramkin arrived. She missed her old partner, but she wanted to follow up on some things of her own.

CHAPTER TWENTY-SIX

The tall, lanky, middle-aged psychologist arrived wearing khakis, a polo, and black socks with sandals. He definitely looked like a fish out of water, but he did not seem to care. Dr. Ramkin was not one to socialize with others much and just wanted to get his work done and leave. Adding new material to his next book was a big motivator for completing an efficient and accurate assessment. He flashed his credentials to the trooper on duty and was taken back to talk with Carolyn. Dr. Ramkin had brought assessment instruments to determine Carolyn's level of cognitive functioning and to screen for psychoneurological issues. Inkblot cards for assessing personality and psychotic tendencies were utilized because it was well believed that Carolyn would be oppositional and defensive; thus, making standardized personality tests useless and invalid.

The mental status, interview, and assessments lasted around five hours. Charlie asked when he would get the results, and he was informed that a report would be completed by mid-day of the next day. Dr. Ramkin was taken back to the complimentary Holiday Inn when he was finished with Carolyn to work on his report.

Charlie remained at the station and caught up on the case. Charlie and Stretchie wondered what had happened to Paisley. They tried calling but it went straight to voice mail. Stretchie and Charlie called Gary and Kansas reported that they had not seen Paisley today. Charlie thought about tracking Paisley's phone but knew that Paisley would find out and be highly pissed about the situation. Both knew that her wrath had no boundaries, so they decided to give her till tomorrow before tracking her phone.

A report was emailed to Charlie the next day, who printed it off and shared copies with Stretchie. Paisley was still at large, and according to Kansas, she had not been to the house that night and she just assumed her mother was working on the case. Charlie and Stretchie were beginning to worry now that something had happened to her. They decided to give her until midday, and then they'd do whatever it took to locate her — regardless, if Paisley got mad at them. To pass the time, they focused on the report.

Highlights of the report identified that Carolyn was possibly schizoid and may have delusional thinking. Her Full-Scale IQ was in the average range and there were no suggested psychoneurological issues. Her inkblot responses indicated a paranoid, insecure, untrusting individual with a deep-seated need to hurt others emotionally with self-esteem issues. The most interesting thing was Carolyn's multiple responses to seeing food and human body parts in most her inkblot responses — ribs, legs, lungs, eyes, and breasts. When Carolyn was asked whether she had ever killed anything, she replied that she had been the one to skin and slice up the hogs and cows on the farm. She had also indicated that humans were no more than animals, and they could be slaughtered just as easily. She added that she would eat human meat if it meant her survival.

"Carolyn is a cannibalistic serial killer? That's a hard one to see coming." Charlie commented while reading through Dr. Ramkin's report. "Yeah. Not sure what to think."

"He's not saying it hundred percent. He does later make a comment that her upbringing may be largely responsible for what she was inclined to see in those ink blots. But ... I agree. It still does not look good for her," Stretchie added.

"Still nothing from Paisley. About ready to ping her careless ass," Charlie threatened.

"The lab results came back this morning. Definitely human remains in the baggies. The freezer destroyed some of the integrity of the evidence. We did get blood type matches for Mona Pragatto and Sara Zinger based on their medical records we pulled from their birth hospitals. Also, definitely, one package was the hip of one of the girls because there was a tattoo of a frog on it," Stretchie reported.

"Why would they even keep part of the flesh?" Charlie asked.

"Maybe it's like some fish that you keep part of the skin to keep the meat from cooking too quickly. It also keeps the meat moist, and locks in the flavor. Hell, I don't know. I ain't no cannibal or much of a cook," Charlie commented. "Carolyn got any family that you know of? Anyone that knows her well enough to help us put this puzzle together."

"No. They're all dead. No children and no friends as far as I know. Paisley's mother might have been her last friend before she died."

"We are going to have to send this up for an indictment," Stretchie added.

"I know. Stretchie, you'll need to formally charge her," Charlie informed him.

"I will," Stretchie responded with some regret in his tone. "I'll do it now."

It was not easy for Stretchie to do, but he told Carolyn what was going on and what the lab test findings indicated. When the charges were read to her, Carolyn burst into tears, and she began yelling at them. Carolyn continued to deny she was a serial killer or cannibal and that she knew nothing about those girls or how those things got onto her property. Although it was suspected that Carolyn was probably working with the BMS, they had nothing tying her to them. Finally, Carolyn calmed down and asked to see her lawyer, who had still not shown.

There was still no word from Paisley. She needed to know about Dr. Ramkin's report and the lab findings, as well as what happened to Carolyn. The question on everyone's mind … Was Paisley alive? Stretchie and Charlie each tried calling her one more time and it went to voice mail both times. Charlie agreed to be the one to ping her phone. He'd pissed her off many times while working cases together and new how to deal with her.

CHAPTER TWENTY-SEVEN

Paisley was unsure how long she had been unconscious. It was already five in the afternoon, and the last thing she remembered was running from a knife-wielding maniac in the woods near the old, dilapidated cabin. She had fallen and rolled down a small hill before stopping at the edge of a thirty-foot drop. Now, her head pounded like a drum being struck hard by a drummer performing a solo at a rock concert. The log above her head had blood dried to it. It was most likely the culprit responsible for her head injury. She didn't believe that she had a concussion, but she wasn't a doctor.

Paisley pulled herself up. She checked for her cell phone. It was nowhere to be found. Then it struck her that it was back at her car — wherever her car was. Looking down near the drop-off, she found a piece of brown tape with writing on it. She looked around, trying to get her bearings. She was not familiar with the area but noted that there was moss to her left, and she heard a stream of water behind her. Given those clues, she decided to go back toward the tall woods toward the large pine trees. She felt this would take her back to Carolyn's farm. With each step, her head pounded. She wished she had something to take to relieve the pain.

--- Hours Before ---

Stretchie's team had been indeed thorough. The basement had been photographed and checked for everything; so, had the barn and house. From experience, Paisley knew that there were things that were overlooked because they looked too natural. She recalled the decapitation case she had in 2009. Forensics had tagged, bagged, and photographed every inch of the victim's home where the victim had been found headless. For some reason, no one cared to look at the missing high school yearbook for 2001-2002. All of the victim's middle school through high school were in order, except her junior year. That meant it was lost, misplaced, or possibly taken by the killer. After investigating and cross referencing classmates from 2001-2002, she found a likely suspect to follow — Paul Zurich.

Paul had dated the victim in high school and was arrested after they broke up for attempted murder and rape. He was sentenced to ten years in prison, and he had been recently paroled. Charlie and Paisley hounded him, and soon Paul's alibi started falling apart. When Paisley and Charlie asked about his whereabouts on the night of the victim's murder, he lied and said he was over two hundred miles away at his dead grandmother's visitation. There was visitation at the funeral home for his deceased grandmother, but Paul was not in attendance. Paul fled, and Paisley and Charlie tracked him to a truck stop where he was killed when he grabbed a steak knife and took a hostage. Paisley did not regret taking the shot. Paul wasn't rational, and she knew that Paul would kill his hostage.

In comparison, there was no library at Carolyn's home and no cookbook for cannibals to be found. It appeared that *The Weekly World News* was the only thing she read. She had a limited supply of food in the refrigerator and what was found was primarily vegetables, including vegan substitutes. The only meat found was a frozen pack of chicken in her refrigerator's freezer dated from five years ago. Something was not adding up. She dug deeper and discovered some recipes for vegetarian and vegan dishes in an old cracker tin.

In a pile of bills, she found several lab results from 2018 -2021, indicating abnormal ranges on most items, as well as a high HDL and Total Cholesterol. Her glucose levels were also above normal at 306. A report from 2020 indicated hypertension and 50% artery blockage. The packages of sucralose and shakers of Ms. Dash further validated that Carolyn was trying to make changes to improve her health.

Why would someone with poor health be adding human red meat to their diet? How would someone with hypertension issues with the risk of a heart attack or stroke be able to wrangle girls and cut them apart? From Paisley's recollection, it takes some brute strength to handle a hog and butcher it. With all these medical issues, Carolyn did not appear to be capable of doing much, except complaining.

Feeling the need to cover the grounds again around the farm, Paisley sauntered around all paths that would have led to the basement or to the barn facing the woods. If someone wanted to be unseen, they could come from there. Forensics had been back there, but nothing abnormal had been observed, and they did not go past the property line. Paisley walked into the forest with her infamous gut feeling leading the way. Leaves covered the path for the most part. However, about half a mile into the walk, she saw something brown that was about three inches long. She picked it up. It was a piece of masking tape with something written on it. It read "201," and the last number appeared to be an "8." *2018? Could it have blown out here? What was it to?* She was no writing expert, but when she thought about the writing on the bags of frozen remains, she was positive it matched the writing on the masking tape.

Now, Paisley felt she was on a roll. Perhaps Carolyn was right about being set up. She followed the leaf-covered trail out to a clearing in the woods. It was a good twenty-minute walk from Carolyn's property, and she was sure that she was now in the national forest. An old cabin with a roof beginning to cave in, and rotting timbers sat there. Someone must have been staying in it from time to time because she noticed a generator on the side. It was old but appeared to be in working order. Inside was a solar-powered freezer. It was empty right now but was still running. *What the hell! What was going on? Who has a freezer and generator in the middle of the woods in an old run-down cabin?*

The first thing that came to Paisley's mind was a serial killer, like one right out of a novel or horror movie. A twig snapped. Something was moving outside. She thought it was a rabbit or deer, but someone dressed in a hazmat suit was standing less than twenty feet from her with their face covered, holding a large cleaver. Paisley reached for her gun, but as she did, the roof began to collapse, knocking her weapon out of her hand and pinning her underneath. Luckily, the beams fell in a manner that left a protective barrier above her body, leaving a space big enough to crawl out from underneath.

As the Butcher made their way toward a potential kill, Paisley pulled herself up and grabbed a large slab of wood. Ten years of Tae

Kwon Do and self-defense classes had taught her to take care of herself. She knew the minimalist's way of defending herself. What she did not count on was her MS beginning to flare. She had already shown some signs when she went to the bathroom this morning. There was some numbness in her ass, and she felt some loss of sensation in her left arm. When the Butcher swung the knife at her, Paisley countered with a broken board, using it to sweep the Butcher's legs, causing the Butcher to fall to the ground. Paisley knew she would lose her advantage at some point because of their size differences and her strength and coordination waning. This would take some of the momentum out of her offense for sure. It was time for flight.

Paisley took off as fast as she could, but the Butcher was already on her. The Butcher grabbed her by the hair and slung her down like a rag doll. The Butcher was incredibly strong. The Butcher tried to squat on her arms and chest like some bully in elementary school, but Paisley gave a swift kick to the perp's scrotum, causing them to double over in pain. Paisley took advantage and began to run again. She ran without any direction in mind. The Butcher was up a moment later, grabbed the cleaver, and started hunting their prey. Although the Butcher thought this one was too old, they might make an exception for causing them pain. They could always marinade them to tenderize the meat.

Paisley ran as fast as she could. So fast that she did not see the log at the bottom of the hill, causing her to fall and strike her head on it before stopping from plummeting over a thirty-foot drop into a rocky ravine. Paisley laid there unconscious, hidden from the Butcher behind the log. Knowing the drop-off, the Butcher went past her in the other direction.

CHAPTER TWENTY-EIGHT

Sirens filled the air as law enforcement vehicles flew onto Carolyn's property with the local search and rescue team. The ping had definitely placed her phone there. Charlie wondered if Carolyn had an accomplice, and Stretchie was just worried if Paisley was still alive.

The property and all the buildings were searched high and low for Paisley. Approximately thirty minutes later after the search began, a rough-looking former Chicago detective stumbled out of the woods looking confused. Stretchie spotted her and was the first to reach her. Paisley was dirty, with matted hair stuck together from dried blood on the back of her head. There was also a sizeable pumpknot that stood out.

"Where have you been? We've been worried about you missing for some time. My God ... You've taken five years off me," Stretchie said like an angry parent whose child needed scolding.

"I'll be alright. Right now, I need some ibuprofen," she responded.

"Tough as nails and alligator hide this one," added Charlie, who led a paramedic with him to examine her. "Sit down. I even brought you a chair, so this fine young lady can check you for any injuries."

"Okay, if you insist. My weapon is back at the cabin. We need to recover it. I need my gun," Paisley insisted.

"Get this. She goes missing, gets hurt, and she's worried about getting her gun back," Stretchie commented.

"Give me a break. I got chased by Jason Voorhees or some psycho back at that old cabin."

"What?" Charlie asked.

"You deaf too. You heard me. Some psycho was there and saw me looking at this old cabin that had a generator and a solar-powered freezer in it."

"What were you even doing out here alone?" Stretchie inquired.

"I'm your consultant, and I can't consult when my gut says there is more than what you all are going to get from some psych report or by interrogating Carolyn."

"You think she didn't kidnap and kill those girls? Dr. Ramkin says she's a nut case. Case closed," Charlie added.

"She might be nutty, but she's no killer. Didn't it strike any of you odd that she'd have primarily vegetables and vegan condiments in her refrigerator at home? Did you look at her medical reports regarding her health conditions in that pile of bills on her table? Did you notice that the last piece of meat bought at a store in the frig's freezer was over five years old?"

Charlie started to say something, and Paisley gave him a look like she had so many times as his partner — shut the hell up and back her.

"Okay, let's say you are right. What else do you have to prove her innocence? The psychopath butcher knife-wielding creep in the woods who tried to carve on me, the cabin being this close that contained a freezer, and this," she said as she handed Stretchie the piece of tape.

"So, it's a piece of tape," Charlie stated.

"Let me explain. I believe if you have an expert look at this, they will see that this writing matches the writing on the freezer bags we found. Get a writing sample from Carolyn and compare them to the freezer bags of the remains and this tape. I don't think that they will match. I believe she was framed. This butcher-waving lunatic ... I think he's the one who killed these girls. How he's involved and whether he's connected to the BMS — that's another question we can start exploring."

"Are you sure this perp you encountered is a "he?" Could be a female," Stretchie commented.

"You're right; it very well could be," Paisley said agreeably. Whoever they were, they were strong. Very strong but could be weightlifting and steroids."

After a clean check by the paramedic, Paisley led everyone to the cabin, which was still burning hot and had burnt nearly down to the ground. They had seen smoke coming from this direction earlier but assumed it was a campfire that someone had been burning. Because of the age and dryness of the wood, the cabin quickly incinerated, ruining any evidence, and probably damaging Paisley's gun.

The ground around the scorched cabin was searched for additional clues, but nothing was found. After the fire burned out, a melted freezer sat destroyed beyond any evidence collection. The generator had exploded, and nothing was left but pieces of blackened metal and melted plastic parts. Paisley's gun was recovered, but the nice Glock 19 was destroyed. Good thing she had a sister to this one at home.

"I'm now mad. We need to make things right with Carolyn." Paisley told her two compatriots.

"It's already headed to be heard for indictment. Judge Salyers will want to hear it and you know the DA. It's an election year for Victor, and he's riding the whole sex trafficking of young girls campaign. A serial killer case — this would really look good for him," Stretchie explained.

"I'll be there for the indictment hearing. Just tell Vic that I'll be testifying in Carolyn's favor. This hazmat sociopath attacked me, and they are the cannibal. They are the "Butcher of Kentucky" — at least that is what I'm calling him for now. Maybe Butcher — I don't know. The Butcher's going down, and that thing can slow roast in the depths of hell. I know the Butcher is responsible for killing these girls, and I think the Butcher is working with the BMS."

"That's silly. Why would a serial killing maniac work for an organized crime syndicate? How are you connecting the two?" asked Charlie.

Paisley scratched her upper lip and calmly replied, "It's a gut feeling, and I know I am right. That's all I can say."

"Not sure how that will go over in the long run," Stretchie added.

"First, we got to catch this Butcher. Not sure how but we'll figure it out," Paisley said before getting in her car to go home for a long-overdue shower.

CHAPTER TWENTY-NINE

The evidence board looked like it had been put together by a group of veteran detectives. Gary stood back and admired his work. The different colored twine and the pictures of probable suspects laid out a pictorial story board full of thoughtful considerations and possible connections. The overall conclusion — the guilty party was someone in law enforcement.

"I don't know, Gary. This is a great board, but I'm in the middle as a possible suspect," Paisley pointed out to her amateur sleuth friend.

"Yes, but you are a suspect as well as Kansas is one too. You were both at the first crime in town. Your mother is also connected to Carolyn, who allegedly killed all those young girls. That gives you a double connection. Hard to ignore, you know. See, I think maybe the BMS — they are the blue square — they are in the middle orchestrating it all. This person ... What do you call them?"

"This picture of Leatherface from *The Texas Chainsaw Massacre* movies?" she asked.

"Yes."

"Butcher of Kentucky for now — at least that what I calling them."

"Why that name?"

"It's Kentucky, and he or she or it or butchers people like they are meat."

"I think the Butcher is part of this, but he's also not part of this," Gary proclaimed.

"Confusing. Just keep doing what you are doing. I honestly haven't had time to construct one of these. It wasn't my thing when I worked in Chicago, but some people I know in law enforcement use them ... I think most are on television."

"Well, I find them useful. So, how's the case going on your end."

"Perplexing and full of dead ends if Carolyn is not involved. I think that I will go back out to the burned-up cabin again. Maybe something will turn up that was missed."

"More importantly, I'm glad you are safe. So, how's the coffee and donut ice cream coming along?"

"I've got Kansas working on that. She's got a knack for ice cream. I tried some the other night, and she was so close to making it feel like you'd just dipped a glazed donut into a fresh cup of coffee."

"I'm a dipper. I'd do it. Might even have it for breakfast."

"Given you told me Doctor Harper says your blood glucose and cholesterol levels are too high ... I don't think he'd give it a thumbs up."

Paisley fell to the floor and grabbed her ribs. Her face displayed an enormous amount of pain. Gary rushed over to her and tried helping her to a chair, but Paisley waved him off.

"MS hug, huh? I'll stay here with you while it passes. Yes, I'll shut the hell up until you can talk," Gary supportively said.

A few minutes later, Gary was allowed to help Paisley back into her chair. Paisley looked at her neighbor and thanked him with a nod, and he sat across from her and winked back.

"Numbness coming back more too in the legs too?" he asked in a concerned tone.

"A little but nothing that I can't handle. I just started a new medication two days ago. It's an injection that I got to give to myself monthly. Supposed to keep the lesions at bay. Side effects would scare you to death, but what don't these days? Safer than the infusion medication that one of my docs proposed for certain. I'll be okay."

"Damn. Wish there was more that I could do."

"You're helping in your own special way. Gary, just stay on it. You are liable to be the one that finds something that breaks the case open."

"I will continue to grow my board. I see the two lovebirds are getting along well. Haven't heard a word about a fight or any disagreements. Can I pick a couple!"

"Listen here, matchmaker dot com. They got a lot of growing up still to do. Before you suggest anyone for me —"

"I know you and Stretchie are starting to consider dating."

"How did — Never mind. We are going to wait until the case is over. It will keep us both focused."

"Boring. But whom am I to say anything. What if one of you gets killed off before it's over?"

"I guess we're both just shit out of luck," she said, patting his hand.

Paisley's cell phone rang, and she excused herself. Gary remained alone. He looked over his board another time. This time, he moved a picture of Carolyn to the consideration pile. From an envelope of cut-out characters, he placed a picture of Sheriff Stone.

"I'd suspect him of stealing social security checks from sweet grandmas and killing them for it. He's local and has power. I'll bet my ass he'd connected," he said to himself aloud.

"Who gave you this phone number?" Paisley asked the person on the other end of the phone.

"Some state police detective guy. Listen, I was just up here doing some night climbing and camping. I was looking out — you know, just getting the lay of the land. That's when I saw this weird thing going on near the river," said the stranger on the other end of the phone.

"First, what's your name, and what are you talking about?" Paisley asked.

"Linus Aspercrest. I'm from Maine. I was at the Gorge and saw some crazy stuff."

"Okay, Linus from Maine. What did you see?"

"It was dark, but the van's lights lit the area up good. It was in a secluded area — maybe a couple of miles off the road. I had this bird's eye view of everything. Night binoculars are cool too. Anyhow, some woman in a van — ugly at that — she pulled a body out and carried it to a canoe."

"That's something you don't see all the time," Paisley commented. "What did you see next?"

"They like paddled up the river."

"Anything else."

"Three hours later, it was light outside. I was taking a wiz off the rock I was staying on, and some Wacko-looking person came paddling up. They looked like some crazy person wearing some wild contamination suit. That's it." he got in the van and drove it off somewhere.

Paisley immediately thought — *The Butcher of Kentucky.*

"Could you show me where this was at on a map?"

"I thought you might want that. Just sent you a text with a map of the area it would have been around — circled it for ya."

"Thanks, Linus. You're a big help."

"Hey, I was wondering, since I liked helped you out, that you could do me a favor?"

"Name it, and if I can do it, I will."

"I hear you own an ice cream shop with delicious flavors. Could I get a scoop for me and my BFF Rocky? He's my canine traveling companion."

"No problem. Just go to the store after three and ask for Kansas. She's my daughter. Tell her I said it's okay for helping me out. Enjoy it."

Paisley now had a lead on where the girls were being dropped off. She'd call Charlie and Stretchie and see if someone couldn't hack into a satellite to get surveillance of the area. If they could find the canoe, they would plant a tracker. Perhaps, they might catch these bastards yet.

CHAPTER THIRTY

The newly elected BMS President Audrey Blunt was not happy. She had just received reports of money losses from the Kentucky chapter of the syndicate. Kentucky's BMS CEO, Lt. Governor Harrelson Gridgewall, was asked to explain the problem at the secure Zoom meeting that included all BMS' territorial representatives.

"We seem to be having an issue at the Red River Gorge operation. I have one of the Chicago operatives working to turn things around. You know how it is with low management," the Lt. Governor said, trying to place the blame away from him.

President Blunt sneered at him, and then she slammed her large coffee cup on the table, shattering the cup into several pieces, causing the hot-filled liquid to quickly spread over the table and run over the sides like a pouring waterfall. "You are still responsible — you piece of shit. It will cost you. If it costs me, it costs you. Everyone vote on the four penalties prescribed now."

Each attending representative had the following choices appear on their screens:

A.   Pay $10,000,000
B.   Pay $20,000,000
C.   Terminate with a severance package
D.   Terminate with no severance package

Lt. Governor Gridgewall was not allowed to vote, so he waited to see his fate. Within twenty seconds, the results were electronically visible to all.

"Terminate with no severance package," said the President.

"I've been loyal these past four years and —" the Lt. Governor tried to finish but was rudely interrupted by President Blunt.

"You know the rules. The vote drives the decision. No recounts or second votes. You need to take action within one minute of the decision, or your family and close friends will pay the price," the President demanded while hiding behind the cartoonish Grizzly Bear avatar representing her in the meeting.

The Lt. Governor pulled out a gun from his drawer, put it in his mouth, and squeezed the trigger. Blood splattered on the screen, and he was disconnected.

Looking at her assistant taking minutes next to her, the president continued on with the meeting. "You know what to do, Kee Kee. Call the press and give them a heads up on the story. Have an email time-stamped and dated going to his family and friends with a suicide note. Notify the next in succession that they have been promoted."

"Yes, Madame President. Consider it done," replied Kee Kee.

"Now on with more business. North Carolina, I see you are up in profits this month. Very good. I'm pleased. But it doesn't make up for last quarter. However, if you keep going in this direction, you will not be terminated. Rhode Island, a little down on the profits but still in the black for the second quarter. Illinois, what's going on with recruitment?"

"We've lost three of our best recruiters tied to the Kentucky connection," said a short, bald, tanned man in his sixties. "It seems the police are starting to pay attention to our baby marketing due to a higher interest in missing teens."

"I see. Tell our Chicago person that they need to start steering the investigations in another direction and to fix this now or, they'll be demoted or worse," screamed the president. "Now, I want some good news. Where are the profits for the young girls we are targeting for our European friends?"

"Sales are up fifty percent. There is a demand for more girls than ever. Some want them as young as five," reported the senior accountant for the BMS.

"We are not pedophile handlers. The girls need to at least be fourteen and up. We can make them look younger, though. Find some with younger faces. I don't care about the two for one as much now. We are getting more for the whoring of these girls than I can for the babies. Increase operations on the street and work with our talent scouts to find beautiful girls looking for adventure. Sell it like an exotic vacation to them. Dr. Wingood, give me the status of the in vitro fertility program," President Blunt demanded.

A rotund, short black man with round spectacles appeared on the screen. "We've successfully started the IVF program in five states. Project "Baby Perfection" has resulted in 90% of subjects becoming impregnated, with 80% of those delivering full term. Adding gene manipulation to create the perfect baby with no negative inherited conditions with controlled physical characteristics has been slow. We are still working on giving people what they want but messing with genes can be complicated."

"What's the problem, doctor? We are behind schedule. This is a lucrative market for us to get into."

"Subjects have been limited. Mostly poor young women looking for money to participate. We need to expand this out. Also, the sperm donor bank doesn't always have a good selection of specimens to use. We need a higher caliber of genetic material to get better results," he responded in a cold scientific fashion.

"Giannelli, work with the doctor. I am sure you can procure more suitable subjects in the name of profit. I expect more progress in the next three months or you know the consequences. We are talking at least thirty to forty million dollars per baby that gives some rich bastard a perfect intelligent, athletic, beautiful little baby with no preexisting medical conditions."

A seedy-looking man in his forties wearing sunglasses responded, "Consider it done. I'll get the doc what he needs."

A large parrot flew over and sat in front of the president's camera. "Rowdy, take your nut and go. We can play later." The bird flew off but not before squawking at the other BMS members on the other end of the video call. "I like that bird. He listens, unlike some of you. You know he scratched the eyes of my predecessor out after I killed him. He has served me well. However, don't think I would not kill him if he did not do as he was told. You know the motto —"

All of the BMS members loudly repeated, "Profit first, profit always, and death to those that hinder profit."

CHAPTER THIRTY-ONE

The bed creaked as Ephrem moved to adjust himself. A soft moan emanated from his partner. Just as he kissed the nape of her neck, a vehicle alarm went off outside, causing the couple to abruptly separate. Ephrem immediately pulled his keys out of his pocket to stop the alarm on his truck.

"Where were we?" Ephrem asked, excited to get back to his girlfriend.

"Stop it, Ephrem. Mom's going to be home anytime. Just glad she didn't sneak back to check on me," Kansas responded.

"My gramps says she's gone to Morehead. She won't be home for some time."

"Having your hand down my bra and the other down my pants is not going to go over well if she walks in."

"If she knew where your mouth and hands were a few minutes ago, she'd probably be unhappy with that as well."

"You're my first. Don't think I'm easy. I'm a curious girl and — I like to think that you think —"

"I know what you are thinking."

"We've been seeing each other for three months now. Patting and touching and feeling. I think I'm ready for you know —"

"You sure?" he asked in a caring tone but with underlying hormonal excitement.

"Yes. I'm not on the pill so we need to use protection. I bought us some condoms. Not a discussion Mom will have with me."

"Okay then. This is my first, too. So, we will do this slow and find out what works."

Kansas and Ephrem undressed each other while slowly exploring each other's bodies. Both were excited to experience the joys and wonders of lovemaking. However, not everything works like in a movie. Within five minutes, it was over with. Ephrem pulled out and rolled over, sighing in exhaustion.

"That felt really good," he said as he hugged her. "How was it for you?"

Being the honest person she was, Kansas responded, "Uneventful."

"What does that mean?" he irritably asked.

"I didn't get off. I didn't orgasm. I didn't see fireworks."

"I did what I needed to. I got off. It's ... I'll try harder. Am I — "

"You think this is about size?"

"Well, I mean ... I heard that ..."

"Not a problem in the size area. You're in acceptable perimeters according to the internet."

"Then what is the issue?"

"It's a problem with endurance," she clearly stated.

"Oh. What am I supposed to do about that?"

Kansas Googled premature ejaculation and sent some links to him. "Read these. Practice these exercises, and maybe we'll try again," she said a little flustered at her first intercourse experience. "I got to clean up before mom shows up. Where's the condom and wrapper? I need to get rid of those right way."

He checked his penis for the prophylactic. The look on his face said it all — it had broken.

"Shit, Ephrem. It broke. It damn well broke. This is not good. I'm ovulating according to my cycle. You better hope that nothing has happened."

"Shit. Me too. Let's just keep an eye on things. Neither one of us are old enough nor responsible enough for a baby."

"You got that right," she sternly replied.

--- SIX WEEKS LATER ---

"Are you sure?" Ephrem said over Facetime.

"Yes. I took a pregnancy test. It says I am ... I am pregnant," Kansas exclaimed.

"What are we going to do?" Ephrem anxiously asked."

"I don't know. If having a baby doesn't kill me, Mom will."

"We have options. There's adoption, raising the kid, abortion," he offered in his solution to the problem at hand.

"None are sounding great. I need time to think," Kansas informed him. "Mom's a good detective. She'll know something is up."

"Gramps is no idiot either. He'll pick up on it too."

Kansas started to cry. Ephrem wished he was there to hold her, but he was in another state visiting his cousin. "I could drive back tonight."

"I would just worry about you being on the road and getting killed if you leave right now. You'll be back soon anyway. We need more time to think before we see each other in person."

"Okay. I'll check into some other things too. Maybe we can find some other alternatives to what we've already talked about."

"Love you, Eph."

"Love you, Kansas."

CHAPTER THIRTY-TWO

Cutting into the flesh of their latest victim, the Butcher smirked under their hazmat hood. The joy of slicing into warm blood created a pleasurable sensation that was almost orgasmic. The Butcher imagined grilling or smoking this tasty young meat with every sliver they carved. They even thought about which wood might flavor the meat the best. Pecan and hickory immediately came to mind, along with a good, seasoned rub. They had learned a lot about smoking meat by watching the *Meat Smokers* television show. As they proceeded to trim the fat and gut their prey, they whistled a tune from their childhood. The haunting melody relaxed them and made them appreciate their grandfather. He had taught them how to properly care for and cook human flesh.

They compared and contrasted how much human meat looked like some other animals once it was processed and wondered why humans were not on the menu in fine restaurants. They grabbed the skinny arms of the young victim, turned the carcass on its side, and took the reciprocating saw to cut the useless parts away. The Butcher thought arms were no better than chicken wings — too much trouble to get what little meat was on it.

The work went fast. The Butcher could fillet, slice, and bag a whole victim in under thirty minutes after removing the head. They always removed the head of all their victims first, so they did not have to see their victim's humanity. It's not that they could not move forward with dissecting their future meals — it just became too connective to the living person that once was, which caused them to hesitate more. They had done the same thing when killing animals and fish as well. Humans were no different.

As far as the Butcher was concerned, it had been a good week for restocking. After planting some of the meat in Carolyn's freezer, their supply was lower. They had been willing to give up some of the older meat to throw the police off their scent and the cabin operation. The Butcher did not care if Darcie and that new bitch were killed, but he did not want to give up their access to a bountiful market. They had liked the quality of the product so far that had been available to them regularly. After all, there were no places to stake out, no concerns about being caught, and a diverse selection of meat.

Marilyn Plainsguard had been an unexpected victim. Brought in a week ago at 37 weeks pregnant, she was ripe for the picking with very little time to wait on the harvesting. The Butcher looked at what little was left of Marilyn. They never looked at the victims in terms of outer beauty. The marbling of their meat and tenderness of the cuts were what they felt were the most important aspect of a person.

Marilyn was a troubled youth with a history of schizophrenia. She had been found wandering in the streets of Louisville when she was picked up by a BMS taker. She kept telling everyone that aliens had kidnapped her and impregnated her. When she asked for help from the wrong person, she ended up at the RRG cabin.

Marilyn was kept chained and isolated from the other girls. Her paranoia had prompted Darcie to keep her in the soundproof bedroom. Her delusions and hallucinations consisted of violence and murder by aliens from another world that clouded her judgment. Although Darcie was aware that Marilyn's child might have a genetic trait for psychosis, she knew another failure meant her termination. However, the Butcher felt that ending Marilyn's life was doing her a favor.

Marilyn's seven-pound and two-ounce baby boy was perfect in every way, except the mother he had. He had been bought for three million dollars by an older couple in Milwaukee that had longed for children but had been unable to conceive surrogate or otherwise. Little Edward Herman Ernesthard II would be living the life of a billionaire's child with no wants or needs instead of in homeless shelters or in foster care.

As the Butcher stripped away Marilyn's skin on her legs, they saved the skin to cook in lard and then season it like pork rinds or cracklins. This would be good snacking during movie time. How they wished their grandfather and father were there to share this feast. The Butcher decided they would go to their new site and smoke a femur and some ribs for tomorrow night's supper. However, before they could go, they needed to inspect the new selection of meat.

"Darcie, where is that psychopath at? We got to let that thing know that it's no longer needed. The BMS is changing their business model. With a larger market for prostitution and the merger with the online porn company, we've got a lot of reasons to continue to let these little ladies stick around," said Ruth Ann Alderman in a business-like attitude.

"That thing keeps whatever hours it likes. I am not its keeper. I wouldn't want to be in your shoes when you tell it," snapped back Darcie.

"You better start being the Butcher's keeper if you know what is good for you. I'm not scared of anyone or anything. Got that," Ruth Ann rudely responded back.

Darcie imagined injecting the old bitch with a sedative and pushing her off one of the nearby cliffs. It would have been easy, too, if Ruth Ann didn't have her two bodyguards constantly watching over her. The two men looked like creepy pedophiles. Even the girls had complained about feeling like they would be raped by one of her thugs because of how they looked at them.

"It's here," stated the more muscular of the two guards who could have passed as brothers by dress, facial features, and height. Maybe they were related, but Darcie didn't care and didn't want to talk to them.

The Butcher came into Darcie's office, appearing grumpy that they had been summoned. The Butcher opened the door with bloodstains on their hazmat suit while wiping a filet knife down with a rag. "You wanted something?"

"Let's get something straight, weirdo. I am not scared of you. Coming in like this doesn't frighten or intimidate me," Ruth Ann pointed out to the killer.

"Don't worry about it. Your meat's too old and boney. Wouldn't make fit stew, even if I simmered you on low for weeks," the

Butcher shot back.

Ruth Ann was taken back by the comment. It was enough to cause the goon that she called Creve to pull out his gun and cock it.

"Tell your bodyguards to not worry. I don't like their meat either. So, let's get this show on the road. What is it?" the Butcher demanded.

"Things are changing. We will no longer be executing or making meals of the young ladies coming here. The company has different business plans which will be more profitable. Your services are no longer needed. Pack up your shit and get ... Today," Ruth Ann informed him.

"The fuck you say. I see. Well, don't expect to have as many of these girls to choose from in the future. You pick up where I hunt already," the Butcher said coldly and distantly.

Ruth Ann gulped and peed a small amount on herself. Her bodyguards were already creeped out and were waiting for Ruth Ann to signal what she wanted them to do with the sociopath.

The Butcher grabbed the door and opened it. "I'm done with doing business with you then. See you in the funny papers."

"You'll do good to remember that we will kill you if you cost us a profit," Ruth Ann again threatened him.

"You don't know who I am. Before these little pissy shits here could pull off a shot, I'd have their jugular veins sliced, and you'd be on the desk getting disemboweled. Don't fuck with me. I can do a lot of damage," the Butcher threatened back.

With that, the Butcher slammed the door and walked toward the community area, where all the remaining captives waited for Darcie to have a group with them. The Butcher pulled up a chair and sat backward in the seat as part of the group's circle, staring at what he considered his cattle.

"I'm leaving, girls. I know you'll miss me. Don't worry. I'll be watching for you. When it's the right time, I'll see you at the slaughter." The Butcher then touched each of their heads as he exited the building. The Butcher's mind was made up. They would clean out any remaining inventory of young girls in the cabin. No one was going to interrupt their perfect meat supply. Ruth Ann and Darcie's days were numbered, and so were their two thugs.

CHAPTER THIRTY-THREE

Rising before three o'clock in the morning to make the trip back to Chicago was daunting for Charlie. He could have taken a flight, but he needed time to decompress in private. Driving alone always seemed to allow him time to talk and convince himself that what he was doing was right. There was no doubt that he was mentally and physically exhausted. He'd been traveling back and forth already for the past two months, keeping up with his cases and trying to manage affairs for his secondary employer. No one in the FBI knew that he had to work a second job to pay his debts. Unfortunately, years of gambling debt and no lady luck on his side had left him in dire straits. He never imagined that his side job would corrupt his soul and slowly eat away at his principles just so he could make bets.

His gambling addiction started when he was in high school. His dad told him that the only way to earn a car was to get a job. Shortly after being given that advice, he began working for a bookie to earn money. Besides learning how to take and collect bets, Charlie developed a taste for betting on sporting events and horses. In the beginning,

Charlie was winning about eighty percent of the time. However, nothing lasts forever.

Charlie's luck seemed to change as soon as he graduated from the police academy. Things went from bad to worse when he started spending more than two-thirds of his paycheck to cover bad bets. It wasn't just money that he was losing — his obsession for betting and winning cost him several relationships. He'd stood up dates, forgot to return calls, and blew off interested women — all in the name of getting the "big win." He was over a hundred grand in debt to Walter "Wally the Walrus" Kelley within no time.

Wally the Walrus broke bones and cracked ribs when money was due that couldn't be collected. Fortunately for Charlie, he had value. Having an inside man in law enforcement was a plus for Wally. It wouldn't pay off all of Charlie's debt, but it would pay off a good portion. By Charlie's account, it would take him at least ten years with interest to pay off the settled debt. Regrettably, Charlie couldn't leave well enough alone. Sure, he let Wally know when a raid might happen, and he was willing to live with letting someone off for illegal gambling, but he didn't want to remain in debt or be caught connected to Wally.

Within months after making a deal with Wally, Charlie had developed a system for analyzing and determining gambling outcomes. He started making bets to test his system with a small-time bookie who knew nothing about him. In the beginning, Charlie's system showed some promise as he won the majority of his bets, but then he got greedy. A twenty thousand dollar bet on a losing greyhound named Flash proved his system was flawed. Now Charlie owed, and he owed big this time to Marcus Spade, who was not as nice as Wally. When Marcus sent a couple of flunkies to collect the debt, they left a reminder of a broken arm that Charlie owed sooner than later. Charlie panicked and became desperate.

Ralph Lilliard was a well-known drug dealer arrested repeatedly who never was convicted due to his connections. Charlie came to Ralph requesting help and did not care what he had to do to get it. Ralph liked a cop owing him a favor. Ralph knew that Charlie already worked for Wally and owed Marcus, so Ralph didn't feel he was getting played. Ralph gave him the number for Terrance, an associate with contacts to some powerful people, who agreed to meet with Charlie.

Before Paisley's husband was killed, Charlie had sold his soul to the Black Market Syndicate. He kept tabs on known targets and passed on any information to benefit the BMS. Charlie also secretly worked with the Assistant District Attorney Plinkard, who had already sold his soul years earlier to ensure the BMS' directives were carried out. Charlie's debt was wiped out in exchange for his services. The agreement he signed with the BMS was considered "lifelong." The only thing that would cancel his deal would be Charlie's death. Unlike other BMS operatives, Charlie would not receive any BMS retirement benefits.

Charlie did what he was asked to do for the BMS without question. However, he felt guilty; his guilt was worse when he was around Paisley. He thought he must have done an excellent job hiding his shame because Paisley never questioned him. He had always been honest with Paisley about everything, but when it came to this part of his life, Charlie was too ashamed that he had let his partner and friend down. The truth was that she was his only real friend, and he was scared he would lose her. He kept telling himself that he would make it up to her and get himself out or eventually tell her the truth. What she didn't know was that Charlie often chased his guilt with a fifth of Don Julio

Blanco.

So, when Paisley retired, and Charlie wanted a change of pace, Charlie applied to the new "Experienced Cops To FBI Agents" program. He was immediately approved without any hesitation. After all, the Associate Director of the FBI was a BMS pay-rolled employee. In the eyes of the BMS, an FBI agent was ten more times valuable than a CPD cop.

--- THE NIGHT OF GREGORY'S DEATH ---

The call came about an early morning shooting in the vicinity of West Main and Parkerville Rd. around 3:30 a.m. while Paisley and Charlie were staking out William Shandly. Shandly was a known thug who had reportedly killed an elderly woman and her six-year-old granddaughter for a bag of groceries and ninety dollars in cash last week, and they were waiting to apprehend him. An anonymous caller had indicated that Shandly was making his way back to his mother's home to grab some quick cash and clothes and steal his stepfather's car. However, they never got to see if he made it to the home or not.

When dispatch gave a description of a deceased male fitting her husband's description found inside an ambulance, Paisley knew something bad had happened with Gregory. She and Charlie arrived only a few minutes behind the first officers on the scene. Paisley ran to the ambulance, knocking Officer Trottell down to the ground. Because Paisley had not identified herself yet, Officer Trottell pulled his sidearm, but Charlie managed the situation and calmed down their fellow officer. Paisley attempted to restrain her emotions but seeing her lifeless husband put her on sensory overload. She buried her head into the chest of her spouse and wept loudly, occasionally stopping long enough to yell out "Fuck" or "No. No. This can't be happening."

It was hard for Charlie to see Paisley in so much pain. Paisley was usually a tough and controlled person. Paisley could only think of the things that had been taken from her, and the things left unsaid; then there were all the things that Paisley thought they still had time to do — the vacations, the restaurants, and retirement. Recently, Gregory had been accepted to nursing school. Now, Gregory would never be able to live his dream. Gregory would also never see his little girl graduate or be there to walk her down the aisle. Worst of all, Paisley had to go home and tell Kansas that the man who hung the moon was dead.

While Paisley grieved with her daughter and close family members, Charlie was pulled into Gregory's investigation in a manner that would have cost his friendship had Paisley known. She might have forgiven him for lying about gambling, disowned him for feeding information to some low-life street thugs, but working with the BMS and doing what he did to impede the investigation of her husband's death was a sure ending to their partnership and friendship. She might even have killed Charlie.

Five minutes after Charlie dropped Paisley off to break the news to Kansas, he was called by his BMS handler — Assistant DA Plinkard. Plinkard said he had put Charlie in charge of the investigation by leaning on the captain. He asked Charlie to take minimal statements and make sure reliable witnesses didn't testify and that any real evidence found did not connect back to the BMS. This was BMS's business, and unless he wanted to join Gregory in the afterlife, he would follow through.

At Gregory's wake, Charlie cried not just for the loss of his friend that he had served with in the military but for the loss of his partner's husband and the father of the daughter he treated like a niece. Underlying it all, he grieved most for his corrupted soul that he felt could never be revealed to Paisley. This is why as much as he loved Paisley from afar and wanted her as a love interest, he knew he was no good for her. By being part of this investigation on the BMS teen kidnappings, he felt that he might rectify some of his mistakes. This time he would manipulate the BMS to protect Paisley and Kansas. He owed her that much and more.

CHAPTER THIRTY-FOUR

Kansas mixed up her final version of Boys In Blue Glazed Donut and Coffee Ice Cream. She tasted it and then handed Deputy Sheriff Tommy Hopple a sample. The law officer savored the flavors and gave an enormous smile.

"Damn good. I swear I was dunkin' a glazed donut into a cup of coffee."

"That's what we are going for," the proud teen answered back. "Here's a large to go on the house. What would I have done without you volunteering to sample every batch being formulated?"

"I guess you'd be working on that firehouse chipotle fudge chili concoction again. Let me tell you — this is why firemen should stick to cooking chili and chasing fires. Next time one of those guys come in here with an idea — tell them "no thank you." They really have no appreciation or sense of what a quality confection is," the deputy responded back.

"See you next time around. Yes, I won't let Sheriff Stone know you are helping me out. I have a lemon pie sorbet recipe waiting to be tried that needs your special tasting capabilities next time."

"Thanks. You know, he really doesn't like your mom. He needs to get over it. To serve and sample. That's my motto."

As soon as Tommy left, she felt a wave of nausea go through her. She had been nauseated several times throughout the day. Crackers and coke had been the one thing that had made her feel better. She remembered her mother telling her how she drank coke and ate crackers when she had morning sickness. She just hoped her mother never put two and two together. Two weeks had passed since she and Ephrem had talked about informing the adults. Neither really felt compelled to move forward with a plan. Kansas knew she couldn't wait much longer. She'd already gained five pounds and was experiencing bloating and soreness in her breasts.

Kansas was a natural writer, and she turned to writing when she couldn't verbally say what she wanted. Taking a break from the customers, she went to the back office and began writing an email to her mother. She would put it on a delay and promised herself that she would not stop it from being sent.

MOM:
I have always tried to be honest with you. However, I find some things that scare me too much to sit down with you face-to-face to begin a conversation about. So, I thought I would start with this email.

I'm around two months pregnant. Ephrem is the father. We did use protection, but protection is not always 100% effective. I don't know what to do. I know all the options, and

I'm scared and confused. I know this is a lot with everything you are going through. I don't want to disappoint you. Let's talk in person as soon as you can about this.

Love,
K

    The delay was set for 12 hours from the current time. She knew that her mother would sit her down at the kitchen table like she had for so many of their talks. She would be ready. She also knew her mother might tell her she was too young, but she also knew her mother advocated for women to decide about their own bodies.

    Kansas skimmed through this week's local trade and sale magazines. On page eight of Trader's World was an advertisement directed toward pregnant teens looking for help. It offered to provide money and assistance. Kansas took the magazine back to the office and closed the door. As she dialed the number, she wondered what they would tell her, what they would do for her, and what their thoughts were about teens having kids her age.

    Gloria Hellman answered the phone and gave her some basic information about the group. She said their organization was part of an outreach program with federal grants. She informed Kansas that they have mobile offices that travel through each state, helping teens decide and finding assistance for them. Gloria promised her confidentiality and that they would not contact her mother unless she gave them permission. Kansas felt at ease with Gloria and wondered if most counselors were this laid back. Kansas was now looking forward to having an impartial person to help her look at all the options before she talked to her mother.

Gloria indicated that one of their mobile units was only an hour away and would be passing through their area in the next couple of hours. Kansas hesitated for a moment and then asked to have one of them meet her in the elementary school parking lot after three o'clock. Gloria scheduled a time for Kansas.

As promised, a van pulled up in the parking lot on time. It was marked as Gloria had told her: "Delphine Frederickson Children's Orphanage Foundation Outreach Program." Kansas climbed in to find a comfy chair and two women in their early twenties waiting on her. They offered her cold water from a cooler. Kansas took a sip, and within minutes found herself dreaming of having a little baby girl named Gregrina.

CHAPTER THIRTY-FIVE

An intense headache causing waves of nausea throughout her body impacted Kansas' ability to see. Each time she opened her eyes, she thought she was going to hurl. Wherever she was, she was moving fast around curvy roads. The motion of the vehicle only intensified the feeling to vomit. She tried to open her mouth to talk or scream, but she could not get anything out. She then figured out that she was now gagged. Her hands and feet were slightly numb, and she noticed that she had been secured by zip ties.

How had she been so stupid? She knew about the case her mother was working on. She was betting these were the people who kidnapped girls who were pregnant. This was just another method of picking up pregnant teens. God, how she wished her mother was here. What had she gotten herself into? She looked for the time and day, but her Apple Watch was missing. She didn't feel her cell phone in her pocket, and she guessed that both had been disposed of to keep her from being tracked.

The brunette driving spoke directly to Kansas while blowing a pina colada flavored e-cigarette toward her. "Wake up, honey. Can't sleep all day. People are waiting on you."

Kansas tried to talk, but the gag kept her muffled. A woman with short-cropped dyed pink hair riding in the passenger's side ripped the duct tape off Kansas' mouth.

"Ouch, damn it! What people?" Kansas responded. How she wanted to tell them that they had kidnapped a former cop's daughter who was well connected with the state police and whose family friend was an FBI agent. She quickly curbed the thought when she realized that bragging or making threats might get her killed and disposed of quicker.

"You'll see," the brunette replied.

"Yep. They have big plans for you. Not a virgin from the situation you are in. I'd say you'll bring a good price. Big blue eyes, sexy hair, and nice tits," said the driver's associate.

"What are they going to do with me?" Kansas asked.

"Don't worry about that. They'll take care of that little bump starting to show. Now shut up. We got to take you on a little off-road adventure," sneered the driver.

They had finally arrived wherever they were going, and Kansas had made it without vomiting. The two women helped her out of the van. Whatever they had drugged her with made it impossible to control her muscles very well. In a foggy state of mind, she tried planning her escape, but her mind kept wandering off. Although she had been trained in various martial arts until she was twelve years old, her current condition barely allowed her to open an eyelid, let alone carry out a roundhouse kick.

Kansas' kidnappers took off the zip ties, replacing them with leg irons. Kansas was led to a canoe hidden in some bushes on the river's edge. Kansas recognized where she was at. She had been here before with Ephrem when they went on long drives to find isolated places to be alone.

Kansas knew her only hope of being found would come from her mother, Stretchie, or Charlie. She would have to leave a clue that she had been here. Grabbing the back pocket of her tattered jeans, she pulled hard, causing it to rip. She let the back pocket fall to the ground when no one looked. She then poked a hole in the box of Nerds that the driver had given her as a snack and let them drop to the ground to create a trail.

Needless to say, it was a lost cause. Before setting out in the canoe, the pink-haired women checked the trail to the canoe, recovered the torn back pocket, and kicked the Nerds in every direction. She used a branch to sweep her footprints to the river away. Now there would be no help for Kansas. For her brave attempt to inform others where she was headed, she was smacked twice across the face by the driver, who told Kansas that was her only warning.

CHAPTER THIRTY-SIX

Knowing she would possibly be stuck all day and night in Morehead working on the case, Paisley had called her daughter the previous morning and asked her to spend the night with a reliable friend. Kansas was supposed to stay the night with Rose and come home to feed the animals the following day. However, Paisley was unaware that Rose had gone out of town with her aunt. Instead of finding another person that her mother would approve of, Kansas decided to stay by herself. Kansas knew that her mother was not probably going to like it when she found out, but she believed in asking forgiveness after the fact. After all, she was almost sixteen and quite capable. Paisley had spent years ensuring Kansas would be a strong independent young woman by giving her shooting lessons, sending Kansas to various martial art classes, and making her take finance classes.

Paisley's phone dinged when she was on her way home from Morehead. It was a message from Stretchie which caused her face to light up like a scoreboard. She knew the message had nothing to do with the case. The night before, she and Stretchie had shared a drink and then a bed with each other. Since they had started working the case together, being around each other had stirred up fond memories of their former high school relationship.

She had not had sex with anyone since Gregory had died. She and Stretchie had never gone beyond some patting and talk about having sex during high school. Things never got too serious, and Paisley went off to college to explore the world and become a CPD detective while Stretchie stayed in the state he loved so much. Why she had waited so long to have sex again or had passed on sex with Stetchie while in high school was still a mystery, if not a missed juvenile opportunity of exploration.

She knew that having sex was long overdue, even if it was a one-night thing. Before he was called out on a homicide the next morning, Stretchie left her a cup of coffee and a donut as a parting gift. The coffee was still warm, and the donut was stale, but the gesture made her feel cared for. Hours after Stretchie left, Paisley was still smiling and felt alive for the first time in a long time. Gary was good company, but he wasn't a person she had any romantic interest in.

Paisley hadn't heard from Kansas since ten o'clock the previous day. The cell phone signals were often hit and miss on these roads. She had her hands-free system read her text messages. Most of them were from her cousin in Buffalo, asking her if she was seeing anyone yet. Paisley lied when she responded because, technically, she was not in a relationship at this point. A text from Charlie asked her to call him because he needed to talk to her about something. She then noticed that she had an unread email. It was from the ice cream shop's business email account. It could have been anyone at the store working, but she saw that the time sent was delayed from the day before when Kansas had been scheduled.

Paisley listened intently to the email being read. She had to play it twice before letting it sink in that her little girl was scared and pregnant. There would be no time to delay. She would call her now. She had three bars, and it was her best chance to dial out without a drop. However, when she tried to call, it went straight to Kansas' voicemail. She tried to call four more times, leaving a message on the last call. She then tried to ping her daughter's cell phone, but nothing came up.

Her gut told her that Kansas was in trouble. Paisley knew she needed help to find her daughter. Years of experience as a cop taught her to be calm and not panic. It was easier said than done when it did not involve your own child. Although she felt a wave of panic, Paisley managed to hold it together to come up with a plan. She contacted her cell phone company to find out the last numbers called on Kansas' phone. One of the numbers was a pregnant helpline. It wasn't just any helpline — it was connected to the Delphine Frederickson Children's Orphanage Foundation, which had just recently been linked to the BMS by the FBI's latest report.

Paisley immediately called Stretchie and explained the situation. She asked him to meet her at the farm to develop a plan. She pleaded with him to not bring anyone else from law enforcement because she did not feel anyone else could be trusted.

She tried calling Charlie, but she only got his voice mail. Charlie, who wanted to talk to Paisley, ignored the call and let it go to voice mail. He had decided that what he had to tell her needed to be done in person. Charlie was only hours away from setting himself free and probably becoming the biggest disappointment in Paisley's life.

Curious about Paisley's message, Charlie listened to Paisley's frantic voice mail. When he heard that Kansas was probably in the clutches of the BMS and they would be selling her and her baby, Charlie sped up. Whatever he needed to tell her about his involvement with the BMS would have to wait. He knew if he called her back and told her anything, she would not let him help. He would have to come clean sooner than later, but right now, he needed to step up to protect his friend and her daughter.

Feeling Gary needed to be informed, Paisley had him come to the house and bring Ephrem. When the news broke, Gary sat in silence, sipping his coffee until he looked at Ephrem and said, "Disappointed in you. Don't love you any less, but disappointed that you never told me, never felt you could come to me, and never had enough sense to use protection. Dumbass is all I can think of."

"Gramps. I ... I ... I ... We did ... It broke ... We were going to," Ephrem stuttered out.

"Let's try to put some things together. We might be able to find her. It seems the call went out about 11:22 a.m. We know that she clocked out of the ice cream shop at 1:15 p.m. I talked to Tommy and he —" Paisley informed them.

"Who's Tommy?
" Stretchie asked.

"Owns that new barbershop that sees everything going on here. Nosy old bastard and charges two dollars higher that the last barber," Gary added.

"Where was I?" Paisley said trying to get things back on track. "Tommy told me that he saw her walking up to the elementary school. He had offered her a ride, and she informed him that she was meeting someone about an afterschool volunteer opportunity. The groundskeeper told Tommy that day that he had seen Kansas get into a van that had some orphanage's name on it. My guess is that they … That they … They took her to the drop-off site," Paisley relayed to them.

"Someone was out there. I just had them pull the satellite tracking information on the canoe. It was gone for approximately 45 minutes from the original site and then returned later," Stretchie added while taking a sip of his coffee and scratching his ear.

"Do we know where it went to?" Paisley asked.

"It traveled up several miles up to this point," Stretchie said as he pointed to a spot on the map. "Looking at the satellite that we had the FBI access for us, we know there is a trail off to the side, but it leads to nowhere."

"Don't be so sure," Gary noted. "Those woods are dense and provide cover to anything built in the middle of it. Besides, if these people are as powerful and influential as you say, I wouldn't put it past them having someone that could be paid to hide all their operations from Big Brother."

"As much as a conspiracy theory as that sounds, I believe that it's highly likely." Paisley supported her friend's hypothesis. "Let's get some backup and go in quietly late tonight under cover of the dark and raid their operation. Only get people you know are honest. These people are sure to have someone looking out for them everywhere."

"I got a few good ones that I can trust. Any word on Charlie?" Stretchie inquired.

"No, but we can't wait," Paisley said in a disappointed manner.

"We're going too," Ephrem shouted.

"I'm with the boy. I'll go grab my shotgun, " Gary said,

supporting him.

"No. This isn't a crime drama we're doing here. This is dangerous. We can't deputize you to help go save the world. You are not trained, and I doubt either of you could take a life," Paisley informed them.

"She's right. I'll make the call. Get things together, and we'll meet at the canoe site around one this morning," endorsed Stretchie.

"Go home, Gary. The best thing you can do is stay out of the way," Paisley ordered.

Gary and Ephrem left without showing disregard for the line drawn. On the way out of Paisley's house, Gary looked at Ephrem and said, "She didn't say we couldn't go opossum hunting, did she. Better get those guns up and other gear we'll need. It's payback time with a vengeance. That's my grandbaby that's being threatened."

CHAPTER THIRTY-SEVEN

Kansas was so glad to be on solid ground again that she could have kissed the ground, which she did because her leg irons caused her to trip when she got out of the canoe and fell face-first into the brown, wet, sandy bank. While she was spitting the dirt out of her mouth, she was jerked up by her two escorts before she could get to her knees. Kansas was then led to a four-seat utility vehicle and buckled in by the pink-haired woman. The trip through the eroded, rutted trails was insufferable. When they finally made it to the cabin, Kansas was ready to puke on the both of them. The van driver saw the signs and pointed Kansas in the opposite direction, however, Kansas could only produce dry heaves.

Darcie came out to greet Kansas. She strode out, trying to look very serious and in control. Kansas looked Darcie over and concluded that Darcie was a has-been person with low self-esteem and confidence issues who did what she was told to do. Kansas was her mother in many aspects — tough, and she knew how to insult someone without trying hard when it suited her. Given her situation, Kansas felt it was better to play the street-wise punk over the daughter of a former law enforcement officer.

"Let me guess — you are going to save my baby and me. Doesn't look like you can save yourself," Kansas analytically stated, trying to get a rise out of her new warden.

"And I can see when someone has an issue with authority. You'll be broken, and you'll do as I say in no time. I've broken many bitches who thought they knew me," she shot back while looking over her newest guest.

"Whatever?" replied Kansas.

"Whatever? It's Ms. Darcie when you are speaking to me. Let's get a better look at you. Teeth look well kept. You're not a bad-looking gal even with those flamingo legs, but we got people wanting girls like you. We'll get you some good therapy too."

"Not for sale, and I'm no who —" Kansas stopped herself from overacting the role.

"You're an irascible one. Aren't you?" Darcie said after paying the two takers some money and sending them on their way.

"Fuck you very much," Kansas responded, trying to appear less sophisticated than she was capable of doing.

"That mouth of yours. You are going to have to learn some manners," Darcie threatened.

"I'm sure you will educate me," snidely remarked Kansas, whose remark was followed up with a whack across the head with a clipboard by Darcie.

It stung, but Kansas shook it off and kept her wits in check. Darcie led her into the cabin, giving her a quick tour. Kansas was introduced to Ruth Ann, who she thought was scary as hell. Ruth Ann looked like she'd suck your soul dry and then come back for more. Kansas decided to cool it and further assess the situation. Regardless of appearing calm, Kansas was worried that her captors would figure out who she really was. She needed to be innovative and think like her mother, who had taught her to assess the situation, look at all weaknesses, formulate possibilities, find the most successful solution, and act without fear. So, Kansas observed all she could before they put her into a room with the most unexpected roommate — Brynlee.

Brynlee ignored them when they entered the bedroom. Brynlee lay on her side, sketching pictures of her and Ephrem by a lake with a baby.

"Here's your roommate. Get along or get punished. You can do the formalities after I leave. Go stand by your bed."

Darcie grabbed a long chain and secured Kansas' leg irons to it. She noted that Brynlee had a shock collar and leg irons. She must have been giving them a pretty rough time if she had both, Kansas thought.

"Don't try to escape. Making sure you and the baby are safe is paramount if you want to collect your money and survive this program. Get my meaning," Darcie stated in a syrupy, uncaring manner.

Kansas nodded in agreement but knew nothing about any money being offered for her baby. She would ignore it for now and ask about it later. Darcie proceeded to explain meal and snack times along with group therapy sessions. As soon as Darcie left, Brynlee jumped up and faced her archnemesis.

"Well, look who got herself all knocked up. I bet Ephrem done run you off — why else would you be here."

"We were exploring options when I was taken against my will. Whose kid are you carrying? Did you pay some dumb freshmen to donate sperm?"

"Screw you, whore. I happen to be carrying Ephrem's little boy. My baby might be your baby's half-brother, but there only needs to be one child that Ephrem wants or needs to be in existence."

"Keeping it real there, drama queen. I bet you made client of the month at the psychiatric hospital. You know Ephrem says he never slept with you. No recognition at all, and we did a lie detector test."

"He might say that, but I got proof in the DNA. He might not have been conscious, but he loves me. Don't you worry about that?"

"Wow. Delusional, aren't you?"

"I think I'll put in a good word about you," Brynlee sarcastically said. "I bet they don't know you're a cop's daughter. I have a feeling you won't be here that long if they know."

"Do it, and I'll make sure that the only way you leave this place is in a body bag," threatened Kansas. Kansas was playing the pufferfish. She didn't want to hurt this poor girl. She was a good five inches taller than Brynlee and could have kicked her ass. However, causing trouble in a cabin housing black market babies and sex trafficking criminals might lead to negative repercussions, placing others at harm. Thankfully, Brynlee backed off when Darcie opened the door and informed them that it was time for dinner.

In the center of the cabin was a large table large enough to seat twenty people. Although none of the seats were assigned, they seemed to be claimed by other girls already sitting at the table waiting to be given the signal to eat. Ruth Ann and her two thugs sat at an adjacent table while Darcie served everyone food. Kansas noted that many of the girls were in the later stages of pregnancy, and some were just starting out like her. If this was her future, she wasn't sure that she wanted it; especially, those having problems sitting down in a chair.

A piece of grilled, herbed chicken with a crown of broccoli filled everyone's plate. Water with lemon was the only beverage of choice. Although the food was healthy, it was bland. Dessert consisted of half of a Little Debbie Cosmic Brownie and a bowl of pureed strawberries. All the girls worked to clear the dishes and do the cleanup chores. An hour of games and reading was allowed before bedtime. Kansas watched for dynamics between her peers. She gathered from their body language and the other girls' subservient attitude toward those in charge that this was not what they had signed on for. Kansas concluded that she could unite these young women by their common despise of their captors. She would start with Brynlee. If she could convince someone who disliked her more than anyone in the world, she would have a chance of getting them all to cooperate and come up with a feasible escape plan. As soon as they were sent to their bedrooms, she began working on Brynlee.

"I know you hate me and wish I'd drop dead. Here's the thing. It doesn't matter if Ephrem loves you or even if you love him. You know these people are going to take your baby away and sell you off or worse. Then all this shit you got against me won't matter. Let's set aside whatever differences we have and focus on saving our babies and ourselves."

"I ain't never going to like you. I'd rather see you dead than alive. But given it would hurt Ephrem if you or his babies came to harm, I guess we need to work together to get out of this place."

"Good. What can you tell me about security? Who else patrols this area besides the two goons, Ruth Ann, and Darcie?"

"The guy in the hazmat. He seems to take care of people disappearing. Some say he kills them for Darcie. I've met him once. Made me almost shit on myself. He's a psycho."

"Heard of him. Going to have to figure this out. Let's start working on a plan. Can I count on the others?"

"Maybe. All of them have been bitching about not getting money and being forced to stay here. Everyone is scared too. Scared they will be beaten or worse."

"I wish I could get in touch with my mom. She could bring the calvary and get us out of here. After rethinking this, I think trying to make a break, given where we are and trying to get out of these collars and chains ... I think we would be a terrible idea. Another thing — pregnant women don't run too fast or well with swollen ankles and extra weight."

"We might be able to contact your mom. Darcie misplaces her satellite phone all the time. If we could watch for her to put it down, you might have a chance to use it. I don't know — they watch us like hawks."

The night was long, and Kansas tossed and turned in the tiny twin bed. The sheets were cheap and felt like a pumice stone against her skin. The following day at breakfast, an opportunity for her to contact her mother materialized when Darcie left her satellite phone on the table when she went back into the kitchen to get some more toast.

The phone was within reach of Kansas, but Ruth Ann kept looking back and forth at the table. Brynlee saw the opportunity as well and decided to create a distraction. She knocked her plate of eggs into the floor, causing the plate to break into pieces and the eggs to splatter under the feet of everyone. Ruth Ann demanded that they clean up the mess; she sent the two goons for paper towels and a broom.

Grabbing her napkin, Kansas covered the phone and made it disappear from the table while everyone was focused on cleaning the floor up. She slid it into her pajama pocket. After the mess was cleaned up and the dishes cleared away, the girls were sent to shower. There was now an opportunity for some privacy. Kansas pulled the phone out and looked it over. She had never used a satellite phone before. It looked simple enough. She hit the power button, and it lit up. She tried dialing her mother's cell number, but an access code for the phone appeared. She tried a few random numbers, and after three failed attempts, she was locked out. Moments later, Ruth Ann pulled back her shower curtain and held out her hand.

"Foolish girl. We get alerted when someone tries to use these without an access code. This is your only warning. Next time you'll find yourself at the bottom of some gorge dead. Now, shower. We have a special place for you to think about your actions."

After drying off, Kansas was taken to a small six by six cabin in the woods with a bucket for a toilet, locked away, and left there. Kansas was not sure if she would ever see her mother again. She was frightened, and she felt foolish because she no longer could help anyone. She wanted to cry but there was no time for tears.

CHAPTER THIRTY-EIGHT

Stretchie left and informed Paisley that he would meet her at the canoe site. He offered to stay, but she needed time to think through the plan and how they needed to proceed. Paisley looked at her daughter's most recent picture from school and then the one when Kansas was six years old, sitting on Gregory's lap dressed as a pirate with a full beard and fake hook as a hand. She wanted to cry and just let things out, but there would be time for that when her daughter was back home. Right now, she had to save her, and any other girls being held captive.

Inside the secret wall in the back of her walk-in closet was a small room containing an array of weapons she had bought over the years, ranging from semi-automatics to .22 caliber firearms. She even had a crossbow. She had learned to use a crossbow as a youth and enjoyed practicing with it. She was as deadly with it as she was with her Glock.

She grabbed two or three handguns and clips along with a shotgun and her crossbow. She placed them in a large duffle bag and grabbed her daughter's picture from the frig. This was her rescue target. She wanted to focus on her.

Within a few minutes of coming off the farm, her car was struck by a large tow truck. The blow from the collision was so hard that it knocked her unconscious and put her car headfirst into a ditch line. The last thing she remembered seeing were the words "Tony's Rescue Tow Co."

Paisley awoke confused and hurting like hell. She found herself in an office handcuffed to a barber's chair when she came to. How much time had passed since the accident was uncertain. Right now, she would have preferred a heavy dose of a pain reliever over escaping. Initially, she was by herself, but Uncle Sturgill walked into the room a few moments later.

"My dear, Paisley. It has been a while since we last saw each other in person.

"Why am I here locked up like some prisoner?" demanded Paisley.

"Simply to keep you safe and out of harm's way. I am quite aware of your little planned raid on the site in the woods. It's not going to end well. Not for those you work with. Seems everybody has a price — even trusted associates of Mr. Bishop Knight."

"So, the BMS has deep connections even with little people like yourself. What would my mother and father say about your interests?" said a wounded Paisley.

"They're dead, my dear, and if they were living, I guess they might be next to you waiting to go on to their reward," he beamed as he swirled his bourbon on the rocks.

"Regardless, I have a function that serves a purpose — profit for the syndicate and me. I am loyal, and loyalty is everything. It means putting your family last. It's just the way life is."

"You know then about Kansas. I guess I couldn't ask you to exclude her from all this."

"That's right. It's sad, but Kansas is also profit."

"If I could shoot you right now, I would," threatened Paisley.

"I would shoot you, my dear, but I don't do that kind of work. I have people for that."

The door opened up, and Paisley's level of trust dropped to its lowest level. There was Charlie, and he was holding a gun.

"Just in time. We have an old acquaintance you've been asked to take care of. I understand your loyalty is outstanding, Mr. Yocum," Uncle Sturgill smugly said.

"Sorry, but profit first, old friend," Charlie said, pointing the gun at Paisley.

"When did they get to you? How long have you been on their payroll?" Paisley then spat at Charlie.

"Since before Gregory died. I'm afraid I got in debt and sold my soul to live. It is what you do when your luck has run out."

"He was your best friend. You were my partner. Kansas is your adoptive niece," she said, trying to guilt her old friend.

"Profit and living are my goals ... But you know, lately, I've had a change of heart," Charlie said as he pointed the gun at Sturgill.

Sturgill reached for a gun under his desk, but before he could retrieve it, Charlie shot him between the eyes. Sturgill fell to the ground grabbing at an old picture of his son and daughter, happily smiling in front of the castle at Disney World. Seems that family did matter after all, but only in the end.

Charlie untied Paisley, who stood up and punched him in the jaw. "You son of a bitch. I trusted you. I loved you like a brother. You betrayed everything ... I'll kill you later. Why'd you kill him and not me?"

"I had to draw the line somewhere. You and Kansas were that line. We got to save her and the other girls, but we need to stop an ambush from happening that'll take out Stretchie and his crew. First, I need you to play dead."

"Do fucking what?" she exclaimed.

"I don't have time. Sturgill's men are outside. They heard a shot, but they think I came here to kill you, not Sturgill. I'll carry you out over my shoulder, and we'll head out to save everyone, but you'll have to play dead."

"No choice. I guess. I'll do this, but I'm holding onto my gun in my pocket so I can shoot you first if you shit on me anymore. Got that?"

"Loud and clear."

"I expect there's a lot more to this than I know about that you are going to tell me. We will go from there."

"Yes, mam."

"Lastly, if we get through this, you are turning yourself in."

"I already planned to."

"Good, now let's get this done."

Charlie picked Paisley up like a sack of potatoes and tossed her over his left shoulder, leaving his shooting hand free to use. They made it to the car, and he had just placed her in the trunk when a man came running from Sturgill's house. Paisley poked her head above the edge of the trunk's interior and fired three shots. Two hit the man in the heart, causing him to fall. Another goon then came charging, firing an AK-47.

The rounds made holes on the driver's side and flattened two of the tires. Charlie went around the side for protection while Paisley shot from the trunk. Eventually, Charlie got a good shot that took the shooter out.

"Damn, hope they didn't call anyone," Paisley yelled out from the trunk.

"Me too. Let's take that truck over there. I saw this one move it when I got here. AK-47 guy should have the keys still on him."

Charlie took the keys, and they jumped in. There was half a tank of gas, and the radio station was stuck on a station that would not change and a radio that would not shut off. The song playing as they left the lot was *Danger Zone* by Kenny Loggins.

CHAPTER THIRTY-NINE

Paisley made several attempts to contact Stretchie. Every time she called it went straight to his voice mail. She knew he was probably in an area that couldn't be reached. If there was a BMS operative in his office, calling to have them radio Stretchie would make things worse. She and Charlie would just have to make it there before anything terrible happened. At this point, the element of surprise was on their side because whoever was sent to take out Stretchie and his associates were not expecting her and Charlie. Charlie had no idea who had been sent. One of the reasons the BMS had been under the radar of the law was that things were taken care of without mass communication and sharing of information.

Charlie and Paisley focused on what they needed to do when they got to the location. The plan was simple and hopefully would pay off. They would arrive before one o'clock and Charlie would go to the top of the cliff overlooking the area where the canoe rested. He would use his nightscope on his rifle to watch for activity and pick off anyone threatening. If he saw anyone that was coming Paisley's direction, he would radio her.

Paisley would enter the backside through the wooded area and watch from there. She had been given Charlie's infrared binoculars to help spot any perpetrators. As far as Paisley knew, Stretchie was supposed to meet her at the site near the canoe and she hoped his plans had not changed. The unknown assailants, whatever that number turned out to be, would mostly likely take a shot at Stetchie and his crew when they stepped out into the open.

There was one more issue to take into consideration. Stretchie had a BMS snitch in his crew that had leaked information to Sturgill. *Who was it, though?* Charlie continued to say he didn't know. He said he would watch for the person that left their vehicle last because a BMS operative would most likely be the one lagging behind to shoot them all in the back.

Paisley warned Charlie again that he'd better not double-cross her, and she'd be keeping an eye on him. Pointing her right dominant index finger at him, she informed him that she wouldn't hesitate to shoot him dead if he fucked up. Charlie just looked ahead and never said a word. They pulled over to a small clearing on the side of the road and backed into a space between some trees a mile from the meeting place. As planned, Charlie took the steep trail up and found a spot to play sniper. Paisley made her way through the wooded area to view the river where the canoe awaited. At 12:58 a.m., two large SUVs rolled in. All the riders waited until exactly one o'clock to step out of their vehicles. Paisley watched and waited, hoping Charlie was still trustworthy enough to carry this off. However, something seemed off.

There were three undercover officers, two men and one woman with Stretchie. Stretchie was the last to get out of the car and was in the rear. Paisley thought: *Was Stretchie with the BMS too? Was he their informant?* A shot rang out from the front of the law enforcement officers in front of Stretchie. Stretchie dropped to the ground and rolled behind a large rock for cover. Two of the three officers with Stretchie fell to the ground. Paisley could not see who did the shooting, who was wounded, or worse. From what she could tell, the shots did not come from the top of the cliff overlooking the water but from the front near the river. Paisley only saw one figure remaining. The figure moved from the brush and thick cane poles near the water.

"Just lay there. Makes it easier to kill you when you don't move," said the figure now standing over Stretchie.

"Dana. You are one hell of an actor. Never would have put you as a BMS bitch in a million years. Maybe that's why," Stetchie responded.

"Is it because I'm a woman?"

"No. You just seemed like a career-driven cop with a family you cared for."

"Fake family. BMS is good at doctoring records. I only care about me. You know you can't live on a cop's retirement."

"You know someone is going to be suspicious when you come back unscathed, and we are all dead?"

"I know. I'll be shooting myself with this little gun here. It'll be a flesh wound. It'll be easy to convince everyone how I defended myself, and then escaped to call for help. You all died heroes. The irony is that I'll probably get a plaque for going above and beyond duty. So sad."

Dana aimed the gun at Stretchie's head. As she started to squeeze the trigger, a shot rang out from above, and Dana went down.

"I guess no flesh wound for you. You are just dead," Paisley said, holstering her gun and offering a hand to Stretchie.

Stretchie gladly accepted the assistance. "So, did you take that traitor down?"

"Charlie did," she said, not having the heart to tell him that Charlie was another traitor in their company. "He's up on the hill doing the sharpshooting."

"I guess I owe him a big thanks. Damn, Jamison and Goldby. She took them out. How did you all know?"

"We did, and we didn't. I got an involuntary invitation to my Uncle Sturgill's, which ended very badly for him."

"What? Sturgill?"

"Seems that he and the dead lady here were on Team BMS. Just as I thought I was a goner — Charlie saved the day. Not before Sturgill did his villainous chatter and told me what was going to happen to you."

"You there, Paisley? Hello!" said Charlie over the device in Paisley's jacket pocket.

"Yeah. Good. No other perps. I believe the plan was to have Dead Dana here to take them all out by surprise. We surprised her ass instead. No survivors except Stretchie," she reported back.

"Coming down. Will be down soon," Charlie responded.

"So, I take it that you all thought that there would be someone else that would be taking us out?" Paisley asked Stretchie.

"We figured an inside person, and I hate to say that I thought that it might be you because you were in the rear. However, we didn't anticipate someone being the perp taking the lead position. Glad you are still with us."

"Time to save your daughter and those other girls."

"That's part two of Plan A which needs to be made as soon as Charlie gets down here," Paisley informed him.

Out of breath and stopping to guzzle from his water bottle, Charlie indicated that he was getting too old for climbing up and down steep hills. Stretchie patted Charlie on the back and thanked him for saving his life. Charlie told Stetchie that he would have done the same thing for him.

There was no need to call for backup. At this point no one outside their trio needed to be involved. To call anyone right now could possibly alert those holding the girls captive. So, they made a plan. Part two of Plan A would involve traveling up the river and then strategically find a way into the cabin with the least risk to the pregnant teens and themselves. It was not without a lot of unknown scenarios that depended on the element of surprise.

Each put on a bulletproof jacket. Everyone received a secure earpiece and com unit to help coordinate the attack. Stretchie opened up the arsenal in the back, where they loaded up on stun grenades. Paisley took more ammunition and a shotgun, Charlie loaded up on extra magazines, and Stretchie armed himself with an extra Glock and more ammunition.

While Stretchie readied the canoe, Charlie asked Paisley if she told Stretchie or planned to tell him about his BMS connection.

"No, it will fuck with the mission. I know what he'll do to you, but I need you to help rescue my daughter and these other girls. You can tell him when everything is settled."

"Thanks," he responded.

"Don't thank me yet. It's far from over."

They loaded the canoe, and up the river, they went.

CHAPTER FORTY

The Butcher watched his next victims from the edge of the woods. Most of them would not be tagged as meat to eat and the others as pests to slaughter. The BMS had invaded their flock and interrupted their supply chain. Now, they would die. In fact, the Butcher had already thought about keeping the cabin and continuing it as a place of their own. They had lost their favorite place to a fire and were still quite angry about the loss. They would install more freezers and a special cooking area outside for grilling and smoking. It would be delightful.

"It's time to patrol the grounds, Crevin. You know how she is if we don't," said the younger of the two men.

"Yeah, I know," replied an annoyed Crevin to his counterpart, Oswald "Ozzy" Humpernickel. "I'll take the east side, and you take the west side. We will meet back in the middle."

"Let's just get it done," a grumpy Ozzy responded back.

As Ozzy made a close pass to the woods, the Butcher threw a rock to the right, causing Ozzy to stop and listen. The Butcher then threw another rock, which hit a tree this time.

"Probably a fucking squirrel, but you never know," he said as he pulled his weapon out of the holster. "Here squirrely, squirrely. You little nut-gathering bastard. Time to meet your maker."

Hearing a twig snap behind him, Ozzy turned around. He was face to face with the psychopath that was fired. Before he could pull the trigger, the Butcher sliced Ozzy's neck like a pig being slaughtered. Ozzy bled out and fell to the ground, while trying to stop the bleeding from both his carotid arteries. His gun fell next to him into a pool of thick red blood.

"You. I will gut and dress you and leave you out for the turkey vultures and other vermin to feed on. That is if they will have you. Now for your friend," the Butcher said to the spasming, soon-to-be corpse.

Crevin had made his two passes and waited at the back entrance for Ozzy to return. After all, Ozzy had the only pass key to get into the cabin; Ozzy was late. Probably distracted by something again. Crevin knew that his coworker had some extreme ADHD at times, and it was a wonder anyone would want to hire him as an enforcer. However, Ozzy was a marksman and great with knives.

Crevin had enough waiting and went looking for Ozzy. Feeling the need to desperately go to the bathroom, he took a break from looking for Ozzy. He dropped his pants and squatted behind a tree in the wooded area. He could see the cabin from there and anyone that might approach it. There were no leaves on the ground, so that meant waiting to clean up at the cabin. He knew the Reuben he had eaten might cause problems, and it was proving him right.

He kept his .38 next to him, so he could quickly grab it. He had taken out many hostiles in Afghanistan while in this compromised position. Silently and as quiet as the flutter of a butterfly's wing, the

Butcher stood behind the squatting target. The Butcher lifted his large cleaver into the air and brought it down hard to the base of Crevin's skull severing the brain stem from the spine.

The Butcher gloated behind their hazmat hood. "Two down. Many more to go. I got time, though." The Butcher grabbed Crevin and drug him to where they had killed Ozzy. In less than thirty minutes, the Butcher decapitated them, hung them upside down by their feet, and poured their internal organs onto the ground. The flies were already gathering, and the sounds of nocturnal creatures catching the smell of a fresh kill were heard.

The Butcher would wait a few minutes before entering into the cabin. They were anticipating others to show that they might also have to kill. They would kill Darcie and Ruth Ann first and use their body parts to make compost for the woods. The Butcher had little patience for these mothers to give birth and they had been thinking how a baby might taste. They thought unborn baby meat might be similar to veal — young and tender. Since working for the BMS, the Butcher felt that their tastes were evolving, and they intended to allow it to happen.

CHAPTER FORTY-ONE

Paisley sat in the middle of the canoe while Charlie and Stretchie paddled to the location where the previous users had stopped earlier. No lights were used to navigate the water, and no one spoke because there was uncertainty about whether the river and trees had eyes & ears. Paisley and Charlie relied on Stretchie's photographic memory and knowledge of the river to get them there. As a youth, Stretchie had paddled and camped on the shores of it many times.

Numbness in her legs and tingling in the seat of her pants were signs that Paisley was getting ready to have another episode. She also felt some stiffness in her right hand, and she was beginning to have some slight blurriness with her vision. She kept lying to herself that it would get better each day to avoid the treatments. She knew her symptoms placed them all at risk, but right now she had a daughter and several other young girls to help rescue and she needed to push herself.

After a lot of paddling, they finally made it to the location on the left side of the river. Directly in front of them was a trail leading into the woods. At the beginning of the wooded area, a sign read "Forestry

Department Only." Shortly after starting the path, they found an ATV hidden under some pine branches.

"If this is a national or state park trail, then I am the president of the United States," Stretchie proclaimed.

"You smell that," Charlie asked.

"Smells bad — whatever it is," Paisley added.

About a quarter-mile into the forest, they came across Ozzy and Crevin. An opossum was inside Crevin's corpse, looking out at them. It took everything to keep them all from hurling their last meal.

"What do you think —" Charlie attempted to finish his question but was interrupted.

"The Butcher of Kentucky is what I know happened," Paisley informed them.

"For real. It's a ... He's a sick fuck," Stretchie added.

"I just hope he's not done anything to Kansas and the others," Paisley said, hoping for the best situation scenario.

The trio continued up the trail until they came to the cabin. They took position on the edge of the woods behind the cabin. It was difficult to tell what was going on inside the cabin due to the shades being closed on numerous windows and some windows being boarded up. Paisley kept thinking about her last encounter with the Butcher. She'd be ready for him this time, and she'd have backup.

Charlie noted the cabin doors required a security card to open them. Even the entry doors that appeared to be rustic wood were deceptive because the wood was just an overlay hiding a reinforced steel door. They decided to check for any unlocked windows, but all the windows were secured.

Although the doors might have been thick, the windows allowed sound to travel. Stretchie heard a girl yelling out who was in labor and motioned the others to listen as well. This was the distraction they needed to sneak in.

Charlie knew about disarming and opening security systems, having worked the burglary division at one time. Like a modern-day MacGyver, Charlie used his cell phone to act as a key card by sending a signal from his phone. The app allowing him to do this came from Burglar Bob, who now worked with the Chicago PD on cases involving high-end robberies in million-dollar homes, businesses, and hotels. Charlie had helped cut the deal so Bob could avoid jail time. Bob was more than willing to turn his life around, share technology, and his expertise so he could watch his twin sons grow up.

They entered the dimly lit cabin with Stetchie bringing up the rear. Paisley went off to the left and Charlie to the right. Stretchie went straight toward the great room where a fire was burning. The smell of sauerkraut and corned beef permeated the air, along with smoke and wood. Paisley found seven doors going down the hallway. She suspected these were the rooms were the pregnant teens were being kept. She tried several doors, and all were locked. It appeared all of them required a keycard just like the main doors.

Using his app again, Charlie was able to get one of the doors to open. Shining her flashlight into the room, Paisley noticed two girls dressed in sweats and tee shirts who were chained to the floor with a limited amount of length to walk within the room. From the smell of it, someone had recently taken a crap. The two girls were not familiar to Charlie or Paisley, but they were obviously very pregnant and appeared frightened.

"It's okay. We're with the police. We're here to help you. How many more of you are there?" Paisley asked.

The shorter brunette responded, "Maybe five or six more of us."

"Do you know someone named Kansas or Brynlee?" Paisley anxiously asked.

"Yes. They have them here. Kansas just got out of isolation," said the tall blonde.

"What's that mean?" a worried Paisley inquired.

"It's a small little shack that stands alone by itself. No heating or cooling, dirt floor to sleep on, and you get a bucket for everything to do your business in. I was told she got in there for trying to make a call," the other girl who was a brunette informed them.

"Shit! Is she okay?" the worried parent asked.

"I don't know," the brunette responded.

"Got anything to get them out of the chains, Charlie," asked Paisley.

"My burglar guy was good at picking anything. I just happen to bring a pick kit," Charlie informed her while pulling a small leather case from his back pocket.

Charlie started working on the chains of the blonde. After five minutes, the brunette looked at him and offered to help him. "I'm a master lock pick. You seem to be struggling with the basics."

"I didn't say I was an expert locksmith," Charlie responded.

"Can you pick your lock and hers and then do the same for the others?" Paisley asked the brunette.

"Sure. Anything to get out of this hell hole," the brunette responded. "My name is Lexa, by the way, and this is Bonita."

"Nice to meet ya. Let's go open all the doors and let these gals do their thing. Have everyone meet us in the kitchen near the back door. We will let the other girls know you're coming," Paisley directed them.

Charlie continued to unlock the doors with his app while Lexa picked the locks on all the girl in chains. Paisley noticed that not all the girls were in chains. Some had shock collars. She was not sure which was crueler. With each new door opened, Paisley expected it would be the one with her daughter. When they finally got to the bedroom with Kansas and Brynlee, Kansas stood up from her bed and stared into the light. Kansas wondered whether it was the Butcher who had come to get her. When she heard her mother's voice and saw her mother move toward her, she tightly hugged her mother and lightly sobbed.

"I'm so sorry, mom. I wish. I wish."

"Don't be sorry. I'm here now. We can deal with whatever after we get everyone safely out of here. Right now, we need you and Brynlee out of these shackles, and we need all of you to go to the kitchen and wait on us. I need to know how many people run this place?"

"I only know of four here now. There was another one. This big creepy person threatened us. Wore some kind of environmental hazmat suit. I haven't seen him in a while," Brynlee informed them.

"He's back. I think that the Butcher took care of two of them for us already. That still leaves two," Paisley said to Charlie.

"Tristine went into labor a little bit ago. I heard her screaming in the hall as they took her to deliver," Kansas added.

"Okay, we will get her. Right now, follow the plan. I love you. We will get everyone out safe."

Paisley left the bedroom. She knew that hovering over her daughter would make her lose focus on what needed to be done. While the girls were being set free, Stretchie found his way to the office and looked through the filing cabinet at the charts on the girls. Some of the charts went back as far as ten years. Just the number of girls that had gone through just this little spot was overwhelming to him.

Paisley and Charlie found their way to the delivery room and listened outside the door. Tristine was laboring, trying to bring a child into this world. Pushing the door open just a crack, Paisley saw two women in surgical attire working with the girl to deliver the baby.

Paisley and Charlie felt it would be best to let the girl deliver rather than rush in. Moments later, a bouncing baby girl was born. The baby was cleaned, wrapped in a blanket, and placed in an incubator. Tristine was told to get used to being not pregnant. In a couple of days, Tristine's daughter would be on her way to a wealthy Canadian heiress who planned on spoiling her new daughter. Not so lucky for Tristine — she was earmarked for a wealthy arms dealer in South Africa who had a personal taste for underage young ladies.

"Don't move," shouted Paisley as she pushed open the door and surprised the two women.

Darcie grabbed a scalpel and ran like a raging bull toward Paisley. Paisley could feel her fingers cramping some, and it took every effort to fire one shot into Darcie's heart before she had to lower her arm. However, Ruth was armed, and she got behind the incubator, knowing that neither would fire toward an infant. Ruth fired two shots at them and told them she was leaving with the baby and they'd better back off.

"Those are warning shots. I won't hurt this little treasure chest, but I will kill mommy if you don't leave the room," Ruth Ann threatened.

Using her best negotiator skills, Paisley responded, "We can't let that happen. You need to give yourself up before this ends badly for you and this girl."

To prove she meant business, Ruth Ann took the baby out of the incubator and secured it in her left arm like some football. She then aimed her gun at Tristine. Soon her threat was lessened because Stretchie had managed to move behind Ruth and now had a gun to the back of her head.

"Go ahead. Take a shot. I'll drop you and catch the baby before you can squeeze the trigger, and the kiddo can hit the ground," Stretchie told her.

"You are a sneaky one. Now drop the piece and take the baby to his mother," Paisley commanded.

Ruth Ann did as she was told. However, Ruth Ann was not one to go silently. As soon as the baby was out of her hands, she reached under the operation table for her spare .22. Ruth Ann was shot by Charlie before she could aim it at anyone.

"Just can't trust anyone these days," Charlie commented.

"You okay, Tristine. We are not here to hurt you. Just trying to get you out of here safely," Paisley informed them.

"Thanks! I like holding this thing. I never thought I would," Tristine said, sobbing and clinging to her baby.

"They are rather special. Do you think we could get you in that wheelchair over there and have Stretchie wheel you to meet your friends?" Paisley asked.

"Sure," Tristine responded.

Once Tristine was squared away with the others, Paisley and Charlie wondered if the Butcher might show. The girls had told them that the Butcher had been fired, but Paisley, Charlie, and Stretchie had seen the Butcher's handiwork on the way up to the cabin. The Butcher was on a killing spree and was probably waiting to kill all the adults and then kill all the girls off for meat. Regardless, the cannibalistic serial killer was there, and she knew the Butcher would be coming for them all.

"The Butcher's a sociopath, and I think it'll kill and fillet us all if it gets a chance to," Paisley stated.

"Me too. What's the plan? I got nothing to lose," Charlie declared.

CHAPTER FORTY-TWO

Charlie and Paisley searched through the cabin, looking for signs of any other BMS operatives. Although the girls might have said there were only four perps, she and Charlie wanted to make sure. The best thing of all — there were no signs of the Butcher. They also did a sweep of the grounds and checked the edge of the woods. There was no indication that someone was out there, but they knew the Butcher was out there somewhere watching them. If they were not careful, they would end up being a buffet for the scavengers.

Indeed, the Butcher was watching them and knew all about the cabin's features, including a crawl space under the left side of the cabin facing toward the river. As soon as the Butcher saw Paisley and Charlie leave the cabin, the Butcher crawled under the cabin and found their way back into the structure through a small trap door that opened inside a large closet in Darcie's bedroom.

The Butcher remained extraordinarily quiet and made their way toward the kitchen. In addition to a knife, they carried a sawed-off shotgun. After all, they were hunting more than just helpless little girls this time. Two girls screamed out, and as Stretchie turned around, he faced the end of the Butcher's shotgun. Caught by surprise, Stretchie thought he was a dead man. Instead of having his head blown off, he got the butt end of the shotgun. Stretchie fell to the ground, now an unconscious victim with no control over his fate.

"Sssssshhhhh, girls! We mustn't make noise and alert the others. Now be good little girls and walk to the first bedroom on the right." The Butcher then kicked Stretchie in the ribs and seemed satisfied of no movement. "If I had the time now, I would add you to the critter feast with the other jerks. I will just have to come back and finish you later."

Fearful for their lives and fearing what the Butcher probably did to the other girls, the pregnant teens followed orders and crammed themselves into one room. The Butcher locked the door and looked forward to the slaughter when they returned.

"Don't make a noise regardless of what you hear, or when I come back, you will be supper sooner than I want. you to be."

This comment creeped the girls out. Like sheep trying to deal with a wolf attack, the teenagers clustered around each other for herd protection. Nothing was said amongst the girls, and it was clear they all feared for their lives. Kansas just hoped that her mother would be back to take this piece of shit down before she ended up a shish kabob on a grill. Just in case, she grabbed one of the chains on the floor to use against the Butcher, so maybe some of them could escape.

Thirty minutes of skirting the woods again revealed no one was out there, at least close to the cabin. Charlie and Paisley decided to join the others waiting on them in the kitchen. However, when they arrived back at the cabin, no one was in the kitchen. They called out for Stretchie and Kansas, but there was no answer. They searched the house and found all of the bedroom doors had been relocked. Charlie started with the first door on his right. He opened it, and no one was in it. Paisley watched his back just in case the Butcher came up behind them.

When Charlie opened the second door, someone grabbed his arm and tossed him against the wall, knocking the breath out of him. Before Paisley knew what was going on, a powerful figure grabbed her hand and smashed it into the door frame, causing the gun to fly out of her hand. The Butcher then picked her off the ground by her neck, strangling her as they lifted her up. Paisley kicked the perpetrator in the groin, but the Butcher must have been wearing some type of protection cup because it didn't cause them to flinch.

Catching his breath, Charlie used the bed frame to pull himself up. He searched for his gun, but he could not find it. He kicked the Butcher in the back of the knee. It still did not cause him to let go of Paisley. Paisley continued to try to loosen his grip on her neck. Her hands were starting to tingle, and she was beginning to feel pain as she coughed and tried to continue to breathe.

Charlie grabbed one of the several oxygen tanks in the corner of the hallway and hit the Butcher in the back of the head. The Butcher fell to the ground where he lay while Charlie assisted Paisley.

"You okay," a concerned Charlie asked.

Paisley nodded her head, trying to breathe again. "The kids. Get kids."

He understood what she wanted.

"Girls. It's FBI Agent Yocum. We got the bastard. Yell, so I know if you are still in the cabin."

The girls screamed out their location. Charlie released them from the room. He found Stretchie in the same room, lying on the floor still knocked out.

"Do you think you girls can drag or carry Detective Knight outside the cabin? We will meet you at the edge of the woods facing the river. We are going to call this in and have the state police send a boat for pickup."

Four girls each grabbed an arm and a leg, with a fifth girl holding Stretchie's head. They carried him outside the cabin. Paisley was now standing, surveying the situation, and rubbing her neck. She knew this would leave a nasty bruise.

"Who do you think it is?" Charlie asked.

"Only one way to find out," Paisley said.

As soon as Paisley attempted to pull the hood of the hazmat suit off, she felt an arm go up, and a knife plunged into her left leg. The Butcher was alert and seemed determined to take both of them out. Neither she nor Charlie had their guns. Because it had worked before, Charlie grabbed the oxygen tank again. It was their only defense.

The Butcher moved toward them with a 12-inch bladed knife Both continued to try to maneuver themselves to a more open area to avoid being stabbed or slashed. Still, the Butcher kept pushing them back toward the wall. Finally, Charlie made a decision — a decision that he knew Paisley would not like.

Charlie rushed the Butcher with the oxygen tank. The Butcher dropped the knife and reached for their shotgun. Paisley immediately thought he was being stupid. After all, Charlie was attacking an opponent who outweighed him, was taller than him, and who had a weapon. The

Butcher pushed back, but Charlie was like an angry pit bull who was not about to let go.

"Paisley, get out of here. I've got this. It's time I paid the price for what I did and all the hurt that I've caused."

Paisley yelled back, "You are not going to get off that easy, Charlie Buchanan Yocum."

Then she saw his plan. Charlie opened the oxygen tank up to the full blast. In his left hand was a lighter. She saw his expression begging her to run. She hesitated for a moment and began her quick sprint from the cabin. As she closed the cabin door, she yelled back with tears rolling down her face, "You are forgiven. You are forgiven."

Paisley was barely out of the cabin when an explosion from the bedroom area rocked the ground. A few minutes later, two other explosions occurred. The cabin continued to burn, and it was almost burned to the ground before the state police showed up. The girls, Paisley, and Stretchie, watched safely from the bank. Paisley wrapped her arm around Kansas. Both sobbed at the loss of their family friend. Stretchie shed a tear as he was someone that he had bonded with and who seemed to care for Paisley and Kansas. Some of the girls seemed joyful that the cabin was gone along with the Butcher. However, many of the teens were now scared more than they had ever been because they would be placed back into a system that often ignored them and tried to return them to homes where the abuse never ended.

After the fire was extinguished, two bodies lay in the middle of a burnt pile of unrecognizable cinders. It would take a while to figure out who the Butcher really was. Paisley recognized Charlie's necklace of St. Christopher around one of the victims' necks. Charlie was definitely dead. Darcie and Ruth Ann's charred remains made it difficult to ascertain who was Darcy and who was Ruth Ann as well.

A BMS satellite operation had been shut down, and the Butcher had been stopped. It was a bittersweet night. Kansas quietly sat by her mother, watching the other girls get processed. She was not sure what would happen to them. Perhaps someone would adopt the teen mothers, maybe they would go back home to family, or they might even run off again. She couldn't worry about them right now. She and her mother had things to settle, and those things would have to wait. Right now, each celebrated the other, surviving the night's ordeal.

Stretchie had sustained a concussion, according to the paramedic, and was admitted to the hospital overnight. Paisley told him to rest, and she would see him soon. Brynlee was the last girl to board the boat. Brynlee looked at Kansas and gave her a new look. The jealousy was no longer there. It was a look of mutual trauma and experience. One that would not make them friends, but shared trauma that would allow bonding.

CHAPTER FORTY-THREE

Results come back, revealing that the Butcher's body was a younger man than believed — between the ages 17 to 24. Additional DNA tests and dental records would be examined, but it would take a week or more for anything to come back. The Butcher was dead, and the BMS had suffered a hit to their profits with their Eastern Kentucky operation being disrupted. Although it was a small win against the BMS, it still took income away from the huge criminal organization and gave some pregnant teenage girls another chance at life. Then there was also the fallout and reality of the situation — a once trusted friend and "uncle" to Kansas who had hidden the truth about Paisley's husband's death was dead.

Charles Yocum would be buried in Chicago. His only living sibling, Diane, took charge of the funeral arrangements. Due to the state of his body, Charlie was cremated. Charlie's mother and father were dead, and only a few relatives could attend. Members of the FBI and Chicago Police Department attended the service. Paisley kept his secret and never told anyone. She let him be a hero because in the end, he was. He was trying to redeem himself.

Many toasts were said at the memorial celebration at O'Hara's Irish Bar and Grill. Charlie's urn and his photo with his lab Oscar were placed high on the special place for those to be celebrated. A round of drinks was on the bar owner, Daniel O'Hara, a friend of Charlie's.

Stretchie had driven Paisley to the celebration. He noticed she was in another world at the reception because she kept quiet.

"A lot to take in, huh?" he asked.

"Yeah," she replied, exhaling.

"I lost a partner my second year. I miss Max. I understand."

"It's more than that. It's just everything. It's the BMS and their control and deep pockets. You know they are not going to let this go. It's Kansas and being pregnant. It's not knowing who this Butcher was. It's dealing with life. It's just fucking everything."

"You're only human, Pastey. Listen. I am here for you. You can let me in. I can be more than just a partner on cases. I can be a confidant who you can rely on and trust."

"Can't always trust those you know …."

"What does that —"

"Never mind. I'm sorry. I've got to go back and talk to my daughter about this pregnancy and what we are going to do."

"Not that easy. Does she know what she wants?"

"Not really. She … She and I are going to see the doctor tomorrow. I think we'll decide afterward. She and I have been connecting again, and it's just slow."

"What can I do?"

"Exactly what you are doing right now."

"Can do," he said as he grabbed her hand and held it.

The drive back to Kentucky was quiet, with the exception of some classic rock playing on the radio. Every now and then, they would sing aloud in a terrible pitch some of the lyrics, which they did not always correctly say.

They stopped in Louisville for gas, a potty break, and coffee. A silver Dodge Ram pulled behind them, driven by a large giant-sized man with an eye patch on his left eye. He was accompanied by a woman in her thirties and a man in his late forties. None of them looked like they had any friends in the world. The woman had a scar on her chin, and the short buzz cut suggested a military background. The male passenger was tall and lanky and looked like a Q-tip. All of them were armed and waiting on two important people.

Paisley's trip to the bathroom revealed more issues with her MS manifesting. Her saddle area was fully numb, and she had a slight mishap and had peed some on herself. It was a good thing she had learned to wear some extra protection because she did not want to do a complete change. While cleaning herself up, she noticed a pair of black military boots go into the stall next to her. Paisley thought she had locked the main bathroom door since it was an option. She watched for a few seconds as the boots stayed there facing the stall door, but no pants ever dropped. Now, her cop instincts kicked in.

She turned her phone on silent mode and texted Stretchie to warn him. Then she grabbed and slid her pants up, trying not to make any sudden moves to suggest she knew something was up. She grabbed the pocketknife from her pants and opened it, and put it under her shirt's cuff, making it ready for access when needed. She flushed and washed her hands. She noticed there were no mirrors right off, so trying to see someone coming from behind would be difficult. Paisley would have to be ready for anything. She would try to quietly take her perpetrator out so the perp would not alert any of her accomplices.

She still saw the boots in the stall. Something seemed off. Why would someone that might be trying to kill her wait so long? They were also compromised being in that stall because Paisley knew she could watch them.

Without any notice, a ceiling tile came down, hitting Paisley on the top of her head, and the assailant pounced down onto Paisley. Paisley fell to the ground face down. Someone straddled her, using their knees to keep Paisley from moving. Paisley was sure she may have broken her nose and maybe chipped a tooth. Not soon after, she felt a piece of cord wrap around her throat while someone increased the tension on the cord, making it tighter around her neck.

Paisley would be unconscious and dead soon if she didn't act quickly. She took her right hand and felt the rope. Using the knife, she cut the cord furthest from her neck. Although the rope was cut, the assailant did not move. Her assailant pushed their knees into Paisley's ribs until it felt like they were going to crack. Paisley just preyed she didn't have an MS hug hit or she would be fucked. Paisley then tried to push herself up from the ground, but the assailant's knees and weight were not allowing it to happen. Paisley took her knife and stabbed the assailant in the legs several times, causing them to finally roll off her.

The assailant appeared annoyed but smiled at the pain that had increased her adrenaline. She touched the blood coming from her pants and put it to her lips and licked it from her fingers.

"Good. I like prey that puts up a fight," the assailant announced.

The assailant retrieved a knife strapped to her leg and attempted to stab Paisley. Paisley quickly rolled out of the way. The knife hit the cold tile, chipping up some of the grout. Paisley took her pocketknife and held it up.

"Is that all you got? It's a knife fight but bringing a pocketknife to this fight is literally like bringing a knife to a gunfight. I'm going to gut you like a fish."

"Don't flatter yourself, bitch. I've killed meaner and better looking with less."

The assailant punched Paisley in the face and then sliced away at her sleeve. She must have nicked the skin because blood began to soak the material.

"Like a cat, I play with my mouse before I kill it," the assailant taunted.

"Obviously, I'm not an ordinary mouse. I may surprise you."

Feeling weak from her first go around with the miscreant and her MS flareup, Paisley relied on her wits to handle her assailant. Grabbing a plunger in the bathroom corner, Paisley used it like a sword. She thwarted several knife thrusts with the toilet device. Feeling frustrated, her assailant decided to rush her, forcing Paisley into the wall. Pushed up against the wall with a knife to her throat, Paisley took the plunger and stuffed it over the assailant's nose and mouth and forcefully plunged. Evidently, there was enough moisture from whatever cleaners, piss, and shit were on the inside of it to cause the plunger to suction to the assailant's face. Maybe Paisley got lucky, or the assailant had a thing about germs because her assailant dropped her knife and attempted desperately to pull the plunger off her face.

Pulling the soap dispenser off the wall, Paisley struck the assailant in the side of the head and then administered a solid right kick to the assailant's left knee, causing the perp to fall onto the hard tile with the plunger still stuck to her face. Paisley removed the plunger from the unconscious assailant's face. It was apparent that whatever was inside the plunger had transferred a round brownish-green circle outlining her mouth and nose.

Paisley unlocked the door to the bathroom. She looked around for Stretchie, but she didn't see him in the store. She tried texting him, and he didn't answer. Peripherally, she saw him with a tall, skinny-looking man in the walk-in cooler. Stretchie looked like he was in trouble. She opened the cooler door near where the stranger was standing and pushed 30 six-packs of bottled beer on the Q-tip shaped assailant, knocking him down on the cooler floor. Stretchie took advantage of the situation. When the skinny man tried to get up on his knees, Stretchie gave him a right hook. The glass-jawed perpetrator was out like a light.

"I think we are targeted," Stretchie yelled to Paisley from inside the cooler.

"I got one in the bathroom. Let's drag both of them into the utility closet, handcuff them to the wall railing, and call this in."

"No, problem. I'll get the keys from the clerk," Stretchie said as he went to the counter of the convenience store and showed his badge.

"I'm betting someone is still waiting on us outside. I think it's the big gorilla in the truck is part of the A-Team. I saw it pull up about the time we pulled in," Paisley commented.

"That's a given. I had the clerk call it in. They'll call me if they need anything. Right now, we got to deal with their muscle outside. I've got a plan." Stretchie began whispering into Paisley's ear, and they both disappeared through the back delivery door."

Pike Muldune was a powerhouse. He was six feet tall by the time he was twelve years old. At thirty-one, he had grown into a six-foot and eight-inch-tall lad, weighing 298 lbs., who could bench press four-hundred pounds. Right now, he was pissed because Talbert and Mia were overdue. They should have snuffed the two targets by now. He never liked either of them and didn't care if they bit the dust. If they screwed up, he'd do like he always did — take care of himself and anyone that was supposed to die.

He would give them five more minutes, and then he would go to Plan B. Plan B would be to put a bomb in the targets' car and then blow it while following them. Pike had been a demolition expert for a construction and mining company and knew how to make things go kaboom. He liked to see a target's car get at least up to fifty before he detonated it.

Pike heard a loud noise, and before he could react, a large forklift slid its forks underneath his truck and lifted it off the ground. Stretchie then used the forklift to push the truck against a concrete retaining wall. Now Pike's passenger side was blocked. Stretchie, who was driving the forklift, pushed the forklift up against the driver's side of the truck. Now he was trapped with no way to escape with all the doors blocked. Unfortunately, Pike was too big to leave the truck through the windows.

Pike threatened them with a gun, but they moved quickly out of the way to avoid being shot. The police arrived moments later, and Pike surrendered. The three were taken into custody and booked for attempted murder. As Paisley and Stretchie spoke with State Police Trooper

Bloomberg, they both realized that the BMS had a hit out on them and that it probably extended to Kansas.

Paisley called Kansas, who answered on the third attempt. Kansas was busy working a long line of elementary school children whose teacher had decided to treat them to ice cream. Paisley asked her to immediately leave and go to Sheriff Stone's office and wait for her there. She explained to Kansas that the BMS most likely had a hit on her too because she and Stretchie had already been targeted. Kansas handed her ice cream duties over to another employee and did as she was told for a change without questions.

Paisley and Stretchie left for Fester and headed to the farm to check for any unwelcome visitors or issues.

"Next steps, Stretchie?"

"We need to find a way to keep from getting killed or going into the witness protection program," he replied.

"Do we have a bargaining chip?"

"Not yet, but we will see."

Stretchie's phone rang, and he put it on the car speaker.

"Hey, it's Joe at the lab. We got the DNA back. This Butcher ... their real name is —"

The cell phone lost its signal, and Paisley and Stretchie kept trying to call back, but there was no signal to call out. All either one could think was — who was the Butcher?

CHAPTER FORTY-FOUR

Kansas sat in the uncomfortable wooden chair next to Deputy Sheriff Jerry Shamble. Deputy Shamble was Sheriff Stone's second cousin who needed a job to pay child support. He wasn't the brightest bulb in the chandelier, but he could read and write well enough to fill out a speeding ticket.

"Now, what did you say you needed?" Deputy Shamble asked the out of breath teen who he was already annoyed with him before she tried to explain the situation.

"My mom is working with the state police, and she says some bad people that work for a big crime organization may be coming after me," Kansas frantically tried to explain.

"You pullin' my leg?"

"No, you ever hear of the Black Market Syndicate?"

"Who?"

"Never mind. Where's Sheriff Stone?"

"This is his day off. He's fishing over at Paintsville Lake. Likes those bass."

"Can you contact him?"

"Needn't bother him. Deputy Cannon will be back soon. We can handle this. Now, what's your name?"

"Kansas. Kansas Hunter."

"Birth date."

"Okay. Shouldn't you be making a plan to help me out here? Serve and protect."

"This form has to be filled out. We keep a record of everything we need to keep up with here. That's another reason my cous — Sheriff Stone hired me for. I keep things organized."

"If you aren't prepared to handle some killer coming through the door, I might as well stand out in traffic," she sarcastically responded.

"Now, see here. No reason for that kind of talk."

"You see here. I've been kidnapped and left in the woods by a bunch of dirtbags trying to take my baby and a serial killer looking to slice me up like a roll of bologna. So, when you are wondering why this is stressing me out ... Take into consideration what I have dealt with."

The deputy sat there, perplexed at what the adolescent had laid on him. Then he rose from his desk, grabbed her by the arm, and led her to the holding cell. Kansas was in shock and resisted some, but Deputy Oaf was too strong. He locked the door and looked at his captive.

"There. No one will get you here. I'm thinking that this is some type of practical joke. Come on. Mafia in Fester or any part of Kentucky is just highly unlikely."

Kansas felt uneasy and anxious now. She had a powerful flashback of being held captive in the little room of the cabin. A rush of petulance escaped her mouth when she spoke.

"You dumb son of a bitch. Really, putting someone who has been held captive into a cell to make them feel safe is one of the stupidest things you could do. It's like lighting a match to gasoline. Do you know what goes through your mind when you're held against your will? Will I live through this? Can I get food, and will I get to use the bathroom? What if no one comes for me? Are you that stupid? I can't believe you. You know what? They are going to come for me, and they will blow you into small pieces, and then they will just shoot me through the bars like a fish in a barrel. When my mom comes — if I am alive — she will give you the chewing of all chewings. After she's done, I'm sure her state police detective friend will chew on you some more. If I die and you live, you might as well make sure your funeral plan is up to date."

"Are you threatening me?" he asked while putting his hand on his holstered gun.

"No, Jerry. She's been under a lot of duress," said a familiar face.

"Gary. I ain't seen you in a coon's age. I didn't hear you sneak up on me," said the surprised deputy.

"Still got it. I can be one sneaky son of a bitch."

"What do you need?"

"I got a call from this gal's mother asking me to take her to my house. She thought I'd be more sympathetic to her needs."

The deputy smiled at having some respite from the annoying teen. Unlocking the holding cell door, the deputy replied back to Gary in a low voice, " Kind of glad. She stresses me out, and I got high blood pressure."

"Glad to take her off your hands."

"How about my phone?" Kansas asked.

"Oh, sorry about —" the deputy started to hand Kansas her phone but was interrupted by Gary.

"Keep the phone for now. Your mom thought the BMS could

hack or track your phone, so she recommended leaving it here to throw them off your location. She said she'll pick it once they feel it is safe. Said she might even get you a new one under a different name."

With some reluctance to leave her prized communication device away and the incentive of a new phone, she climbed into Gary's 1987 F-150, and they headed back to the farm.

"Where's Ephrem? I haven't seen him in a while. Can't call him. I hated that he had to go back to Ohio to visit his Amish cousins. I guess that I could send him a letter like you old people do," Kansas said trying to find a way to talk to her baby's daddy.

"Don't underestimate the power of a letter. Can't believe that there are no cell towers closer than town to get a signal. He went to the grocery store yesterday and called me from there. He said to tell you he misses you, and he's thinking of you and the baby."

"Why did he have to go so soon? He was gone before I got checked out at the hospital. I so wanted to see him. I have so much to talk to him about."

"Time to be honest. About those Amish cousins — they ain't none. You might as well know the truth. Ephrem is up in a psychiatric hospital in Indiana. Didn't have any places open here. He got all upset when you were taken and when they wouldn't let us help rescue you — he became suicidal. I had to get him committed because he was over 16. Kept threatening to kill himself. Said he was going down to the middle of the square and splatter his brains."

"Mom never said a thing, and it's been weeks. Why lie?"

"We didn't want you to worry more about anything until Ephrem had his head screwed back on more."

"Can't I visit or call him?"

"They aren't recommending it. I am the only one they are allowing at this time."

"I hate this. I really, really hate this," Kansas cried out, and she began to softly sob. Gary placed his hand on hers to provide comfort and then patted it. She smiled and just looked out the window at the clouds, trying to make sense of her life and the mess she was in now.

The storms had rolled in fast, and it was pouring down the rain. Gary asked if Kansas would help him feed the cows and put a few things up before getting into the house. She offered, and she felt it would be good to take her mind off everything going on. The newly installed LED barn lights usually lit the entire place up, but they had to resort to battery lanterns when a lightning strike hit a transformer causing an outage on the farm. Kansas looked outside toward her house. The house was still dark; it looked like no one was home. She wondered how much longer before her mother and Stretchie got there.

Stretchie. She thought that her mother was having a relationship with him. What if she was? Was it really any of her business? She questioned whether she'd ever call him stepdad if her mother married him. Then she started thinking about raising a baby at her age. All the things that she'd miss. What about Ephrem? Was he really that mentally ill, and would that be something that would pass onto the baby? Would he make a stable and reliable father?

The rain downpour was so hard outside that they were forced to wait in the barn for the storm to let up. Gary grabbed a couple of waters for both of them from the barn frig, and they sat and drank them, watching the storm. Kansas felt tired. Maybe she was just tired from being pregnant, or perhaps just all the stress she had dealt with. With the sound of the rain hitting the barn's tin roof, she found herself being lulled to sleep. She stretched out over two bales of hay and was out within a few minutes. Gary was there. Gary would protect her. After all, he was her mother's good friend and the great-grandfather of her child.

CHAPTER FORTY-FIVE

Sheriff Stone felt like his ass was being continuously chewed out and handed back to him. He couldn't get a word out of his mouth to save his life. Paisley tore into him like a hungry wolf ripping a lamb apart.

"Why in the hell did you let my daughter leave here?"

"Gary said you sent him here to get her," Deputy Shamble sputtered out.

"I would know if I told my daughter about any change of plans. So, where did they say they were going?" she asked while pointing her finger at the deputy's nose.

"I — I — I don't recall," said the ineffectual deputy.

"Just hold it a minute. You can't come into my office and start raising hell with my deputy," Sheriff Stone said, trying to protect the integrity of his office.

"Some deputy. I should charge you both with endangering a minor, releasing her to a wrongful custodian, interfering with an investigation — most importantly — being dumbasses," Stretchie added.

"I don't think some of those are legitimate charges," Sheriff Stone shot back.

"I'm a state police detective. Don't think I won't make it easy for you, especially if something happens to her daughter," Stretchie said, making threats to the two-county law officers.

"Do your job, Sheriff, and put out a BOLO on my daughter. Stretchie, let's check my house and Gary's," Paisley said as she walked out the door.

A few seconds later, Paisley opened the door again, grabbed her daughter's phone off the inept deputy's desk, and walked out, slamming it again. Sheriff Stone raised an eyebrow and ordered his deputy to put the bulletin out. Pouring himself a cup of coffee, Sheriff Stone turned to Deputy Shambles and said, "Blood ain't thicker than water. When you're done with doing that BOLO, you're fired. I should have never listened to Mama when I hired you."

Stretchie and Paisley drove like they were taking laps at the Indianapolis 500. Nothing much was said, and the news they had gotten from the medical examiner was not good. It added another layer of trouble, and they just hoped the BMS was not waiting on them when they arrived.

When they pulled up to Paisley's farm, they noticed the security light was out, and her and Gary's houses were both dark. They went inside her house first, anticipating an ambush or worse. The dogs' water bowls were full, but the dogs were nowhere to be found. Paisley wondered if they had been let out to roam the farm, but her gut said something had happened to them. Paisley and Stretchie went to each room and checked for any intruders. They just hoped they didn't get blown up. After the house was cleared, they checked the property and the barn. All things seemed in order, including the barn critters. They found Popeye, Olive Oil, and Duke in one of the barn stalls. Food and water had been put out for them and they seemed content.

They weren't sure what they would find at Gary's. Paisley was feeling her hand numbing up, and she was having some problems thinking through the situation. Her MS was expressing its ugly self again, and this time it was definitely the wrong damn time.

Paisley knocked on Gary's door. There was no answer. The door was unlocked, and Paisley and Stretchie entered with caution. After checking each room, they found no one at home. They tried to search the basement, but the door was locked. Paisley felt for the key on the trim above the door. It was where most people kept locked doors in the country. She unlocked the door, and they went into the basement. A washer, a dryer, several canned goods, a freezer, a sump pump, a water heater, and a furnace were all that were found. They were expecting to find body parts, or worse, but when they looked into the freezer, they found nothing but actual meat and vegetables.

The barn was the only other structure left to search on the premises. Because the barn was so dark, they pulled Stretchie's car to the front of the barn and turned the spotlights on. All of Gary's animals seemed to have been recently fed and watered. It was pretty quiet except for a low, muffled noise coming from behind the hay bales on the top of the barn. Stretchie climbed up the ladder to investigate, and there was Kansas, gagged and tied up. Before he could get a word out, a shadow raised a shovel and whacked him hard in the head, causing Stretchie to fall off the twelve-foot drop and onto the straw-covered ground.

Paisley heard someone fall and began yelling, "Stretchie! Stretchie! Is that you? Are you okay?"

She began to walk toward the direction of the fall, shining her flashlight as she went. There was Stretchie all stretched out. She checked for a pulse to make sure he was breathing. He was breathing, but he wasn't conscious. She cocked her gun and shined her cell phone's flashlight around the barn.

"You'd better show yourself. I've taken on you BMS bastards once and kicked your asses, and I'll do it again," she shouted with her hand trembling.

A figure stepped directly out into her cellphone light. It was not who she expected. She thought that she'd be facing some goon that was sent to waste her and her family or maybe Gary, who might have been overzealous to help or who was really a BMS operative — but what she saw was a surprise.

"You're dead. You died in the fire and explosion with my old partner. You are not real. The examiner confirmed you are dead!"

The Butcher of Kentucky continued to stare at her through their hazmat suit. Paisley screamed at the serial-killing cannibal, "Show me who you are? Face me, you chicken shit!"

With little hesitation, the Butcher removed their hood.

"No, No, No. You. What kind of sick game are you playing?"

"Never a game, my darling neighbor. A man's got to do what a man's got to do to eat," Gary informed his next victim.

"We just found out the Butcher was Ephrem. How can —."

"Be two of us. It's a family tradition. Ephrem was learning the ropes and the cooking. He got a little too zealous in the end. Loved that boy. Sadly, his death ends the family line. But that little girl of yours …

In about six months, there will be another one to raise in the ways of my family. We've been human meat consumers since the late 1700s when meat was scarce one winter. It might have been for survival to eat those neighbors, but it was good eating according to my ancestors."

"You're a sick fuck. Where's my daughter?" she screamed as she raised her gun, trying to hold it steady.

"You're not going to be shooting me. Kansas is getting a bird's-eye view of everything. She's okay for now. You want me to tell you everything like those villains do in the movies? I know how you think — you think like a detective who has to know every detail. So, here you go since I like you enough to give you my time. Since you got here, I've kept tabs on you and this investigation. Pays to know how the other side thinks.

I've been working with the BMS for a little while as a freelancer, but I had my own thing before discovering them. Then, I had to hunt my prey and pray I didn't get caught. I worked hard to hide who I was from everyone. I started wearing this here outfit to conceal my identity in case someone saw me. Life was good for a while until you got too good at your job, and the BMS changed its business practices. When things were going my way, it made for a steady quality meat supply with a lower risk for me of getting apprehended. It was literally like going to a grocery store or a buffet."

"You're nothing more than a monster, Gary."

"That's your perspective. I'm just thinning the herd. Anyway, where was I? As you know, things went south. Got a little overzealous and planted that stuff on Carolyn. Thought for sure, she'd be enough distraction to keep you away from me and the operation. I saw that falling apart and when these idiots fired me — I knew it was time to leave here and start some new place else. Unfortunately, I had to tie up some loose ends — Darice and that bitch Ruth Ann. Let's not forget you and Stretchie.

Just so happens I recently worked a deal with the BMS to move to Indianapolis — contingent on me getting rid of you and Stretchie. See how the stars align when people make the same wish. You know, some of BMS top management had heard about me and were quite the fan of my disposal methods. Made me blush. Really hated losing Ephrem in this. I loved that boy, but not all is gone astray. Like I said, I'll have a new Ephrem … or Ephremma to raise."

"You play hell. You'll slaughter my daughter after she gives birth," she said while trying to steady her gun.

"MS acting up. I've been tracking your MS since you moved here. I bet your arm and hand strength has dropped significantly in the past couple of days. I know right now you're quite vulnerable and trying to squeeze that trigger would be like lifting a semi-truck for you. You're not physically capable of shooting me."

"I can still squeeze off one shot to take you out. To think that I trusted you," she indignantly responded.

"Never trust those closest to you. They just want to break your heart and eat it too. Oh, don't worry. You're too old for my taste. You and tall boy will be taken to your home and burned after receiving a tap through your skulls. The fire has some irony to it, given that's what took out Ephrem."

"That only accounts for us. Won't they be looking for Kansas too?"

"Actually, they already found a dead ringer for your daughter's size and body weight, including being pregnant to take Kansas' place. It'll look like you are all dead, and no one will be looking for her."

"You're sick. I can't believe I ate and had coffee with you every morning."

"I can't believe I did either. I rather hate neighbors."

"You won't get away with this."

"I already have," he said while putting his large filleting knife back into its sheath.

Gary was right. She could not pull back on the trigger. Her fingers had no sensation in either hand, and she was experiencing some visual issues. Gary came toward her, and she was able to move out of the way, but she dropped her gun in the process. Now she had nothing. He came again, and she dove out of the way, rolled into a stall, and pushed the door behind her. She was now cornered with no escape. Gary slowly opened the stall. His knew his prey was trapped with no place to go. It would be over soon.

Pulling out a .38, he pointed at her and said, "You're fucked as they say. But I'm not all that bad. I'll let you say goodbye to each other then we got to get you and police boy to the house to wrap up your last and most fatal case. Now come on."

Paisley got up. Not only were her hands and vision causing issues, but her legs were also feeling numb. They were all tingling, and if someone stabbed or shot her in her legs — she wasn't sure she could even feel it.

"Get him up. He's only slightly out. I saw him stir a minute ago."

"Stretchie. Get up. It's over with."

"What's over with?" Stretchie asked.

"The Butcher. There were two. Ephrem was in training. Gary is the real Butcher."

"I see. What's in it for him?" Stretchie asked.

"More human flesh, money to raise my grandchild, and a free ride from law enforcement," she piped up.

"What's in it for us?" Stretchie asked.

"Being killed to make it look like someone was hired by the BMS," she responded.

"Sucks to be us," Stretchie commented.

"Up, you two. Say goodbye to Kansas from here."

"Don't you think people are going to gossip or be suspicious of you disappearing after we died?" Paisley snapped.

"It's just gossip. Just like everyone thinks I got heart problems. Utter bullshit spread by me to make people think I'm weak. Besides, I've been telling folks for the longest that if the right deal came along for the dairy farm, I'd move away. Doesn't hurt there are new hunting grounds," the Butcher nonchalantly said.

"I can't hug my daughter. I want to hug her."

"No. She can hear you. Just think she'll be joining you in the afterlife in about six or so months, and you will have eternity to spend together. On the downside, I have to eat her meat within 12 months to avoid freezer burn."

"You really are one sick bastard. Kanas, I love you. I'm so sorry all this has happened. I'm so sorry. I will always love you. I promise I'll find you and save you," Paisley yelled out to her daughter while tearing up.

"Lies. Why tell her lies? Kansas, your mama and Stretch boy, will be dead before you and I leave for the promised land. See ... She has nothing to say."

"She would if you hadn't gagged her," Paisley replied.

"Let's go, you two. I've got to get moving. New owners take over tomorrow. They get the house and all the furniture and the barn with all the animals. Got a nice spread with a butcher room for me waiting on my new ten acres."

Gary prodded them along. He had them walk no more than six feet in front of him. He would shoot them dead before they got to Paisley's house if he needed to. Paisley needed a plan. It would have to be believable. Gary was no fool. She'd have to fool Stretchie as well so that he would follow along naturally without any signs of deception. Collapsing to the ground, Paisley made it appear her legs gave out.

"Get up," Gary ordered.

"I can't, dumbass. My legs. I've been having symptoms all day that something was going to happen."

"My tracking says that you had a few more days before this might happen."

"You're fucking tracking is flawed like you. I can't walk. You're gonna have to shoot and drag me there."

"Paisley. I can carry you," Stretchie offered.

"That'd work. Shooting here would leave a blood trail," Gary said, nodding.

Stretchie picked her up with some exertion.

"Now march," Gary ordered.

The walk was longer than Paisley remembered, or maybe it was just the fact they were walking to their death. It seemed now Gary was convinced that she was no threat to him. Paisley's plan hinged on having an opportunity to surprise Gary and overpower him somehow without getting shot. She patiently waited and watched for when that time would come, knowing that Stretchie and Kansas depended on her to get them out of this situation.

Stretchie sat Paisley down on the porch and opened the door to the house as instructed by Gary.

"Why are the dogs in the barn?" Paisley demanded to know.

"They are going with me. I know your daughter will need some companionship. Anyhow, I think innocent animals do not deserve to be killed. Humans, on the other hand — are expendable."

Stretchie placed Paisley on the couch. Gary motioned for him to sit in the chair across from the sofa.

"Let's see here. I gotta shoot ya. Then I'm going to use kerosene to get the party started. Any last requests?"

Stretchie firmly stated, "Let us go."

"Request denied," Gary quickly replied. "And you neighbor?"

"Go to hell!" Paisley informed him.

"My dear. Hell is not living, and I'm living."

Gary turned and faced Stretchie. He cocked the .38 and pointed it toward Stretchie but was interrupted by Paisley, who jumped onto his back. Stretchie grabbed for the .38 but was shot in the chest in the struggle to pull the gun from Gary's hand. Stretchie fell hard to the ground. Paisley was not sure he was dead, and she was losing her grip on Gary.

Paisley fell at Gary's feet, and Gary started to shoot her when she kicked him hard in his kidneys, causing Gary to double over. She ran as fast as her numb legs would allow her. If she could get to her barn, she could get her shotgun she kept loaded there. Gary didn't stay down long. He was on her ass and was closing in. Paisley worried about Stretchie and her daughter, but they would have to wait until she could contain the situation to help them. She made it to the barn and found her shotgun, but it was not loaded. She had forgotten to load it from the last time she used it. Gary swung open the barn door.

"Maybe I will eat you, Paisley. Perhaps all this energy and

stamina you've got makes old meat like yours tender. I can serve you to your daughter for the next five months and then look at the expression on her face after I tell her that I've been feeding you to her right before I kill her. What a joy!"

"Go ahead. Do what you like? You will not get away with it. I'll fight you before I let you kill my daughter or me."

"Always have that sense of humor with an unrealistic outlook. You're screwed, my dear. So, why don't you just let me take you down without a fight? It'll be much easier on you."

"Fuck you, Gary."

"Such witty banter. I shall not forget it."

Paisley grabbed the barrel of her shotgun and began waving it like a baseball bat. Gary smiled and looked into the eyes of his prey. Although it was dark, Paisley could see the bastard's cold, piercing eyes preparing for the kill. She knew the odds were against her. Saving her daughter was still her first task, and now that appeared to be an impossible task.

Gary grabbed the shotgun with his left hand as Paisley swung. With his other hand, he pulled the fillet knife from its sheath. He planned to slice her across the jugular and maybe use her head to make some souse. He had till the morning to be out — plenty of time to trim up some meat.

As the knife came toward Paisley, she left her eyes open to meet death, but then something stopped the blade from touching her. She looked at Gary and noticed four metal prongs protruding through his abdomen. The prongs disappeared and reappeared this time through his chest, piercing his heart. Gary collapsed to the ground. Gary lay on the ground with the pitchfork standing up in the air. He was dead as a doornail. Standing over Gary was his killer — Kansas.

CHAPTER FORTY-SIX

Cleaning up after a cannibalistic serial killer is never fun. It took the state and county police working with the FBI over a week to clear the scene. Just as Gary stated, home buyers showed up the next day. Needless to say, Oneida and Terrance Crumble were quite upset when they showed up only to find their new home surrounded by tons of law enforcement combing over the property. When the Crumbles learned their home belonged to a serial killer, they called the realtor, who was more than happy to get their money returned to avoid negative reviews.

Neither Paisley nor Stretchie helped with any of the physical investigation. Stretchie spent two weeks in the hospital recovering from his gunshot wound. Paisley required an infusion because her MS symptoms had become more progressive. For once, she didn't balk at having to spend four hours in a chair. Within a week, she felt a lot better. This also allowed her time to recover from her injuries and contusions.

For Kansas, things were more complicated. She found out that she was never pregnant. Her test had been a false positive all along. Her symptoms were considered psychological in nature, mimicking the symptoms of pregnancy. When Kansas found out that Ephrem was the Butcher, she freaked out. After calming down, Kansas was thankful that she was indeed not pregnant with a psycho's child, but at the same time, she still grieved the loss of the boyfriend that she thought she knew.

Kansas was a strong person — just like her mother. With her mother and Stretchie supporting her, along with her therapist Mildred Pierce, Kansas began working through her own personal trauma. Family therapy with her mother helped both of them deal with the loss of her father, which had been long overdue. They were also able to reach an agreement about Paisley continuing to consult on cases and trying to communicate better on all aspects.

Carolyn was released with extreme apologies from the Kentucky State Police and FBI. She seemed to understand, at least on the surface. Two months later, she filed a lawsuit against them for one million dollars for wrongful arrest and defamation of character. It was settled out of court for $350,000. Carolyn moved to Arkansas, where no one knew her name.

Brynlee decided to have Ephrem's baby. Brynlee planned to move to Ohio to live with her aunt and raise her son. Even though she knew about her sperm donor's killing nature, she was convinced her little Ephrem would be different because he would be raised by a loving and caring mother who would be there for him. However, her plans fell through when her baby was taken and placed for adoption within two days of being born. The reason — Brynlee's father would not allow a child with those genetics to be considered his grandchild. Sadly, Brynlee tried to kill herself because she had nothing left to live for in life. She was admitted to a psychiatric center for eight months and then placed in a Catholic girls school in Nebraska.

While recuperating, Stretchie was kept apprised of the progress of the investigation. Paisley continued to consult on Stretchie's request to help close the case. To encourage her new boyfriend to get better, Paisley brought him all the ice cream he could eat and let him know how she and Kansas were doing.

    The police tore Gary's house apart looking for any evidence to connect him to any missing teens. A secret panel had been discovered in Gary's basement leading to a butcher shop. The shop was clean, and there was no DNA evidence of any human remains. However, they were lucky to find a truck rental receipt from Frazier's Moving Company that led them to a truck that Gary had housed in a storage shed. Inside the back of the truck was a freezer, and it was being kept cold by a propane generator. Inside the freezer were various packages of meat — all human. It would take months to figure out if any of the body parts in the freezer belonged to any of the missing girls. They had the evidence, but their perpetrators were dead. The Butchers were gone.

CHAPTER FORTY-SEVEN

BMS President Audrey Blunt looked over the financial reports. The adoption and sex trafficking in Kentucky were hit hard. Over thirty million in projected revenue in the next month, not including the exposure to their organization and growth in those two areas, were lost for now. Audrey was not a woman to cry over spilled milk, but she was one to clean it up and pour a fresh cup of milk.

She had sent an ensemble of contractor killers to take out Paisley and Stretchie, but it had only caused more problems. There was talk about the BMS President's decision-making capability and gossip of a coup among her associates. Getting thrown out as president took a majority vote but not everyone played by the charter rules. A third-party contractor from a nonparticipating country could be used to take her out. She knew this and had increased the security around her home. The only thing making her safer than her predecessors was technology. Not having a meeting in person changed the game. Remote meetings using the Safe Meeting Video Conferencing application, developed by a top-notch programmer known to be hackproof across the globe, ensured no leaks online, or pinging her physical location. Moreover, she also had the power to play God with stocks, companies, and the lives of all those working for the BMS if they tried fucking with her.

There was more than one way to hurt or get rid of someone. An ice cream company seemed like a good investment. Who doesn't like ice cream? Audrey had always wanted to own one. Perhaps destroying Paisley's ice cream business would make life a little sweeter. She knew a distributor that the BMS owned that could maybe run Paisley out of business. She might even bribe the local health department to close Paisley's shop. There would be no profit in being vengeful but getting rid of that pain-in-the-ass retired CPD detective would make her happier. She could also arrange for a certain state police detective to be killed on duty. Payback would come, but it would be unexpected, painful, and slow.

Audrey's thoughts were interrupted by a phone call from her investment/marketing specialist. A new business was now officially online in Kentucky with the possibility of earning more money than the black marketing of babies and teens. In the past, counterfeiting had been an easy scheme, but eventually, the Treasury Department caught on, but this time the BMS had real mint plates and the right paper— thanks to an inside person. Even distribution of the counterfeit bills was carefully planned and included countries outside of the United States. Profit — it was the most important thing after all.

CHAPTER FORTY-EIGHT

The door read "Private Investigator/Police Consultant Paisley Hunter" in huge gold letters large enough to be read from across the road that faced opposite of the sheriff's office. On the large glass office door of the 1932 building, Paisley's motto "What cops can't or won't do, I will" informed prospective clients of her commitment. She was proud of her new office and ready to open shop.

Her decision to open a detective/consulting agency did not happen without significant debate. She had spent several months in family therapy with Kansas before an agreement was reached on how to conduct business that ensured Paisley's medical condition was kept as the number one priority. After that was settled, Paisley let Kansas decorate and supply her office. Paisley even gave Kansas a small side office to manage the ice cream shop and do her homework. Kansas saw it as an opportunity to learn the other family business. She didn't want to admit it, but maybe being a cop was in her blood too.

The unexpected thing that made things possible came in the mail from Charlie. It came a week after his funeral from his attorney. Charlie wrote a long letter explaining why he did what he did and apologizing. The funny thing about his letter was that it was dated two years before he died. Evidently, he had wanted to tell her for some time but had not been able to tell her. Accompanying the letter was a lottery ticket from Kentucky that Charlie had bought his first time to visit Paisley's farm worth two million dollars. Paisley was flabbergasted and overwhelmed. Although the money helped pursue her interests, it could not replace Charlie. She had forgiven him for his involvement with the BMS and covering up her husband's death, but she would not forget what had happened. It had made her feel more suspicious and untrustful of others, especially after finding out about Gary and Ephrem as well.

From across the street, Sheriff Stone watched with envy and annoyance as the little business came to life. He initially never knew that Paisley was going to be the one staring at him from across the road until the final letters dried on the glass window. He was not happy about someone who might take away any glory from cases that would get him recognized and reelected. He didn't want to jeopardize his big plans in politics. After all, he might be mayor of Fester and then governor of the state of Kentucky one day. Truth be told, most people were unaware of his ambitions. Some would have laughed if they knew about them. Sheriff Stone knew that he was not the most respected person in town, but he did want to help people. Sometimes, his pride and being jealous got in the way — eighty percent of the time.

Paisley had no set office hours and met with clients by appointment. She had set up shop, and in less than a month, she already had a missing dog case, a misplaced Last Will and Testament, and three cases to consult with the state police on — thanks to Stretchie. The license for being a private detective was quite simple to obtain. Her extensive experience in law enforcement made it reasonably easy. Stretchie just asked that she not kill anyone or have any shootouts with the sheriff across the road.

Life was looking up for Paisley and Kansas. Stretchie and Paisley had reconnected, and Kansas was healing. The Boys In Blue Glazed Donut and Coffee Ice Cream ice cream was a hit. Paisley had been offered to market her product nationwide, but she chose a regional rollout. Ten percent of all Boys In Blue Glazed Donut and Coffee Ice Cream went to the Law Enforcement Family Fund that helped down and out families who lost spouses and parents in the line of duty. To show those she served with that she hadn't forgotten them, she sent a whole case on dry ice to her old Chicago Police Department, who were asking for more ice cream by the end of the week.

Paisley was adjusting to life without her neighbor. She had let her guard down. Sometimes she looked in the mirror and asked herself how she could have been so dumb. Over time, she realized that you don't know people until you really know them. She had only looked at common interests to connect with Gary, such as crime solving and farming. She remembered he did all the probing and seemed to monitor her medical condition. He indeed was a good investigator, but his intentions were not good.

Looking across the field at Gary's old farmhouse, she wondered what possessed a man to take others' lives and then to proceed to carve them up like a Thanksgiving turkey. He was a cannibalistic psychopath, and she and her daughter were almost one of his statistics. She knew about serial killers and had spent time in Chicago chasing a few. She had moved to the quiet country life to get away from these things but had only managed to find danger here. She still had many things that bothered her about the case that kept her up some nights.

She would probably never know who killed her husband, but now she knew the BMS was responsible for his death and stalling her husband's murder investigation. Now, she was pulling Stretchie into her life. What did she really know about him? Did he have secrets, and what were they? What of the BMS? They tried taking her and Stretchie out, and they had come close. Would they ever give up? How would she protect her daughter and those she loved from something so powerful?

Deep down, she knew that she would answer for the damage she caused to that organization, and she would have to be ready for payback when the time came. For now, she would help those in need and try to be the best mother she could be. She prayed her MS symptoms would continue to take a hiatus and allow her to live life and explore love again.

Case closed — for now.

COMING SOON!

The next book in this series continues with a new case for Paisley Hunter that tests her skills and pushes her limits as she takes on a serial killer who strangles and crucifies his victims and the BMS's counterfeiting ring while dealing with an unexpected relative she never knew existed. Watch for updates and release information for *The Paisley Hunter Detective Files: Skeletons In The Closet* at https://www.alanhounshell.com. The first chapter has been provided within this book for patrons to preview.

Paisley Hunter Detective Files: Skeletons in the Closet
CHAPTER ONE

A stranger watched from the distance as Shelby undressed in her bedroom. Shelby always kept her curtains open that were facing the woods. Who would be out in the middle of Bum Fuck Egypt watching her anyhow? Her well-developed bosoms and her soft skin on her delicate frame made him want to be inside her. She wanted him — she just didn't know it yet. She was just like her — the woman who had scorned and abandoned him. The one who ignored him. Shelby would love him and beg for his love when it came down to it.

He approached closer and peeked into the window. She was now in the bathroom and stretched out in her garden tub full of bubble bath. The bubbles covered her nipples and crotch, but he knew what they looked like. He had looked at her nude already using the camera that he had installed the last time he was in her house. She would be his soon enough.

Right now, he needed to get back to Leesa before she felt too alone. It was quite a drive back to see her. So many women; so little time to absolve them of their sins and save their souls. He so hoped that one of them would be worthy enough for him to love.

When he arrived back at the little shack he had built in the woods, Leesa was still tied up and gagged. How pretty her blonde hair and blue eyes were. She was almost perfect, but not quite as perfect as she had been. He gave her another injection causing her to pass out. He untied her and gently carried her to his bed. He stroked her hair and touched the areas of her body that he had read were considered erogenous zones. Leesa did not respond. Maybe he had sedated her too heavily?

Trying to stimulate himself, he rubbed his condom-covered penis against her, but after several minutes of not getting an erection, he knew she was not the one. None of them seemed to be. This was the fourth girl since she had left him.

He took out the synthetic fiber-based braided fishing line that he had cut from his newest spool and wrapped it around her throat. He could feel her pulse traveling up the line. It gave him the erection that she could not. He was hard now. He just needed to wait before he tightened the line more before he got off.

His victim stirred, indicating that he did dose her just right. Now alert enough to know she was in trouble — Leesa began to struggle to free herself from his stronghold. The fishing line dug into her neck's flesh, causing her to bleed. The warm blood oozed over her perfectly firm breasts. She needed to be fully awake to experience her death.

Leesa was no match. None of his victims had been. They were all smaller and weaker than him, and that's the way he liked it. As she let out her last breath, he ejaculated into the condom that he wore to collect any evidence of his DNA. Her killer thought if Leesa had only been able to arouse him earlier, she might have been spared.

He gathered all evidence of his existence and made sure he marked his prey. He pulled out a scalpel from a small pocket case, removed her eyes, and placed them in a small glass jar with clear fluid. Her eyes were so beautiful. Although being similar in appearance to his greatest love, her eyes were what drew him to her in the first place.

He was lucky his job allowed him to travel and meet new people. It supported his drive to find the perfect woman — his next soul to save would be Petina. Due to so many women disappointing him, he always made backups. Besides, God's will asked that he seek out those needing salvation.

As killers go — he was anonymous, and yet he wasn't. Police had mentioned little to nothing about his efforts to cleanse the earth of sinners. He made those women sinless. Leesa was just a faceless person to the world before he found her. He had just made her feel special and unique when he cleansed her. Before he left his saved souls, he needed to ensure they died like Christ to show his respect to the Father.

Leesa's body was loaded into his car and then taken to a large pine tree near the service roads leading into the Morgan–Monroe State Forest. He lifted her up and propped her against the tree. Using a hammer, he drove a 12-inch spike into each shoulder and one into her heart. The silver stakes with their gold heads would purify her soul. He smiled at his good work and then walked away. It was time to get on the road. Time to spot more loves that needed saving. First, a stop at McDonald's for a coffee and apple pie. He always liked something bitter and sweet after sex and saving as soul.

Paisley and Stretchie hadn't finished their main course at Jazon's Steakhouse before Stretchie got a text regarding a new case.

"Funny money being circulated," he mumbled to his date. "Secret Service would like me to work on this with them."

"Really. Nothing funny about it to me. What's up with counterfeiters?" Paisley inquired.

"They seem to be flooding the state parks, theme parks, and tourist towns across the United States," Stretchie added.

"Do we need to bring them some ink or new plates? What's the deal?" she asked in her most sarcastic manner.

"I've been asked to get on it ASAP. You interested in consulting?"

"New ice cream flavor going out the door tomorrow. I think I need to focus on that. Also, Mr. Bradshaw has me spying on his new girlfriend. I knew I'd get those types of cases. Comes with the territory."

"I know Jim Bradshaw. He's lost more honest girlfriends with that paranoia of his. I guess having two ex-wives cheat on you will do that. Did you say the new flavor is called Cinnamon Red-Hot Rolls?"

"Yep. Kansas came up with it. Odd, but it tested well."

"I don't know. Red hot candies mixed with cinnamon rolls in vanilla ice cream. Makes my GERD crawl. I didn't say I'd eat it. But if there is a market for it, then who am I to stop it?"

"You been following the Forest Strangler case?" she asked.

"Some. He's not dropped into Kentucky yet, but we got enough on our plate. I'm still whirling from good old Gary the cannibal."

"As bad as it was, you bought his place pretty cheap. You are a little bit of a peculiar neighbor, but I can get used to you," Paisley replied while grinning.

"Problem is since I moved in ... I spend more time at your house than mine."

"About that. Having another person over more and eating food over at the house — raises my expenses. Might have just to kick you to the curb," she jokingly said.

"Perhaps we can play musical houses. I got chores that you can help with at my house as well," he said.

"Really. You sold the dairy cows to me so I could make my cream, and the other animals have moved to my barn due to being refugees."

"I do donate food for them."

"Pretzels and beer do not count, nor are they healthy for them. I'll help you with the case at the end of the week. I'm raising my rates by another five an hour. I need feed money for the new animals."

"I believe I can make that happen."

After consuming a large meal, both decided to stop by the ice cream shop for something sweet. A blonde-haired, green-eyed woman walked into the store while Paisley dropped a triple scoop for Stretchie onto a waffle cone. The stranger immediately came up to Paisley.

"Excuse me. Are you Paisley Hunter?"

"Yes. I am. Who are you, and how can I help you?"

"I'm Marletta Worm. You may not believe this, but I'm your sister, and I'm in trouble."

ABOUT THE AUTHOR

Alan grew up in the rural areas of Breathitt & Wolfe County, Kentucky. Before writing books, he wrote dinner theater plays, writing parodies of shows from the 50s and 60s. Saturday Night Live, the 70s and 80s movies, and living in a small community motivated Alan to channel his imagination into writing. Alan has been writing and publishing novels since 2016.

Alan enjoys writing fiction (science fiction and fantasy). He embraces being a Trekkie, attending comic cons, and watching superhero movies (DC and Marvel). This is his sixth novel, with more in the works.

Alan graduated with a master's degree in clinical psychology from Morehead State University. He currently lives in Lexington, Kentucky, with his wife Lenore and their critters. Alan is working toward retirement so he can have more time to write. Alan asks that you donate to your favorite charity and if you don't have one, consider the National Multiple Sclerosis Society or the Humane Society.

Made in the USA
Middletown, DE
18 July 2023